EDEN MERCER THRILLING MYSTERY SERIES
BOOK ONE

SHATTERED
SILENCE

PAIGE
BLACK

GET SECRET WITNESS FOR FREE

In the misty town of Nightfall, rookie officer Eden Mercer races against time to solve a decades-old mystery and save a missing woman.
Get Secret Witness now and uncover Eden Mercer's first gripping case!
www.paigeblackauthor.com

BOOKS BY PAIGE BLACK

Eden Mercer Mystery Thrillers

In the fog-shrouded town of Nightfall, Oregon, Officer Eden Mercer confronts dark secrets and hidden dangers. As she battles her cult past and tackles chilling cases, Eden is determined to uncover the sinister truths lurking beneath the surface.

Shattered Silence

Deadly Lessons

Lethal Lines

Treacherous Depths

Twisted Pursuit

CHAPTER 1

"We're lost."

The words had been bouncing around in Jenna Morales's head for the past hour. They started as a quiet whisper, but as the minutes and miles stretched on had grown to a panicked shout.

She planted her aching, numb, wet feet and glared at John's back. "John." He didn't even turn around. "John!" she tried again, louder this time, sharper. She swiped the rain from her forehead. "We need to stop and regroup."

Finally he spun around, raindrops peppering his reddish beard. "It's cool."

Jenna frowned. Things were definitely not "cool."

He pointed. "I see the lights of a town up ahead." His unyielding confidence grated on her last nerve.

She shook her head, unconvinced. What town? Had John's "shortcut" veered them closer to the coast than she'd realized? She squinted, barely making out the faint golden light peeking between the tall, straight trunks of the pines.

"I don't think that's a town." For one thing, there weren't *lights*. Just one. Still, maybe they were closer to civilization than she dared hope.

As he'd done all day, John ignored her misgivings and tromped onward. "I'm going to climb the hill and check it out. It's definitely a town."

She rolled her eyes at the back of his rain slicker and muttered to herself, "Of course he knows better than me. That's why our day hike has turned into this six-hour death march." She leaned back against the rough bark of a towering pine, sheltering under its branches for a bit of respite from the steadily pouring rain.

Her hands were numb with cold, and she could no longer feel her nose or toes. This was January in coastal northern Oregon.

Sunset came early this time of year, and the light had already grown soft and gray with dusk. Well, even softer and grayer than it'd been when they'd started their hike midmorning. This was Oregon, after all. Gray skies were the norm this time of year.

Jenna set her jaw, torn between annoyance at John and fear. They had maybe an hour at best before they found themselves stumbling around the forest in the pitch-black with little more than half a bottle of water between them and a couple of power bars stuffed in their packs.

At least she'd had the foresight to pack her raincoat and wear proper hiking boots and thick socks. But when the temperatures dropped after sunset, would the cold grow life-threatening?

She shook her head at herself. Jenna had grown up in the Pacific Northwest. She knew her way around the wilderness. And yet she'd allowed her not-even-boyfriend John Sinks to convince her to take a shortcut he promised would lead to an amazing viewpoint. Only now, they were far, *far* off the trail with no clue how to find their way back.

Lost. Her throat tightened. She'd allowed herself to be led astray by this doofus who wouldn't even commit to calling her his girlfriend, despite the fact that they'd been seeing each other for almost three months.

She let out a heavy sigh, unsure if she was more frustrated with John for getting them into this mess or with herself for letting him.

He'd already climbed the hill out of sight, and she decided it was time she take the lead in getting them back to the car. If only she could figure out where they were.

One positive—she'd taken the time to study the posted map near the entrance to the trail. She closed her eyes, picturing it in her mind.

Had they stuck to the trail, they'd have veered west toward the coast, then headed north and looped back around to the starting point again.

But where the trail had begun to veer north, John had suggested his "secret shortcut."

They'd continued west off the trail, toward the coast. If he really had spotted the lights of a town, it meant that they were nearer the ocean than she'd anticipated. She slowed her breathing, and as her heartbeat quieted, she closed her eyes and listened.

A few birds squawked in the distance. Leaves rustled—probably a squirrel darting through the underbrush. Raindrops pattered the leaves and branches overhead.

And below it all came a quiet, rhythmic *whoosh… whoosh*. She opened her eyes. *Waves*. They were near the coast. *Damn*. They were worse off than she'd guessed. And they need to be careful, too. If they were close enough to hear waves, that meant they were near the steep, tall cliffs that lined much of the coast.

They needed to watch their footing lest they inadvertently drop off the edge to their deaths. Hot anger flushed Jenna's chest. If she died following this dude around the forest, she would come back to haunt him so hard.

Refueled by her anger, Jenna oriented herself so that the sound of the waves came from behind her. If they kept the sound to their backs, they'd be heading east and likely meet back up with the trail or at least the highway. If they found the road, they could hitch a ride back to their car or into the nearest town.

"John," she called. She got no reply. No way was she going to bother climbing that tall hill in the opposite direction of where they needed to go in search of him. Instead, she began picking her way over wet, matted leaves, fallen logs, and curled ferns.

"John," she called again over her shoulder, but still he didn't answer.

Teeth chattering and shivering with cold, Jenna hiked her way through the underbrush, vowing never, *ever* to follow some guy out into the wilderness again. She knew better than to go off the path, but John had seemed so confident, she hadn't wanted to seem like she was second-guessing him. She shook her head at herself. She'd risked her life so as not to hurt this dude's ego; never mind he'd had no trouble stringing her along for months, hurting her own sense of self-worth.

She scanned the tree trunks for any sign of the path or the highway. As she approached a steep slope down, her gaze landed on something unusual amidst the forest floor—a bright splash of red.

She came to a halt, unease flooding through her. "John," she called again, more uncertain this time.

"Yeah?" came the muffled shout.

She spun toward the sound, her annoyance with him momentarily forgotten. Her heart thudded against her ribs—a mix of fear from the eerie silence around her and relief that she wasn't alone in it. "John, come here."

"Hold on."

But Jenna didn't wait. She crept toward that odd, unnatural color, which stuck out among all the green and brown of the forest. As she neared, her throat closed, and the hairs rose on the back of her neck and arms. She squinted. The red appeared to be the fabric of a shirt, or a sweater maybe, peeking out from under a pile of stones.

Heart racing, she edged closer, picking her way with sideways steps down the slope. She kept her eyes on her steps, careful not to lose her balance. It wasn't until she'd reached a small shelf of level land that she looked up.

There, mere feet from her, lay a small hollow nestled on a flat stretch before the hill continued in a sharper drop. Her gaze darted around the confusing sight. A tangle of matted blond hair. Unnaturally blue hands with blackened, chipped nails protruding from the sleeve of the red sweater. A leather strap binding the hands together with a metallic, rune-like pendant resting on top. Stones piled on a body. The head... not where it should be. Rose-colored crystals had been placed over the eyes above the leering, gaping smile.

Jenna's piercing scream echoed around the forest. Wings flapped as birds took flight from nearby trees. She didn't even realize the sound had come from her own mouth for a good couple of seconds. She shrieked again, her throat hoarse.

"Jenna! Jenna, what's wrong? Are you okay?" John's voice drifted down to her from overhead.

Before she could answer, Jenna's stomach lurched at the putrid smell of rotting flesh that flooded her nostrils. She spun away from the macabre sight and retched. She spat what remained of her breakfast onto the dark, rich earth, and stood bent over, trembling. She covered her nose, trying to breathe through her mouth.

John skittered down the slope beside her. He put a hand on her back. "You okay?"

She shook her head. No—she was far from okay. But as her stomach still threatened to upturn again, she couldn't speak and merely pointed behind her at the corpse.

"What is that?" John wandered over to the body buried

under the pile of stones. It took him longer to realize what he was looking at.

"Holy shit!" He stumbled back, lost his footing, and tumbled down the steep slope below the body, screaming as he fell.

Jenna lurched upright, filled with fear. "John!"

CHAPTER 2

The alarm on my phone blares for the third time this morning, and I fumble around in the bedsheets till I tap the right part of the screen and turn it off.

Beside me, Shadow groans, and I drag my hands across my eyes. *I feel ya, buddy. I feel ya.*

The curtains are drawn across the big windows in my bedroom that overlook Evergreen Street below. When they're open, I have a partial view of the town and the ocean beyond. But right now, it's pitch-black outside.

It's 5:25 a.m. in January, which means it'll be another couple of hours before the sun rises. It seems cruel that I have to be up before the sun. Then again, at least I'm not working the overnight shift anymore.

I pad down the hall, sticking to the carpet runners and hopping over the bare wooden planks of the Victorian in between the rugs. The old floorboards creak like crazy, and my sister, Hope, is sleeping down the hall, but also the bare wood is freezing this time of year. I take a quick shower, huddling under the warm stream of water in the clawfoot tub, then dress in my neatly pressed uniform.

Grandma likes to say the dark blue really sets off my blond hair, but considering my shoulder-length waves are pulled back in a tight bun 99 percent of the time, I'm not sure how much that's doing for me.

I quickly brush my hair back in its typical style, throw on a little mascara, dab on multipurpose lip balm and blush, then dash downstairs to the kitchen. Grandma's already up, and Shadow's gulping down the food she set out for him.

"Thanks, Grandma," I call as I tug open the fridge. She's sitting at her usual spot at the eat-in table with its wrap-around wooden bench seat.

She's half-turned toward the bay window, where the twinkle of the town's lights are the only bright spots in the pitch-black. She's got a book in her hand, her readers perched on the end of her nose, and a steaming mug of coffee in her hand.

She gives me a warm smile. "Of course. Can't let my baby go hungry."

I smirk as I grab the carton of milk. "I thought *I* was your baby."

She chuckles. "You wish."

I quickly down a bowl of microwave oatmeal, then carry my empty dish back to the deep farmhouse sink. I dart a quick glance at Grandma Gloria, who's lost in her book, and then pour some of the coffee she's brewed into my Nightfall PD branded travel mug. I crinkle my nose—*extra* burnt this morning.

It's my and Hope's secret that Grandma's coffee is notoriously undrinkable. I don't know how she manages to consume the sludge herself or how my grandpa did for decades, but neither my sister nor I have ever dared criticize it openly. Grandma seems particularly proud of her coffee... if one can call the dark brown mud beverage coffee.

I help my massive German shepherd fur baby into his police-issue harness and then grab the leather leash from the hook by the heavy wooden door with the inset glass window. "See you tonight, Grandma."

"Have a good day, Eden," she answers. "And be safe out there." I grin to myself as I zip up my puffer coat. She says the same thing to me every day, even though my day-to-day involves writing traffic tickets or, for a dash of extra excitement, ushering drunk partiers off the beach.

Nightfall is a sleepy town. We get our fair share of tourists during the summer months, but otherwise it's a small place where nearly everybody knows everyone else. I lock the door behind me, and Shadow tugs me across the porch, down the steps, and along the crooked sidewalk toward town. The world is dark and quiet… and drizzly.

I don't bother pulling the hood of my coat up. It's just spitting, but my nose and ears have already gone cold. At least Grandma's terrible coffee is helping keep my hand warm where I hold the travel mug.

We stroll past historic Victorian homes like the one I live in with my grandma and Hope, their yards shaded by tall, sturdy trees with branches shifting in the wind. I inhale the fresh, salty scent of the ocean and can hear the distant crash of waves when I reach the bottom of the hill.

I stop at a little patch of land near a small tidal creek and pop the lid off my travel mug, dumping out the coffee. It's a daily ritual, and Shadow knows to wait. As soon as I finish, though, he's tugging me forward. And I know the reason for his eagerness.

Instead of heading straight to the station, we make a slight detour downtown. Most of the little shops and boutiques on Main Street are still shuttered, their lights dark. All except for the Daily Grind, whose warm golden light spills out onto the street, beckoning me in like a moth to a flame.

The little bell over the door tinkles as Shadow and I step into the blessedly warm cafe, my nose filling with the rich, earthy aroma of fresh brewed coffee. As usual, Maya Cooper, owner of the Daily Grind, looks up smiling from behind the wooden counter, her dark eyes sparkling.

I raise a chilled hand in greeting. "How do you always manage to be so cheerful at this time in the morning?"

She chuckles and comes around the counter to kneel in front of Shadow, ruffling his black and tawny fur. "I've already had six shots of espresso."

I scoff, jealous. "Well, that'll do it."

Maya scratches behind Shadow's big, pointed ears as my goofy canine grins. "The usual?"

I nod, and instead of getting up to make it herself, Maya shakes her dark wavy hair over her shoulder and calls to the back, "Matty! Customer!" A couple of moments later, the lithe guy with gauged ears and a bright smile pushes through the curtain from the kitchen, wiping his hands off on a striped kitchen towel.

"Hey, Eden."

"Hey, Matty." I slide him my now empty travel mug.

His blue eyes study my face for a moment before he peeks over the counter to grin at Shadow. "Hey, buddy."

My dog's fluffy tail swishes over the wooden floor. "The usual," Maya instructs as Shadow flops onto his side, giving her easy access for stomach rubs.

I roll my eyes and shake my head at my K-9. "Shameless. This is hardly professional police dog behavior."

Maya tsks. "You're not on duty yet, are you? Are you, good boy?"

I dart a glance at Matty and find him staring at me before he looks back down to the milk he's foaming for my latte. My cheeks warm, and I keep my eyes glued to Shadow.

Matty is a couple of years younger than me; I'd guess maybe twenty-six. He plays in a local band, The Band She's, and Maya sometimes lends them a corner of the cafe for performances. I have to admit he's a good musician and their frontwoman is fantastic. He's not a bad barista, either. Maya's nudged me a few times over the last couple of years, hinting that he has a crush on me. I fold my arms across my chest and shift on my feet. The mere thought of it makes me uncomfortable.

At twenty-eight, I've never had a boyfriend and only been on a handful of dates. My younger sister, Hope, is always encouraging me to put myself out there, and even Grandma Gloria not so subtly hints that I should wear my hair down more. Apparently, that's what the young men like. *Eye roll.*

But I don't have any interest in that, not right now at least. My focus is on my career. Besides, once anybody got to know me past the initial pleasantries, they wouldn't be interested anyway. Not once they found out about my past.

Matty taps the pitcher of foamed milk a couple of times on the counter as the espresso machine hisses.

Maya rises and pulls a bone-shaped dog biscuit out of a dish on the counter. Shadow snaps to attention, sitting perfectly still, his pointed ears perked and his intelligent brown eyes laser focused on the treat in her hand.

I chuckle. This is the reason he drags me down the hill to the cafe every morning. "You've got to tell me where you get those." Shadow eagerly chomps down the treat. "We've been working on our cadaver dog training, and he's doing pretty well but could use a little extra motivation."

Maya winks. "I bake them myself."

I blink, surprised. "Seriously?"

She chuckles as she gives Shadow one more scratch behind his ears before walking behind the counter and washing her hands. "Sure. I'll make you a batch." She uses tongs to put a chocolate chip scone into a paper bag for me, the other part of my usual order, and Matty slides the travel mug across the counter to me.

I hand him my credit card. "I'll pay up the tab." They usually let me ring up a couple of weeks' worth of orders before I pay it off all at once. As he charges me, I inhale the heavenly aroma of the freshly brewed coffee and chocolatey scone. I bid them goodbye, then pluck up Shadow's leather leash and drag him away from Maya, one of his favorite people in Nightfall. I have to admit I like her warm, welcoming personality too, but I suspect some of his affection has to do with those home-baked dog treats. The bell tinkles again as I step back onto the cold, dark street.

I wait for a car to pass, its headlights sweeping over us, then step out from under the awning and jog across the street. The rain has picked up, pattering against the top of my head and beading Shadow's black-and-tan fur. Luckily, we don't have far to go. Just across the street and down a couple of buildings on Main Street stands Nightfall's Police Station.

It was originally built in 1892 as the town's jail, and though it has been remodeled a couple of times since then, it retains most of its vintage charm. We duck inside, and I note a middle-aged couple sitting on the polished wooden chairs in the lobby.

I raise my travel cup in greeting to Linda Park, one of the administrators who works behind the front desk. I think of her and her counterpart, Joan, who often works alongside her, as some of my few allies in the station. Linda winks and gives me a warm smile.

"Morning, Eden. Morning, Shadow."

"Morning, Linda." I push through the low swinging door that divides the lobby from the rest of the station, accessible only to those who work here. I step closer to Linda and lower my voice, tipping my head at the couple in the lobby. "Everything okay?"

"Psht." She waves off my concern. "I've got this under control. Easy peasy." She shoots a look at the grumpy couple, their arms folded, brows furrowed, then lowers her voice. "They're apparently angry that the neighbor's cats keep pooping in their yard. Stepped in some on their way out this morning."

I fight to hold back a snort. "Good luck getting the cats to stop."

Linda tugs her camel-colored cardigan tighter around her, then wiggles her fingers at Shadow. "Cats can't be trained quite like you smart little puppies, can they?" she coos. She taps her lips, growing thoughtful. "Police cats. Now that'd be something."

I smile in spite of myself. "I'll stick with the K-9s for now."

I wind my way back to the locker rooms. During the last remodel in the '90s, they put in a ladies' locker room, though at the time there weren't any female officers at the station. Now there is a grand total of one: me. Of course, there are Joan and Linda, who work as administrators, and a few women dispatchers.

But I'm the only officer, so I have the locker room to myself.

I slide out of my puffer coat, store my keys and a few odds and ends, and then make my way out to my desk in the bullpen.

I sit at the worn wooden desk and run my fingers along the polished scratches. I love the history of the building and the town. My eyes land on the pile of paperwork stacked in the corner. I do *not* love the paperwork. I unclip Shadow's leash, loop the leather band a few times, and tuck it into a drawer of the desk.

Dutifully, he curls up in the gray dog bed beside my desk. I take a sip of my deliciously frothy latte and pop a bite of the warm chocolate chip scone in my mouth. I close my eyes and resist the urge to moan.

I generally try to be one of the first into the station in the morning so I have time to settle in. But there are still a few officers finishing up the night shift. I nod hello to Officer Barnes and Officer Simmons. I don't know them well. Really, I don't know a whole lot of the officers well.

Even though I've worked here for four years (and volunteered under my grandpa's tutelage for years before that), most of them still seem to expect me to quit at any moment. At least that's how it feels. Like they don't bother getting to know me because I won't be here the next day.

My best (and only) friend on the force, Officer Nathan Brooks, strolls in.

There's just something about Nathan. Maybe it's his bright blue eyes or floppy sandy golden hair. It's probably his bright grin and double dimples, but he has this boyish charm that wins everyone over.

"Morning, Eden." He's one of the few here who calls me by my first name. To the rest of the officers, I'm simply Mercer.

He passes behind my chair, pausing to squeeze my shoulder and wiggle his fingers at Shadow. "Hey, little buddy." Shadow perks his ears up and swishes his tail. Nathan always seems to brighten Shadow's mood too. "That looks good."

I roll my eyes but dutifully hand over a chunk of my scone.

"You're the best," Nathan sings as he strolls back to the men's locker room to stash his belongings. I shake my head. He's another one who is unnaturally peppy at this time of the morning.

One by one, the other officers on the day shift filter in, including my least favorite person—Bulldog. That isn't his real name, but Officer Mark Jensen has earned the nickname not only for his bulky, droopy-eyed physique that reminds all of us of a bulldog, but also because he has about as much charm and intelligence as one. Okay, maybe that's just my interpretation—he claims it's because of his toughness and courage. *Sure, Mark.*

I glance down at Shadow at my feet. That's probably not fair to bulldogs, though. I'm biased, after all. I mean, I love dogs, *all* dogs, but I can't help feeling like Shadow, a rescue

German shepherd, could run circles around most other canines in terms of intelligence. In fact, Shadow could probably run circles around Bulldog, too.

I keep my eyes down as he and his two buddies, Officers Larson and Garcia, make their way to the locker room.

His very presence annoys me, though I try not to show it. Bulldog barks out a laugh, disturbing the quiet peace of the morning, and slaps Larson on the shoulder so hard, he staggers. "I showed her my badge, and she was practically drooling."

Garcia sneers while Larson guffaws.

Charming. I keep my gaze down, hoping to avoid being a target this morning. As he walks behind me, Bulldog suddenly lurches over my shoulder, yelling, "Boo!" I jump, sloshing coffee onto my desk, then gasp as the men laugh. Pressing a hand to my suddenly racing heart, I say flatly, "Morning to you, too."

"Oh." Bulldog pouts. "Don't be grumpy."

"Careful." Garcia snickers as he raises both hands. "She might shoot."

Bulldog sneers, which tugs the corner of his thick mustache up. "That's right, we wouldn't want another repeat of New Year's Eve." Heat flashes up the back of my neck, and my stomach churns. Suddenly that scene feels like it might come right back up again.

Luckily, Chief Jamison steps out of his office.

The older man is nearly 60, tall, with short-cropped graying hair that contrasts with his dark skin and a sturdy build. His commanding presence demands respect from all, and he gets it too.

They sober up some—Bulldog, Garcia, and Larson—but still snicker as they make their way to the locker room. At least they're leaving me alone. I shoot the Chief a grateful look, and he merely nods.

Chief Jamison treats everyone fairly but firmly. He started

on the force as a young man and worked alongside my grandpa for many years. I suspect he has a bit of a soft spot for me, considering his long and loyal relationship with my grandfather.

Bulldog and his lackeys pass Nathan on his way back out of the locker room. Nathan, too, tries to arrive early to avoid running into those idiots in the locker room. I'm the only one he's come out to at the station. And I've promised, of course, to keep his secret until he's ready to share it.

But that doesn't prevent Bulldog and the others from suspecting. They tease Nathan for being so well-groomed, for his mannerisms, for being friends with me. I can't stand bigoted people. Never mind the fact that Nathan is one of the best officers on the force, despite being the youngest.

Nathan glances back as the idiots disappear into the locker room and then sidles up beside me, perching on the edge of my desk. He rolls his eyes. "Ignore them." I have to admit, my heart is still pounding.

Bulldog's reference to the incident on New Year's Eve shakes me up more than I want to admit, but I give Nathan a weak smile. "Thanks. I was gonna say the same to you."

He grins, flashing those double dimples, which helps put me back at ease. Within fifteen minutes, the rest of the day shift has arrived, and Chief Jamison calls us all to the briefing room for the morning update.

I sigh as I take my seat in the row beside my friend. "What do you think; more traffic duty today?"

Nathan gives me a little nudge with his shoulder. "You never know."

I smirk. "Except we do know." Nightfall is a small town of about eight thousand people. My days consist of giving out traffic tickets, sometimes patrolling the signage shopkeepers put out, and, during the summer, following up on car break-ins. I joined the force to become a detective like my grandpa and to make a real difference, investigating serious crimes and helping those in need. I know I have to be patient, put in the work, and stay consistent. But it eats at me, the tedium of the day-to-day work.

I wait for Chief Jamison to dole out assignments, fully expecting I'll be on traffic duty for the umpteenth day in a row. Instead, he stands at the head of the room, next to the whiteboard and American flag, and folds his hands in front of him.

Gray light is just beginning to shine outside the paned windows, and the fluorescents overhead gleam off the polished wooden floors. As everyone settles, Chief Jamison clears his throat.

"Officers, two hikers named Jenna Morales and John Sinks were lost yesterday in the forest outside Nightfall."

I sit up straighter, my curiosity piqued. Do we have a missing persons case?

"The male hiker, Mr. Sinks, fell and suffered an injury to his ankle. The pair are currently at Nightfall Clatsop Regional Hospital."

Any hope of an interesting day sinks, and I slump in my seat. No missing persons. Just some injured hikers. I mean, I'm glad they're safe and relatively unhurt, but selfishly hoped for a chance to prove myself.

Chief Jamison shifts on his feet and continues in his deep, measured voice. "However, before his fall, the pair discovered what they describe as the remains of a woman."

It's as though the rest of the sounds of the station go silent. The phones ringing, the little shuffle of people in their chairs, the murmur of conversation, the hum of the heaters—all of it fades away.

"The body was buried in what they describe as a ritual fashion. Highly unusual."

My breath catches. Now this is something. A body? In all four years on the force, there hasn't been a single murder in Nightfall.

And now we have a ritual burial out in the forest.

No way that this was an accidental or natural death.

The chief clears his throat. "Detective Hanks is already on his way up to Warrenton for his weekly task force briefings with the other detectives from neighboring towns. So in his absence, I need a couple of officers to head over to the hospital and take these hikers' statements."

Nathan bumps my knee with his. He knows how badly I want to make detective. I've confided in him about my ambitions many times. I don't dare look at him. I keep my eyes glued to Jamison, willing my name to come out of his mouth.

"Officer Jensen."

I set my jaw. The chief is the only one who doesn't call him Bulldog. And of course he'd send *him*. Bulldog isn't quiet about anything, much less his own aspirations to make detective, though I can't think of anyone less qualified for the position.

My grandpa taught me that detectives need keen skills of observation and have to be talented at finessing information out of people. The role takes creative thinking and being able to see problems from lots of different angles to find creative solutions. Bulldog, on the other hand, seems to solve all of his life problems with brute force and bravado.

Chief Jamison's gaze shifts to me. "And Officer Mercer."

I gasp.

"I'd like the two of you to head over to the hospital as soon as this briefing is over. Take their statements and get as much information about the location of this body as you can." His expression grows grim. "The hikers are unfortunately unclear on where these remains were found. We'll send out a task force to look for the body as soon as possible, so any details they can remember that might help us locate this body are essential."

Chief Jamison doles out other tasks for the day, reminds us of Nightfall's upcoming lunar eclipse watching festivities, which will inevitably draw hordes of tourists here this weekend and require everyone on deck, and then dismisses us.

I leap to my feet, and Nathan is right beside me. He squeezes my hand. "Eden, this is your chance."

CHAPTER 3

Shadow leaps up into the back seat of the white Ford police utility vehicle. I close the door behind him and then slide into the passenger seat, avoiding making eye contact with Bulldog. Of course, he snatched up the keys and decided he was driving without any discussion. He turns on the engine and pulls out onto Main Street, from which we head north towards Nightfall Clatsop Regional Hospital in silence.

That's fine by me. It's a definite improvement over having to listen to his machismo-filled stories or insults.

Shadow's big furry head settles onto my shoulder, and I grin in spite of myself. I reach up to ruffle his fur, which sends some tawny hairs flying. Bulldog, with his droopy-eyed expression, looks over and shoots me a disgusted look. "Can't believe you're bringing the dog."

I press my lips tightly together to keep myself from retorting that the dog has a name and is more of an officer than he'll ever be.

"Unhygienic," he sneers, his voice dripping with disdain.

I shoot him a pointed look, but keep my mouth shut, despite the retort at the tip of my tongue. Unhygienic? A big accusation for a man who never washes his hands in the bathroom. The other guys have teased him about it in the breakroom, and Bulldog seems to view it as a point of pride. I shudder and make a note to wipe down the SUV's steering wheel before I drive it next.

He cranks the radio, which blares twangy country music. At least it keeps me from having to make conversation with the brute.

We park in front of the sprawling, new-ish hospital, and he insists on marching about ten feet in front of me with his barrel chest puffed up and beefy shoulders squared. I'm surprised he can still fit through doorways.

Thankfully, Chief Jamison has picked up on our mutual dislike for each other and almost never makes me work with Bulldog. In fact, he and I probably would have killed each other by now if we'd had to spend much time on the same patrol. But the chief also knows that both of us are interested in making detective, which is why I suspect he assigned the both of us to do the interviews this morning.

The kind lady behind the lobby desk points us to the emergency department and we head back through the double doors. Our shoes squeak along the white linoleum floors, and a woman's muffled voice sounds over the loudspeaker, paging a doctor to surgery. Medical equipment beeps as we pass rooms until we reach number 107. The curtain is open onto the tiny room and Bulldog announces our presence by clearing his throat.

A woman in her mid to late twenties sits huddled on a chair beside the young man laid out in the bed. She looks up, and dark bags hang under her large eyes. Her black hair is a tangled mess around her pale face. She hugs the sky-blue hospital blanket around herself. Most people who don't regularly deal with police officers find us a bit intimidating… especially Bulldog.

But when the woman's eyes alight on Shadow, her expression softens and a grin tugs at the corner of her mouth. I give her a gentle smile. Shadow is my K-9 partner, so I'd have brought him regardless. But I know the effect he has on people. Most people love dogs, and it helps put them at ease —which should make it easier to glean information from them.

"Jenna Morales and John Sinks?" Bulldog booms. I try not to wince. He's speaking way too loudly for the quiet hospital at this hour of the morning. But he either doesn't notice or doesn't care. Probably both.

Jenna nods. She has a few light scratches on her arms and face, while her companion, John Sinks, has fared worse. A butterfly bandage spans the deep scrape across his cheek, which runs into his thick red beard, and his arms and hands are mottled with red abrasions and dark bruises that slice through his intricate tattoo sleeve. His left foot lies on top of the blanket, a splint wrapped around his ankle. He blinks at us, his eyes slightly unfocused and dazed.

"I'm Officer Jensen with Nightfall PD." I expect him to introduce me, but of course that's too much courtesy to hope for.

I smile at John and Jenna, trying to hide my annoyance. "And I'm Officer Mercer." I gesture down at my K-9, who sits patiently beside me. "And this is Shadow."

Jenna smiles at my dog. "Hi, Shadow."

"Hi, Sladow," John parrots in a slurred voice.

Jenna shoots us an apologetic smile. "He's on some pretty heavy pain medication and kinda out of it."

I gesture at his ankle. "Bad injury, then?"

Her expression grows flat. "It's just a sprain."

"A bad sprain," John interjects, a belligerent edge to his voice.

Jenna lowers hers to stage whisper, though John can clearly still hear her. "He's been pestering the nurses since we got in last night for more pain meds. They said he should be fine, but he claims he's in excruciating pain."

"I am," John insists.

I look between the two, slightly amused. I wonder if their disagreements will carry over to their recollection of the body's location.

Bulldog, who towers above me, bulky and scowling, folds his hands in front of him. "We have questions about the remains you found in the forest."

I tug the curtain closed behind us to give us some semblance of privacy and then pull out my phone. "Is it alright if I record the interview?" They both nod their agreement, and I hit the red start button on my phone's recording app.

"Can you tell us a little bit about what happened last night? Why were you out in the woods in the first place?"

"It was a date," John explains, his head lolling to one side.

"So, you two are... dating?" I gesture between them.

Jenna crosses her arms and sets her jaw. "For the moment."

Hoo boy. There's some not-so-subtle animosity between them—at least on Jenna's side.

John lifts his palms, which are as scratched up as the rest of his arms. "We went for a hike and then got lost."

Jenna shoots him a dark look, then turns back to Bulldog and me. "John insisted he knew of a shortcut that would take us to what he promised would be a beautiful view. Instead, we ended up lost."

John, clearly high on painkillers, drops his chin to his chest and chuckles while Jenna shakes her head in annoyance.

I try to steer us back on track. "What time did you head out for the hike?"

John shrugs, but Jenna answers, "I think it was about ten thirty in the morning."

"Talk us through the day," Bulldog orders.

Jenna takes a sip from the plastic cup on the rolling table beside her, then clears her throat. "We followed the trail at first."

"Which one?" I ask.

"It was right off Highway 101—Pine Crest Trail, I think." She pulls her phone out of her pocket and opens her browser to a hiking website I've used myself to find new spots. She nods and holds the phone out to show us a photograph of tall pine trees surrounded by lush ferns. The title at the top indeed says Pine Crest Trail.

"Great, thanks." I know the area well. As an avid hiker myself, I've explored most of the trails around Nightfall. They lead through beautiful old growth forests and more often than not offer glimpses of hidden waterfalls and gorgeous views over the bluffs to the ocean below. I've hiked Pine Crest a few times.

I glance over at Bulldog, whose lips are pressed together and eyes narrowed. He turns to John, who seems to be barely tracking the conversation. "That's the right trail, sir?"

I frown and tip my head toward Jenna. "She *just* said it was."

He holds a hand up to me without taking his eyes off John Sinks. "Just verifying."

My nostrils flare with annoyance. What more could I really expect from such an open misogynist? Of course he needs the man to tell him where they were hiking—no matter the fact that the guy is barely conscious.

John nods, his head lolling to the side. "Yeah- wait, no I'm not sure."

Bulldog nods as if siding with him. I glance at Jenna whose eyes are narrowed and mouth open, clearly offended that my partner is questioning her account. I jump in to keep from losing her.

"When did you leave the trail?"

She glares at Bulldog for another moment before turning

to answer me. "Where we would have looped north, John suggested we keep heading west."

John shakes his head. "No, no, no." His words still come out slurred. "No. We were still, we were heading north for at least a mile or two before I headed west."

Jenna frowns at him. "That's not true. I remember."

"Psh," he scoffs. "Well, you remember wrong."

Bulldog smirks, which sends hot anger flushing up the back of my neck. Just when I think he can't get more annoying and frustrating, he manages to surprise me.

I let out a heavy sigh, then address the hikers. "Alright, so you disagree about when, but at some point, instead of following the trail, you veered west." They both nod. "Then what?"

The young woman folds her arms. "We wandered around aimlessly... for hours."

John rolls his eyes, then winces as if it hurts to do so. "Look, I swear there's a shortcut, but it looked... different." He shakes a finger at me before letting his arm plop down beside him. "Must've been because when I went last time it was spring."

"Right, that's it," Jenna mutters, turning away from him.

"So you realized you'd gotten lost," Bulldog growls, clearly losing patience for their back-and-forth. "When did you stumble upon the body?"

Jenna's expression grows pained. "It was cold and raining. And even though John insisted he knew where we were going and that we were almost there—"

"I did," he whines.

But Jenna ignores him and continues. "I decided it was time I take things into my own hands and get us back on track. So, I headed in the direction I figured would lead us back to the highway. And I spotted something red on the ground." The crease between her brows deepens, as if she's reliving the moment.

"It looked out of place. So I went to check it out. I walked down this slope, and when I got to this level bit about halfway down, that's when I–I found her." What little color she has drains from her face.

"Can you describe what you saw?" I prompt gently. Shadow's ears perk up, and the young woman looks at my dog, gathers herself, and then nods.

"It was horrible. I've never seen anything like it. She was buried under this pile of stones."

"She?" Bulldog interrupts. "How do you know it was a she?"

Jenna's throat bobs, and she shakes her head. "I don't know, I guess it was the clothes? She had on this red sweater and jeans. And long blond hair. She was kind of"—she grimaces—"decomposed, so I'm not positive. I just got the impression it was a woman's body."

I nod, suspecting she's correct. Sometimes we observe things we don't consciously process.

"The stones," I prod, "did they look like they'd fallen on top of her?"

"No." Jenna sits straighter and shakes her head, emphatic. "Definitely not. She was lying on her back. I..." She licks her lips. "Her hands had been bound together and there was this strange symbol resting on them." She holds her hands close to her chest with her wrists pressed together.

I raise my brows. This situation is rapidly growing more strange. "Did you recognize the symbol?"

She shakes her head. "The stones looked like they'd been placed on her. Sort of to hide the body."

I nod. Or perhaps to keep predators from ravaging the remains. Interesting. If someone killed the victim, why would they have gone to the trouble of burying her so neatly and arranging her hands in that way?

"She's not telling you the worst part," John interrupts. He turns an odd shade of gray green like he might be sick. His nostrils flare, and his chest heaves under his hospital gown. "Her head." The muscles of his neck tense, and he gags. "It was between her *feet*."

Bulldog shifts and folds his arms across his massive chest. "As in, she was bent over? Like doing a yoga pose or something?"

"No."

I wonder if I should call the nurse. John looks like he's about to retch.

"No, her head had been removed and placed there," Jenna clarifies. She looks down at her feet. "It was horrible."

"I can't imagine." What in the world had these two stumbled upon? Nightfall hadn't seen a homicide in years, and now all of a sudden we had a beheaded woman found out in the forest?

"What happened then?" Bulldog pushes on.

"Well," Jenna muses, "I lost my lunch."

"The smell was disgusting," John finishes for her. "She screamed, and I ran to help but got hurt."

Jenna snorts. "He got so freaked out he tripped over his own feet and fell the rest of the way down the hill."

I suck on my lips to keep from chuckling, and Bulldog clears his throat, clearly fighting the urge himself. "And that's, uh, how you hurt your ankle." He gestures at John's splint.

The poor guy nods. "Yeah."

"What time was this?" I ask.

Jenna sucks in a breath. "Uh, just before dusk. We were starting to lose the light, and I was afraid we were going to be wandering out in the woods in the dark all night." She rolls her eyes. "Which we were."

I frown. "When did you get into the hospital? And how did you get here?"

Jenna splays her palms over the knit blanket. "I found him a walking stick, wrapped his leg up with a spare shirt as best I could, slung his arm over my shoulder, and we hobbled in the direction that I guessed the highway lay. And eventually, after lots of whining from this one—" She jerks her head toward John.

"Hey, my ankle hurt, okay?" He blinks bleary eyes. "It was scary."

"—we finally found the highway, flagged down a trucker, and he gave us a ride into town to the hospital."

"Wow." I look at the petite young woman with even deeper respect. "That must have been really difficult."

She snorts. "You have no idea. I almost left him behind and went for help myself, but he begged me not to leave him alone in the dark."

Bulldog scowls at her, as if he doesn't believe her, even though John offers no arguments in defense of himself.

Jenna sounds like she has a cool head to me, and the fact that she successfully steered them back to the highway suggests she had a decent sense of her surroundings.

"Do you remember where you found the remains of the body?" I prod. This is the heart of why we are here.

Jenna sighs, shaking her head. "Honestly, not really, sorry. We were lost at the time, and then it got dark, and I was so focused on just finding a way back to civilization, I didn't think to note where the body was."

John shrugs. "Yeah, could be anywhere, really.'"

Bulldog rolls his eyes and grumbles, "This is a waste of time."

I do my best to ignore his negativity and focus on Jenna. Again, all of us observe things that we don't always consciously note. It might take a little more effort to recall, but I have a feeling Jenna can remember something that might help us find the body.

"Think back to what was going on when you found the remains. What clues gave you a sense of where you might be, or where the highway might lie? How long had you been walking off the trail? Did you hear or see anything unique?"

She holds up a hand. "Wait a minute, yeah." Jenna's eyes dart from side to side as though she's casting back in her memory. "John saw a light up ahead that he thought was a town."

He pats the bed next to his leg. "That's right, I did. Yeah, it was definitely a town."

Bulldog edges closer to John's side, his interest piqued. "Could have been Nightfall." In a rare moment, he addresses me as a colleague. "Bet they were on the bluffs right above town."

I frown, skeptical. I know Pine Crest Trail. It's not only on the other side of Highway 101, but about fifteen miles away from the trails above Nightfall. "Are you sure you saw the lights of a town?"

Jenna shakes her head. "No. In fact, it was just one light. I didn't think it looked like a town at all."

Interesting. "Can you remember anything else?"

"Yeah—I could hear the ocean. Not super close, but not too far off either."

"Alright." I give her a smile. "That's really helpful, thank you."

We ask them a few more questions and get their contact information in case we need to follow up. Just as we're about to leave, a nurse pulls back the curtain, popping her head in.

"Oh, it's a party in here."

I shuffle aside as she lifts a clipboard off the end of the bed and reviews the notes.

"Would it be alright if we ask the nurse about your medical treatment and some details, like when you arrived at the hospital?" I ask Jenna and John.

They both nod, and the nurse clarifies with them, "I have your express permission to share your medical details with these officers?"

Again, they give their consent, and after Bulldog and I

thank the two hikers, we pull the nurse aside down the hall a bit from their curtained off room.

"Can we just confirm a few details with you?"

"Sure, shoot." She tucks a stray strand of blond hair behind her ear, her round face open and smiling despite the weary bags hanging below her eyes.

"Can you confirm the time Mr. Sinks and Ms. Morales checked into the hospital?"

She glances down at the clipboard. "2:15 a.m. I was here when they came in."

I give her a sympathetic smile. "Long night."

She chuckles and tucks one hand into the pocket of her olive-green scrubs. "Tell me about it."

"What were they treated for?"' Bulldog asks.

"They were both dehydrated, so we gave them some fluids." She scans the notes again. "Both had mild hypothermia, so we got them warmed up. Ms. Morales was in better condition, but Mr. Sinks had an injury to his ankle. So we ran some X-rays to rule out any fractures, and it came back as just a sprain. He had a few minor abrasions as well."

"Do you expect them to be released today?" I ask.

An expression flashes across her face faster than I can interpret it. She clears her throat and looks down. "They would have been released already, except Mr. Sinks insisted he stay for observation and more intense pain management. He's been very…" She trails off as she searches for the right word. "…vocal about his needs."

"Got it." I smile, and she flashes her eyes at me. I take that as code for obnoxious, which seems to jive with what I've seen and what Jenna has described as well. "Thanks so much."

The nurse nods and heads back down the hall to the hikers, greeting Jenna and John while Bulldog and I head out, Shadow trotting along at my side.

"Well, that was interesting," I mutter, forgetting for a moment that Bulldog is my archnemesis at work.

He scoffs. "No kidding. That lady sounded bitter. Wanted to take all the credit, like she was some kind of hero or something."

I scowl at him. "Are you serious? Jenna Morales is the only reason they made it out of there alive. If it weren't for her, they'd still be lost out in the woods, following that dude's imaginary shortcut."

Bulldog merely rolls his eyes, muttering, "Women," as he marches his way out of the hospital, leaving me trailing ten feet behind.

CHAPTER 4

FOUR YEARS AGO, SIMI VALLEY, CALIFORNIA

Joy Ackerman eased her way down the hallway, careful to avoid the squeaky floorboards. This wasn't the first time she'd snuck out of the house in the middle of the night while her mother slept. It probably wasn't even the hundredth time. She grinned ruefully to herself. You didn't become a pregnant seventeen-year-old without learning how to successfully sneak out of the house.

But really, what else had they expected, raising her so strictly? Obviously she was going to rebel.

Now her dad was gone, passed away a few years ago, but it hadn't softened up her mom at all. She was just as militant, just as harsh, and more judgy than ever.

Joy hoisted her sleeping four-year-old son, Clay, higher up on her hip and winced when the two backpacks slung over her other arm scraped against the wall. She froze, listening, but heard only the steady tick-tock of the clock in the kitchen and the hum of appliances.

Joy let out the breath she'd been holding. She adjusted her own heavy backpack, filled with as many clothes, toiletries, and shoes as she could stuff in, as well as the small child's backpack she'd packed for her son. She'd made sure to include his favorite teddy bear, a couple of picture books he liked, and some of his own clothes and shoes.

She'd considered sneaking some snacks earlier, but she knew her mom would have noticed missing food and asked questions. That was the most annoying thing about her mother. She couldn't just mind her own business. Sure, Joy was glad they had a roof over their heads and that her mom covered a lot of her bills.

But it came at a price. And that price was her mom constantly judging and nagging and lecturing Joy about what she should be doing with her life, who she should be spending her time with, and how she should be parenting her own son.

Joy had been so convinced that she'd be out of her parents' house the second she turned eighteen. And now here she was at twenty-one, stuck in the same boring northern California town, under the same roof with her mother.

That's why she wasn't leaving Clay behind.

Yeah, she could have made a brand-new start of it without him. And she knew her mother would have taken care of the little guy. He currently slept peacefully against her chest, freckles sprinkled across his cheeks and nose, his tan skin a beautiful blend of her own pale shade and his father's dark skin. Not that Clay had ever met him or seen a picture of him. The moment Joy had gotten pregnant, Clay's dad had left town and cut contact.

Clay also had his father's curls. Strangers constantly complimented her about what an adorable, sweet little boy he was.

And while Joy now looked forward to enjoying her youth, partying, being free, and living her life on her own terms, she had enough maternal instincts to care about what happened to her son. Of course it would've been easier to leave him behind. But she couldn't bear to leave him with her mother.

She knew he'd be fed and clothed, of course.

But she was also sure he'd bristle under her mother's overbearing rules just as she had. Clay was her son, after all. And though he was sweet and polite and well-mannered in a way she had never been, even at his age, she also saw some of her own spark in his curiosity, his easy laugh, and the little kid jokes he often cracked. No, Joy couldn't leave him to be smothered in her mother's oppressive household.

Joy steeled herself, heart fluttering against her ribs as she tiptoed past her mother's bedroom door. She paused just outside it, listening. She thought she could make out slow, heavy breaths.

She eased past, anxious not to wake her up. If her mom woke up now, it would ruin everything. She'd try to stop her and Joy couldn't handle that. This was her chance to escape.

Joy's plan had been in motion for weeks, but the seething resentment had been bubbling under her skin for years. It was now or never.

Tension eased out of Joy's shoulders as she made it down the hall and around the corner into the foyer. Still, she wouldn't breathe a sigh of relief until she was in her friend's car and on her way.

Joy crept toward the front door, streetlights slanting in through the narrow windows on either side. She paused as her gaze landed on her mother's leather purse beside the door. She hadn't stolen from her mother since she was a teenager. After all, these days all she had to say was she was buying Clay some toy or a new pair of shoes, and her mother willingly forked it over, even if Joy did use the cash to splurge on herself half the time. One last time wouldn't kill her mother.

Again, Joy shifted Clay on her hip, bit her lip, and carefully reached inside. She fished around until she found her mother's wallet, popped the button open, and thumbed out as many bills as she could find. She held the wad up to the light, spotting several twenties in the mix. Not a bad haul. She stuck them in the back pocket of her jeans. And now, here was the tricky part—slipping out the front door. She turned the deadbolt slowly.

And then she turned the knob. Joy pulled up on it as she opened the door—a little trick to keep the hinges from squeaking. She hurried out into the cold night air and eased the door shut behind her.

Clay stirred, his little brow furrowed, and nestled tighter to her.

There, across the street, her friend Laura Steen's boxy green Volvo sat idling. She'd turned off the headlights, but Joy could see her bright grin by the light of the streetlamps. Joy hustled across the street to her.

Clay shoved his thumb into his mouth and sucked on it, still mostly asleep. She hurried to the back passenger door and tugged it open, which turned on the dome light in the car.

"You made it!" Laura beamed. She smiled brightly, her wide brown doe eyes taking in Clay. Joy had told her all about her son, but her friend had never met him before, seeing as the two knew each other from yoga class. "Aw, this must be Clay. He's adorable."

"Thanks," Joy muttered, still too focused on her escape to chat. She got Clay situated in the back seat and buckled his seat belt. He slumped halfway over, mumbling and sucking on his thumb.

There was just enough room in the back seat to fit the small boy. The rest of it was crammed with Laura's belongings. A laundry hamper sat on the seat next to Clay, piled high with clothes. Jugs of water littered the floorboards, along with odds and ends like shoes, a coffee maker, and a healthy-looking spider plant.

Joy tipped her head toward the bags slung over her shoulder. "Any room in the trunk?" she whispered.

Laura winced. "No, sorry."

"No worries." Joy closed the door, then hopped in the passenger side, shoving the stuffed backpacks under her feet. Her knees bent halfway up to her chest, but who cared? She eased the door shut behind her, wincing at the noise.

"Let's go!" Joy hissed.

Laura giggled. "I feel like the getaway driver."

Joy scoffed as she looked out the passenger window. Laura flipped on the headlights, pulled into the street, and drove away.

Joy glanced back, watching the modest ranch house she'd grown up in fade into the distance. With any luck, that would be the last time she laid eyes on the property. As she looked back, she noticed Clay stirring and rubbing his eyes with his tiny, pudgy fists.

"Mama, what's going on?" he murmured in his tired little voice.

"Hi, sweetie!" Laura said brightly, grinning at him in the rearview mirror.

Joy winced almost instinctively. Even though they were now safely on the road, part of her still felt tense and on edge and like Laura's chipper tone didn't match her mood.

"I'm Laura. I'm your mom's friend!" She turned to Joy. "He looks so cute in that little dinosaur onesie. I'm telling you, Source is going to go nuts over him."

"Most people do." Joy unzipped her son's colorful backpack and pulled out his teddy bear, handing it back to him. He blinked a few times and hugged the stuffed animal to his chest. She knew he'd be back asleep soon. It was the middle of the night, after all.

"We're going on an adventure to Oregon," Laura said in her sing-song voice.

The little boy's eyes drooped for a moment before his head

rolled sideways and he slumped back off to sleep. Joy spun around and finally breathed a sigh of relief as Laura drove them through the dark streets, heading north toward the highway.

Toward a new life.

Finally, Joy was getting out of this town.

CHAPTER 5

Back at the station, Shadow and I follow Bulldog and Chief Jamison into the conference room.

I raise my brows in surprise when I spot Detective Hanks in his tweed blazer lounging in one of the wood chairs around the long table, his feet kicked up on the seat of another chair.

Shocked as I am to see Hanks, Bulldog is the one who voices his surprise. He scoffs as he steps in the door, stopping so suddenly I nearly run into the back of him, which would be about as pleasant as smacking into a brick wall. "Detective?"

Detective Gordon Hanks is experienced, weathered. Some call him grizzled.

He merely raises a brow in answer to Bulldog's challenge.

"Chief said you were up in Warrenton."

Nightfall and our neighboring coastal towns of Astoria, Seaside, and Cannon Beach are all so small, each force only employs one detective. They meet at the sheriff's station in Warrenton to give each other support on big cases and work together on several joint task forces dealing with homicides, child abuse, arson, and other serious crimes.

Detective Hanks, probably in his midfifties, presses his lips together, which only deepens the lines etched into his face.

"This situation with these remains is the most exciting thing any of us have going." He lowers his feet to the floor and sits up straighter, then continues in his deep, gravelly voice. "We rescheduled so I could get back here to lead the search."

We file into the room and gather around the long wooden table, Detective Hanks rising to his feet. Chief Jamison lays a topographical map out, smoothing out the creases with his big hands.

He grabs a red marker from the sill of the whiteboard and makes a circle on a northern stretch of coast. "Here's Nightfall."

He turns his intelligent, deep brown eyes to me and then Bulldog. "What did you two find out? Did the hikers have any idea where these mysterious remains might be?"

I open my mouth to speak, but of course, Bulldog jumps in first.

His deep voice is so loud, I almost wince at the volume. "They found her over here." He jabs a massive, stubby finger just to the east of Nightfall, on the bluffs overlooking the town. "The male hiker, Mr. Sinks, saw the lights of the town through the trees just before they located the remains."

I lace my hands behind my back and bite my lip. My natural inclination is to hold my tongue. But Nathan's voice echoes in my head. He's always encouraging me to speak up, to voice my opinion. And considering this search will be one of the biggest operations in Nightfall PD's recent history, I know I'll be kicking myself if I don't express my concerns that Bulldog is literally miles off.

Detective Hanks frowns, the lines between his brows creasing as he stares down at the map. Chief Jamison looks up, his eyes meeting mine.

"Is that what you got from the interviews too, Mercer?"

I avoid looking at Bulldog beside me but step closer to the table with Shadow hugging my side. I clear my throat. "Respectfully, sir, I believe we'd have better luck looking at a different location." I trace my finger along Highway 101 until I locate the bend in the road that approximates the head of the trail.

It lies north and slightly east of Nightfall, far from the location Bulldog has suggested for the search. I trail my fingertip westward.

"Ms. Morales indicated that they were hiking the Pine Crest Trail. She says where the trail loops north, her partner, Mr. Sinks led them off trail farther west toward the coast."

Bulldog scoffs beside me, bristling. I can feel the irritation radiating off him.

My throat tightens, and I clam up, but Chief Jamison gives me an encouraging nod.

"You believe we should search further north?"

I bend over the map. A strand of blond hair tumbles forward out of my bun, and I tuck it behind my ear. "Miss Morales said she heard the sound of waves, so I believe they got very close to the coast." As my finger drifts west, right to the very edge where the land meets the blue sea on the map, I note the location and can't help but grin.

"This is actually really close to the old Nightfall lighthouse. I bet you that was the light that they both spotted, not the lights of the town." The old lighthouse is still in operation, though it's automated now, and the old keeper's house, perched on a winding stretch of rugged coast, has been turned into a quaint B and B.

Bulldog scoffs, his disdain for me clear in his tone. "They said it was the lights of the *town*, Mercer."

I lick my lips, irritation burning in my chest. "No, *Mr. Sinks* said that. Ms. Morales noted she only saw one light and didn't think it looked like the light from a town."

The chief and Detective Hanks are both staring at me, and my stomach clenches with nerves. My first instinct is to acquiesce to Bulldog's point of view, but I tamp that down and press on, lifting my chin. "Ms. Morales seems cool-headed and calm and was the one who got them rescued from the situation. I have more confidence in her account than Mr. Sinks's."

"Oh, well if *you* have more confidence," Bulldog snarls.

Detective Hanks's perceptive gaze darts between the two of us, clearly taking in the animosity.

Chief Jamison makes a thoughtful noise and studies the map. "Hanks, what do you think?"

The detective straightens his tie and plants his hands on his narrow hips.

"I think it'd be best if we searched in both locations, just to be safe."

Jamison shakes his head. "We're a small department, and I'm not sure it's wise to divide our resources."

"Agreed," Hanks counters. "But with such differing witness accounts I'd hate to put all our eggs in one basket, only for it to be the wrong one."

The chief sucks in a breath over his teeth, thinking it over, before nodding. "Alright, Hanks, we'll do it your way." He gives the detective a long look. "Now, I'd like you to choose one of these officers to assist you with the case."

My breath catches. This could be the opportunity toward becoming a detective I've been hoping for. Shadow nuzzles my hand, reassuring me. He always picks up on subtle cues that let him know when I'm feeling heightened emotions.

Detective Hanks scoffs. "I think I'm plenty assisted by the other detectives from the coastal towns."

"That wasn't a request," Chief Jamison presses in his measured, deep voice. "You're going to need local help on this one. We've got a strange homicide that looks like it might have been a ritual killing. This is shaping up to be one of the biggest cases Nightfall's ever seen, and I'm putting as much manpower into it as we can spare."

He rubs his forehead. "It'd be best to get this wrapped up, or at least well underway, before the media gets a hold of it. What with the lunar eclipse this coming weekend and all the events scheduled around it, we're going to have thousands of tourists flocking into Nightfall. And the last thing I need is people questioning our department's competency."

The detective scowls but keeps his lips pressed tightly together.

Chief Jamison raises a dark brow. "Detective Hanks, which officer would you like to work with?"

Hanks grunts and shrugs out of his blazer, tossing it over a chair. He rolls up the shirt sleeves of his button-up chambray, the hem neatly tucked into his jeans. As a detective, he gets to wear plain clothes. I don't know if he's intentionally dragging out this moment, but I pray that he'll make his choice quickly so I can breathe again.

The detective strokes the dark gray stubble on his chin as a sly grin tugs at the corner of his mouth. "How about this." He taps the two spots on the map—the area Bulldog indicated, and the spot near Pine Crest Trail where I suggested we look. "Whoever's search team finds the remains gets to work the case with me."

"Fine." Chief Jamison turns to Bulldog and me. "Mercer, Jensen, assemble your teams. I want you out there ASAP."

Bulldog mutters out of the corner of his mouth, "Good luck, Mercer. Try not to have a meltdown."

I bristle at the jab. I'll never live New Year's Eve down. Then again, a part of me isn't sure I deserve to.

His insults only rankle so much because I know there's truth to them. And I've been down on myself for the grave error I made for weeks. I'm harder on myself than he or any of the other officers could be. Of course, Chief Jamison has been understanding.

I know my late grandfather filled him in on my and my sister's history, so he knows better than most what I've been through. Still, he doesn't have all the details, and even so, he's extended me grace. Just the fact that I'm still on active duty is generous of him, though I did have to go through a medical exam. Everyone knows it, too--so embarrassing. What they don't know is that even one more similar incident, and I'll be put on desk duty and sent to mandatory therapy. I am grateful for the second chance, but also not sure that I'm deserving.

But this isn't about me. This is about finding the remains of this woman and seeking justice for her. And while I sometimes have trouble standing up for myself, it's a lot easier to defend others.

"Sir," I address the chief, "I'd like to bring Shadow with me. We've been working on his cadaver training, and I believe he could be a great asset on this case."

Jamison nods. "Sounds good to me."

Bulldog and I bow our heads and thank the chief and Detective Hanks for the opportunity. As we leave the conference room, Bulldog shoulders me out of the way.

"Good luck working alone," he sneers. "No one's joining your team."

CHAPTER 6

FOUR YEARS AGO

Clay woke up and rubbed his eyes It was really dark, and his neck hurt from sleeping all funny. He yawned a big yawn because he was super tired. They had been driving for so long, he thought maybe they were driving to the end of the world!

He wanted to ask Mama, "Are we there yet?" but he remembered that she got kinda grumpy when he asked too many times.

Mama's friend Laura was always nice to Clay though. She had a big smile and told him he was going to really really like the place they were going. Mama and Laura tried to explain to Clay what was happening, but it was confusing. All he knew was that they were getting a new family, whatever that meant.

Clay looked down at his feet. He was wearing his dinosaur pajamas again with the footies. Grandma usually got him dressed in his pj's for bed. He didn't want a new family. He missed Grandma. Clay hugged Teddy, his favorite stuffed animal, and looked out the window. He couldn't see much except for the dark sky and bright stars.

Really bright stars. He had never seen so many before. His mouth fell open in awe, and he shivered, suddenly aware of how cold it was. The car was bumpy, like they were going over potholes and rocks, and they were rolling along slowly, slower than when they were on the highway.

"Where are we?" Clay asked, his small voice quiet.

His mom glanced back and grinned. "We're finally here, bud."

Clay sat up straighter, interested. He stretched himself to his full height and tried to look out the window, but he was so small he could barely see anything except for all those stars in the big black sky and the branches of trees bouncing overhead.

"The mothership," Mom's friend Laura said quietly.

"Mothership?" Clay asked. They had never told him they were going to a ship.

"Wow." His mama giggled. He hadn't seen her so happy in a long time. "There's a lot of people here."

"Mm-hm," Laura agreed.

Clay leaned against the car door as they turned and then rolled to a stop.

"They've been calling for people to join. New members are coming from all over, just like us." Laura glanced back at Clay and flashed her bright smile, then spun around, turned off the car, and grinned at Clay's mom. "Let's leave the luggage for now. We can come back to get it later."

They unbuckled their seat belts, and then Mama opened Clay's door. Cold night air flooded in, raising goose bumps on his arms and legs. She undid his seat belt and picked him up, resting him on her hip. Clay leaned his head against his mom's shoulder, holding tightly to her and his teddy bear.

They slammed the door shut and walked toward the big

house. Pebbles and rocks crunched under their feet, loud, so loud in the quiet. Clay had never been to a place this quiet or this dark before. There was no sound of airplanes, or cars, or anything else.

The big house stood in front of them, and it seemed like every single light was on, shining brightly behind curtains. One window flashed red, then purple, then green, then blue.

As they neared, a new sound hit Clay. Music, and talking, and laughter.

Mama laughed again. "Sounds like a party."

Laura skipped along beside them, barely able to contain her excitement. "It is; a welcome party." She was smiling so hard, it almost looked like it hurt.

"Hell yeah," Mama cheered. "I thought everybody would be asleep at this time of night."

Laura shook her head. "They've been broadcasting online. Lately it seems like it's a party every night. They have so many new people coming."

Clay wasn't sure he wanted to join the party. He was tired. He wanted quiet. He wanted home. He wanted Grandma. But Clay didn't have a choice. Mama carried him up the stairs onto the porch. The wood planks creaked beneath her and Laura's footsteps. It was cold here. Clay's breath fogged the air, and when he glanced back over Mama's shoulder, he noticed lots of other cars and lots of other buildings. Some were trailers, and some looked like teepees. He had never been anywhere like this before.

Mama raised her fist to knock on the front door, but Laura just laughed. "We don't need to knock. We're home now." She turned the knob on the door, and it swung open, unlocked. A rush of sounds and smells and lights hit Clay, and he gasped.

If he thought the outside of the house was strange, he was utterly shocked by the inside. People, so many people.

A man played a guitar while a woman sang.

The place smelled like incense and something spicy, almost like a skunk.

Christmas lights, like they put up on their tree, were strung everywhere around the room, flashing different colors, while colorful sheets and wind chimes hung from the rafters of the ceiling. It was a big cabin, with a fire crackling in the fireplace, and it was warm, wonderfully warm inside.

"Welcome!" A pretty young woman with long blond hair like Mama's jumped up from the couch and rushed over, wrapping Laura, Clay, and Mama in a big hug like she knew them.

Clay had never met her before, he was sure. And he didn't think his mom had either. Had she? He looked to his mom for guidance, but she just laughed and set him down on the floor. He didn't want to be on the floor; he wanted to be in her arms again. He hugged tight to her leg and tugged at her shirt, but there were more people rushing over, men and women, old and young, all tall, all adults, hugging Mama and Laura.

"Welcome!"

"You made it."

Mama was laughing, and Laura was laughing too, even though she was crying. Clay couldn't tell if Laura was happy or sad. They were hugging everyone, and then they noticed Clay. An older woman with short gray hair who kind of looked like Grandma chuckled and crouched down in front of him.

"Well, hello, little fellow." Clay hugged tighter to his mama's leg, though she was ignoring him. She was too busy talking to the other adults. Clay hid his face against her jeans.

"You don't have to be afraid. I know this is a lot. But you're going to be very happy here." She made a thoughtful noise and fished around in her pocket before pulling out something crinkly. Clay peeked at her with one eye, unsure.

"Would you like a candy?"

Clay's stomach rumbled and ached. He couldn't even think of the last time they ate. When he asked for supper, Mama had said just to wait because they were almost there.

Still, he was unsure. The old woman smiled, and the corners of her eyes got lines like Grandma's. He reached a small hand out and took the candy from her.

"You can call me Terra. If you need anything, you just come and find me." She patted her legs and then stood up, her long flowery skirt swishing around her ankles. Clay closed his fist tightly around the candy but didn't eat it yet. He didn't want to let go of Mama.

But Mama reached down and peeled him off her leg. "Wait, no!" Tears sprang to his eyes, but Mama pushed him away.

"Laura, can you keep an eye on Clay?"

"Of course," Laura sang, still surrounded by all the new grown-ups.

"I'm gonna go hit a joint," Mama said with a wink. She left Clay and joined some other adults in the kitchen. Hazy smoke hung in the air. Clay didn't like the smell.

"Oh, look, another little boy," Laura said.

Clay followed her finger as she pointed at a little boy hiding behind one of the couches. Chairs, couches, and beanbags were scattered around the big room with the tall ceiling.

Some people sat on them, playing songs and singing. Others were beckoning to him and Laura to come join them.

"Why don't you go play? He can be your new friend." Laura gently pushed Clay toward the other little boy. He didn't want to go. He didn't want her to leave him too, like Mama had. He didn't know any of these people.

But then again, maybe another little boy would be his friend. Maybe they could play. He walked past the new adults. They smiled down at him. "Oh, you're so adorable."

"Welcome, little man." A tall guy with a long beard gave him a fist bump, which Clay hesitantly returned.

Everyone seemed nice. Clay walked past the warm fire. It made him feel even sleepier. But he went, like Laura said, and stood beside the boy. The boy was frowning at him. He was taller than Clay and a little older. He didn't have Clay's freckles or his curly hair. Instead, his hair was straight and brown.

And unlike his and Mama's eyes, the little boy's eyes were dark and brown.

"Hi." Clay hugged Teddy tighter to his chest, like his stuffed animal could protect him. The other little boy continued to frown at him, but the woman standing next to him gave him a little nudge.

"River! Aren't you going to introduce yourself to our new family member?" The woman crouched down beside the little boy, her arms around his shoulders. She was wearing a long, flowy shirt and tall boots with tassels. "I'm Luna. And this is my little boy, River. Say hi, River." River continued to scowl at Clay. "Why don't you two play?"

There was a red toy truck on the ground in front of River. Clay crouched down, holding Teddy and the candy in one hand, and reached for the truck to play with River. But the boy shrieked, snatched the truck away, and clutched it to him. "No. I don't want to play with him, Mom."

River's mom gave him a stern look, her eyebrows pinched together. Clay backed up. That was the look his mom gave him when she was mad at him. But instead of spanking or yelling like his mama would do, Luna's face softened into a smile. "Oh, River, go on." She pushed the scowling little boy away and then crouched down again in front of Clay.

"I'm sorry. Sometimes River can be a grump. He's up way past his bedtime. I bet you're pretty tired, too." Clay kept his lips pressed together but nodded a couple of times. "What's your name?" She tipped her head to the side, like a bird.

It took Clay a moment, but he found his voice. "Clay."

"What a cute name." Luna gave him a big smile. "I can't wait to find out what your new name is." She stood up and turned away, joining some of the other adults in conversation.

Clay lingered beside the couch, hugging Teddy tight to his chest. New name? He was going to have a new name?

He didn't want a new name. He didn't want a new place. He wanted his old room and his old grandma.

He looked for Mama, but she was still in that smoky kitchen. He looked for Laura. But Laura was laughing and talking and crying with a group of adults and didn't even look over at him.

Clay's stomach hurt, and not just with hunger. He didn't feel good here. He wished he could just climb into his bed and close his eyes and wake up back at Grandma's house.

But he was also cold. So Clay wandered back over to the fireplace.

There were some grown-ups sitting in a circle in front of it. An old man gave him a big smile. He was missing some teeth.

"Hey, kiddo. Welcome to the mothership."

Clay frowned. "Where's the ship?"

All the adults started laughing, which only made Clay feel worse. He didn't understand the joke or what was so funny.

A woman with curly white hair gave him a tight smile. "Welcome night is always confusing for all of us. It's gonna get easier. We just call headquarters the mothership because it's our home. And someday, the big mothership in the sky is going to pull Source up in a beam of light, and all of us with her, and we're gonna live in a brand-new, wonderful world."

Clay had no idea what she was talking about. None of this made sense. He didn't want to get pulled up in a ship, and he didn't know who Source was, either. He said nothing and turned away, crawling up onto the warm stone bench that surrounded the fireplace. He hugged Teddy tight to his chest and tucked his feet up under him.

There were some big pillows and cushions on the bench, and he leaned into them, closing his eyes. The noises of laughter, music, singing, and talking blended into the crackle of the fire. Clay's eyes grew heavy.

He didn't want to be here, but he couldn't stay awake any longer.

When Clay opened his eyes again, the room was quieter. He didn't know where he was at first. He jolted upright and looked around, panicked. Where was Mama? Where was Grandma? His bed, his room?

"Shh." He looked to his left, where a tall, thin woman with yellow hair and blue eyes stared down at him.

"Hello, little one."

Clay didn't know what to say. Who was she? Where did she come from? Where was he? The room had gone quiet. Everyone was staring at him. No, they were staring at the woman next to him.

Mama was standing in the doorway to the kitchen. And Laura was drawing closer, her hands clasped together, tears running down her face. She was staring at the woman next to Clay like she was in love with her.

Clay turned back to the woman beside him. She was wearing a long, flowy white dress, and he was struck by how much she looked like figures from their Christmas decorations. Maybe that's why they had Christmas lights all over the house.

He gazed up at her. "You look like an angel."

The woman laughed in a pretty way. When the woman laughed, everyone else in the room laughed too. Even Clay couldn't help but smile.

"I'm Source." The woman placed a hand against her chest. She smiled down at Clay, her eyes dancing. "And what's your name?"

"Clay." Something about this woman made him want to answer right away. Like she could see through him, like she already knew him. She smiled. Her teeth were white and straight.

"Welcome, Clay. Welcome to all our new family." She spread her arms wide, and as she did so, placed a hand on Clay's back.

Her hand was cold, really cold through his clothes, but it felt good now. He had warmed up, sitting beside the fire, and now he was almost too hot.

Source's hand slid to his shoulder and tugged him closer to her. He didn't dare resist. Even though she was very thin, she was very strong. Her hand clamped down around Clay's shoulder.

"Welcome, all, to the Ascendant Light Fellowship. Welcome to your new family." The adults cheered and whooped and clapped. Someone played a drum with his hands. Clay felt excited and nervous. Scared, but also happy.

Maybe he would like this new place. Maybe it wasn't so bad.

"By joining us," Source continued, her long hair flowing in waves over her shoulders, "you leave your old world and your old life behind. Here, at the Ascendent Light Fellowship, we relinquish our ties to the outside world, to the material, and commit instead to ourselves, our family, and the true source of all good and life in this world."

This time, instead of cheering, the others nodded their heads or bowed them, murmuring their agreement, kind of like they did in church when Grandma took him. He frowned. Did giving up his old life mean he had to give up Grandma too? But he missed Grandma.

Source smiled down at him, and some of the unease in his stomach relaxed. "In welcoming you to your new family, we bestow upon you new names, which have been told to me by the Elders." She looked toward the ceiling, lifting her palm as though she was being showered in rain or catching snowflakes.

She looked at Mama standing in the kitchen. "Welcome to Joy Ackerman. You are hereby known as... Gaia." The room broke out into loud cheers again. Mama looked happy. She smiled and pumped her arm in the air.

Could Clay still call her Mama?

Source turned to Laura, who had wandered directly in front of her. She was on her knees, tears running down her face and hands clasped as though she was praying.

"Laura Steen," Source said, "You shall now be known as Rainbow."

Laura sobbed. Was she sad?

She shook her head. "I love it. I love it. Thank you." She lowered her forehead to the colorful rug on the floor, bowing down to Source.

Clay looked at the blond woman beside him, confused. Who was this woman? Should he be bowing?

Source looked down and met Clay's eyes. Her bright blue eyes seemed to glow.

She had a nice smile, but something about it made Clay feel weird inside. It kinda looked like the scary smiley cat from the Alice story Grandma read to him sometimes. The cat that knew secret things. "And you, Clay Ackerman, I can sense in you something special. Something beyond." The room got quiet, and Clay felt shy. He hugged Teddy higher so that just his eyes peeked above the little bear's ears.

"You, little one, are destined for greatness. You have been noticed by the Elders."

Laura gasped and covered her mouth. Her gaze darted between Clay and Source. Clay didn't understand what any of this meant.

"You, little one"—Source squeezed Clay's shoulder tighter, so much it almost hurt—"shall now be known as Chosen One." Gasps sounded around the room.

And then it went so quiet that the crackling of the fire sounded loud. "You are the Chosen One. You have been chosen by the Elders and the cosmic forces to play an important part in Earth's redemption."

Laura now turned toward Clay and again lowered her forehead to the rug. The others gaped at Clay with wide eyes.

Had he been chosen for something? For what? What was this woman talking about?

Source stood, and with her hands still tightly clutching Clay's shoulder, guided him off the bench and onto his feet.

"As always, we have an initiation ceremony, which involves symbolically letting go of what ties us to our past, to the material, false world. Gaia, Rainbow, please come forward."

Mama handed something that looked like a cigarette to the man next to her and weaved her way through all the others gathered in the big room with the tall ceiling. Clay reached out for her hand, but Source gently tugged him away, out of reach.

She gestured at the burning orange fire in the fireplace. "Like all before you, I invite you to sacrifice your IDs. Let go of who you once were and embrace your new life… with us."

Laura fished around in her pocket without hesitation, pulled out her wallet, and then took out her license with her picture on it. She tossed it into the fire, and Clay watched as the edges turned black. The plastic peeled back in layers, and the whole thing crumpled in on itself, melting. The people in the room cheered and made a lot of noise.

Mama didn't act right away.

She frowned at Source. "Seriously? We have to burn them? What if I want to drive somewhere?"

Source smiled, but her eyes weren't smiling. "We have an understanding with local officers. Besides, we're pretty self-sufficient out here. You're not going to need to go anywhere."

After a moment, Mama shrugged, pulled her own wallet out, and threw her license into the fire. Everyone clapped and whistled.

Then Source turned to Clay. "And now it's your turn, Chosen One."

Clay frowned, and the room quieted down. "But... I don't have one."

Source crouched down in front of him so that she was staring at him, eye to eye. Her eyes were so blue and so icy it seemed like he could see into them, like one of his glass marbles. "Chosen One. It's true, you don't have a license. But you have something tying you to your past, to your life before us, and you must let go of it."

Clay stared at her and blinked, confused. He didn't know what she was talking about.

She raised her eyebrows and then looked down, right at Teddy.

"No." Clay hugged Teddy tight to his chest. He loved Teddy. Teddy had always been with him. He always slept with him. He had always had him, as long as he could remember. When he was scared or sad, he whispered to Teddy, telling him all his problems and secrets and fears and wishes.

Teddy was his best and only friend.

"It must be done," Source said. She was smiling, but her face was frozen.

Clay's chin trembled. He looked around. All the adults were staring at him. The other little boy, River, was laughing at him. Tears rolled down Clay's cheeks. "No, not Teddy."

He looked to Mama for help, but she just looked away. He looked to Laura next. But she just gave him a big smile and a nod. "It's worth it, Chosen One, I promise."

He couldn't do it. He couldn't.

But Source took him by the shoulders and turned him around. She grabbed him behind the elbows, and she was strong, her fingers digging into his skin. She pushed his arms straight, forcing him to hold Teddy to the fire.

"No!" Clay cried harder now. He wouldn't let go, but as Source forced him to stretch his arms toward the fire, the flames heated his hands, burning him, so that he was forced to let go.

As soon as he did, Teddy dropped into the flames, and Source tugged Clay back out of harm's way. He tried to run forward to rescue Teddy as the flames licked at his fur, making it clump together, melting his big brown eyes, but Source held him back, pinning him to her.

"No," Clay screamed. "No." He was crying now, sobbing. He dropped to the ground.

Source gently patted his head and dropped down beside him, whispering soothingly in his ear. "It's alright, Chosen One. It's alright. I promise you, your sacrifice will not be in vain. I'm taking you under my wing, little one. You're ours now."

CHAPTER 7

Nathan, Shadow, and I walk along the soft dirt path, our footsteps nearly silent on the wet leaves and earth. I'm filled with adrenaline and excitement and have to keep reminding myself to pace myself. This is a marathon, not a sprint. Likely we'll be out here searching for hours, if not days.

And excitement is probably the wrong word. One should never be *excited* to find a dead body in the forest. But I am driven. I want to find this woman, whoever she is, and get justice for her.

I also want to win. I so badly want to work this case. I need it. I need a chance to prove I have what it takes. Not only to Chief Jamison and the other officers, but to myself.

Back at the station, Nathan and I reviewed maps of the area, delineated a grid, and punched it into our GPS. I reviewed the terrain, noting areas I thought might match Jenna's description of the slope on which they found the woman's remains. It turned out that Bulldog was right about one thing—nobody wanted to join my team, except for Nathan.

I was chagrined, sure, but I'd expected as much. While

Bulldog and his cronies bullied me, the others weren't exactly hostile just...distant. It was partially my own fault I hadn't made stronger connections on the force. I didn't go out with the others for drinks after work, and I was naturally a bit reserved and tended to keep to myself. Plus, it didn't help my case that I was the only woman at the station and everyone knew my history as the weird cult girl.

I shrugged it off. So what if no one besides Nathan wanted to join me. It'd only make it all the more gratifying when we discovered that woman's remains before Bulldog's team.

From there, we'd called the park ranger, who closed the trail to the public, and headed out. Jenna and John's dusty Jeep still sat alone in the lot. We scanned the otherwise empty gravel parking area for evidence but didn't find much aside from some candy wrappers and cigarette butts. Still, we can't be too methodical, so we bagged them all up and locked them in the SUV.

Now, we plod along the first leg of the Pine Crest Trail, eyes scanning the wilderness and Shadow sweeping the ground with his well-trained nose. Though the tall pines that close in above us help shield us from some of the rain, it patters steadily against the hoods of our raincoats, wetting and darkening Shadow's fur. It's been raining since last night. There's almost no chance of spotting footprints, but we still keep an eye out for them. And luckily, Shadow and his amazing nose aren't inhibited by a little water.

I'm a big fan of continuing education and take every course I can convince the chief to let me attend. I'm especially keen on training Shadow. I think of him as my secret power. Ever since I rescued him from a life of neglect, he's been bonded to me, step by step, always by my side. That's why I named him Shadow. It's what my grandma started calling him—my little shadow. Though right now, he trots along ahead of us on his long lead. We use a different one than his normal leash for searches, so he has more room to explore, but we're still linked. It's more for his safety than anything. Out here in the wilderness, especially, it's easy to get hurt with sharp drop-offs and wildlife.

That sweet, malnourished little puppy has now grown into a beautiful, intelligent, loyal dog. I love working with him. Not just for his great nose, but for the emotional support he always lends me. And he's not the only one I have to be grateful for.

I glance over at Nathan. His blond hair is matted to his forehead from the rain. And maybe it's just the filtered light trickling in through the gray clouds, but he looks pale.

I give him a little smile when he turns and catches me staring up at him. "Hey, just wanted to say thank you."

He grins, which brings out his double dimples. "For what?"

I snort. "For being here with me and Shadow."

Back at the station, Detective Hanks had explained the situation to the other officers, setting Bulldog and me up as team captains, more or less.

"I'll leave it up to you officers," Hanks had announced, a smirk tugging at the corner of his mouth. "You decide who you want to join in the search."

Every single officer, every last one aside from Nathan Brooks, had joined Bulldog. If it wasn't for Nathan, I'd have been entirely alone out here. A hawk screeches in the distance, its cry echoing out over the treetops, and tall ferns line the path, their curling fronds bouncing in the rain.

Nathan gives me a disbelieving look. "Of course, Eden. What was I gonna do? Join Bulldog?" He scoffs. "He'd probably have made me go march in the opposite direction just for a laugh." He shakes his head, and I give him a rueful grin.

"You're not wrong."

He nods. "Besides, I think you've got it right about where to search."

I gesture at the winding path ahead of us. "We're miles

away and on the other side of the highway from where Bulldog claims they were. There's no way they would have made it all the way to the bluffs above Nightfall without noticing that they'd crossed the highway."

"Exactly," Nathan agrees, his hands shoved in the pockets of his rain slicker. "Besides, I trust your instincts."

I have my misgivings there, but don't voice my doubt. I need to be a leader here. Nathan has put his trust in me, and I need to prove that he's been right to.

We slow as we reach a bend in the trail, which curves north, away from the coast. I stop, and Shadow, out on his long lead, comes trotting back to stand beside me. He gazes up at me with his ears perked and dark eyes curious.

I consult one of the many maps stuffed into my pockets. One shows the terrain, another holds the grid we've marked out, and the one I unfold is a trail map. I tap at the page, then look up at the dirt path curving in front of us.

"Jenna Morales says that where the path curved north, her partner, Mr. Sinks, indicated he knew of a shortcut. They'd continued to head west toward the coast, heading off trail." I look to my left, and Nathan follows my gaze into the dense forest.

"All right." Nathan clears his throat, his voice notably hoarse. "Let's go." I stuff the trail map back into my raincoat's pocket, then pull the grid map out of the other. I once again try to get the app on my phone working, but I have no reception out here. I've been trying since the parking lot without any luck. The GPS device isn't much better. Ideally, we'd be marking our progress via GPS. It's more accurate and it can't get ruined in the rain; but unfortunately we can't seem to get any signal at all, whether via phone or satellite connection.

I shake my head, frustrated, and stuff my phone away. "Paper map it is." I pull a red pen out of my pocket, uncap it with my teeth, and make a little X in the corner of the map.

"Quadrant 1, here we go."

Nathan reaches into the messenger bag slung across his broad shoulders and fishes out a bright yellow flag on a thin wire. He hands it to me, and I slide it into the ground right at the edge of the path, marking the beginning of the first quadrant.

We step into the forest. The already dim light immediately grows darker as we thread our way between the dense trees, leaving the trail behind.

Jenna gave us her bandanna so Shadow can track her scent, if any lingers after all the rain. We also attended a training for cadaver searches and I've been working with my dog on picking up the smell of human remains. I let Shadow out maybe 30 or 40 feet ahead of me, to give him room to sniff and follow any trails or scents he might pick up, but keep him close enough to stay out of danger.

That's my main job, after all. To keep Shadow and Nathan safe on this rough, uneven terrain. I shake my head again, thinking of the hikers.

No wonder Jenna was pissed at her maybe-boyfriend for getting them lost out here. It's more dangerous than most people realize. What with the rough terrain, the cliffs over the sea, the cold and rain—it's easy to get disoriented, lost, and succumb to the elements.

While we search for the dead woman, we have to make sure not to end up sharing her fate. Biting wind blows through the tree trunks, rustling the leaves and sending down a shower of cold raindrops.

I shiver, stick my free hand in my pocket, and tromp on, climbing over pine needles, fallen logs, and skirting ferns and brush.

This is going to be a long day.

CHAPTER 8

EIGHT WEEKS AGO

Joy Ackerman trudged across the muddy field that divided her yurt from the mothership. Compared to her primitive living conditions, which lacked electricity, running water, heat, or even a bed, the giant cabin where Source and her inner circle lived was practically a mansion.

Resentment burned in Joy's throat, making it grow tight. She threw the hood of her jacket over her head and wrapped her arms around herself, pulling the sleeves over her frozen hands. Shivering, she dodged a muddy puddle as rain pattered down.

During the summer, Oregon was beautiful, all perfect weather and sunny blue skies, but in the middle of November, it was nothing but rain and cold and more rain, and if you were lucky, snow. She huffed. *I guess at least it isn't snowing… yet.*

As she stomped up the wooden steps to the porch, she passed a little clique of Source's handmaids and serving men, as she called them. Joy fought not to roll her eyes. Her former friend, Laura, who now went by Rainbow, stood among them.

Source required them all to go by the names she'd given them. But in her own private mind, Joy couldn't bear to think of Laura as Rainbow. She sneered as she passed her fake former friend. Laura had dumped her practically as soon as they'd arrived to serve Source, and serve she did.

Laura was practically Source's slave. She spent morning to night documenting everything Source did in reams of notebooks. Everything she ate, everything she said, every time she sneezed, and every time she farted.

Joy rolled her eyes. She threw open the screen door and pushed into the house.

She'd never been that devoted to Source, which was probably why she was constantly doing penance for challenging her. She sighed and stomped her feet. At least it was warm in here. A fire crackled in the fireplace, though the big room sat mostly empty.

She inhaled the heavenly scent of bacon wafting in from the kitchen, and her stomach rumbled. When was the last time she'd eaten? Sure, they'd had some meager morsels last night, but when was the last time she'd *really* eaten? Only Source and the inner circle got luxuries like bacon. The rest of the fifty or sixty poor saps living on the compound had to make do with oatmeal, porridge, and scrambled eggs... when they got lucky enough for some protein.

She wrapped her jacket tighter around her. The garment had felt tight on her when they'd arrived four years ago, but now she was swimming in it. She didn't know how much weight she'd lost, as there weren't scales or mirrors on the compound. But she knew she was thin. Everyone here was thin. No one had enough to eat.

She dragged her feet to the small closet under the stairs and glanced up the staircase. Somewhere up there, probably in Source's room, where all the inner circle hung out, was her little boy. She only caught glimpses of him when everyone gathered here in the mothership.

Maybe that was what she deserved. She'd never been a great mom, if she was honest with herself.

Joy opened the little cupboard, fished out a bucket, some rags, yellow rubber gloves, and cleaning powder and liquid, and hauled them over to the bathroom, kicking the door closed behind her.

She stuffed her hands into the yellow rubber gloves that reached nearly to her elbows. This punishment, as she saw it, was probably deserved. Four years ago, when she, Laura, and Clay had first arrived at the compound, she'd viewed her son as a burden.

But now she missed him.

In fact, she was now doing this penance of cleaning all the bathrooms in the big house for challenging Source about wanting to spend more time with Clay.

But Source never let Clay out of her sight. Not since her revelation that first night that Clay was the Chosen One. Since then, Joy had barely had two conversations with the little boy alone, and that had been years ago. Now she barely recognized him. He'd grown so much since then.

He'd gotten his tan skin from his father, along with his tight curls, but still had her freckles across the bridge of his nose and cheeks. She always saw him with a book in his hands. How had he even learned to read? Had Source taught him? Laura? She set her jaw, grinding her teeth as she fished the toilet brush out of the bucket and began to scrub away at the bowl.

How had she ended up here?

Things had started out so great. When they'd first arrived, everyone had hugged them. They'd shared food, drink, good weed, and greeted them as if they were long-lost friends. It had been nothing but love, acceptance, and partying. It was the escape she'd needed. When they'd first arrived at the compound, the Ascendant Light Fellowship had felt like a breath of fresh air, like heaven on earth.

And here she was scrubbing toilets, always in the doghouse, shunned and isolated by Source and her inner circle.

All that love and acceptance and friendship at the beginning, and now? She felt constantly isolated and lonely. She couldn't even get close enough to her own child to give him a hug.

She'd leave, but Joy had no money. She'd given it all to Source when they'd arrived. Hell, she didn't even have a license. They'd burned that.

Maybe she could call her mom? Her stomach tightened at just the thought of it. No way. It would be too embarrassing to go crawling back to her. She'd never hear the end of it.

Joy channeled some of her frustration into scrubbing at the toilet bowl.

When she finally got the thing shining, she stuffed the brush back in the bucket and grabbed a rag to wipe down the sink.

But in those quiet moments between tasks, she heard the whisper of voices filtering in through the vent. One voice she recognized—Source. She frowned and listened.

"...plans for the boy must be kept quiet until it's near."

Joy's mouth dropped open. She quietly closed the seat of the toilet and climbed on top of it, straining to bring her ear closer to the metal vent high up in the wall. More whispers.

"He's been chosen."

Her heart pounded against her ribs. What was Source talking about? Did she mean Clay? She rose on her toes, straining to catch the quiet words.

KNOCK KNOCK KNOCK!

She jumped and nearly tumbled off the toilet, slamming into the wall behind in her panic.

"Hey, I need to get in there!" came a man's deep voice.

Joy's chest heaved as she fought to catch her breath. "I'm almost done," she managed to mumble. She stared up at the vent.

What was Source planning?

―――

Later that night, Joy leaned against one of the big timber poles that supported the cabin's exposed beams. She lingered in the back of the assembled group, a loosely woven blanket wrapped over her shoulders. A meager defense from the cold. She scowled. Seemed like it was always cold here. Of course, it was warmer in the mothership at least, but she dreaded returning to her yurt with its thin sleeping pad on the dirt and the cold night she'd spend shivering, trying to sleep with her four yurt-mates.

Source, who stood beside the river rock fireplace, was droning on about something or other related to the group's online crystal sales. It was all made-up hippie stuff in Joy's mind, but Source and her right-hand man, Orion, were always pushing more sales to help fund the group. He stood beside her now, hands clasped behind his back, his dark hair slicked back. Not like Joy saw any bit of the profit, so what was her motivation?

The only reason she paid any attention was because of her son. An orange fire crackled in the fireplace, casting Source and Clay, beside her, in red light. Joy shifted on her feet and glanced around the crowded room. How was everyone so entranced by Source? Was she the only one who didn't think the woman was truly a divine being? Was Joy the only one who saw through her bullshit?

Sometimes it felt like it. Anytime Joy tried to hint at her feelings with another member, they would scowl at her or look shocked. And inevitably, word would get back to Source, and Joy would find herself doing penance… again.

Just like she'd been doing this morning when she cleaned the bathrooms in the big house. She'd had an uneasy feeling in her stomach ever since then. Well, an uneasy feeling layered on top of the constant gnaw of hunger. They'd all gathered this evening for the nightly communal dinner. Source and her inner circle ate first, with generous servings of pulled pork and sweet-smelling cornbread, while the rest of them got meager portions of canned soup that was more broth than anything.

Joy's stomach grumbled, and she pressed a hand to it. Her ribs pushed through from under her T-shirt.

It was the silence that made Joy look up. For once, Source wasn't going on and on. The woman loved the sound of her own voice. Instead, she was staring with those piercing blue eyes out at her followers, her eyes skimming over each one. She even met Joy's gaze for a fraction of a moment. She stood limned in the golden light of the fire, which made her blond hair shine.

For a moment, Joy could understand why so many saw her as divine. But any feelings of reverence she might have had dissipated as soon as her gaze landed on the little boy beside Source, hiding in her shadow.

Clay stood there, his head hanging. Some book—it was hard to read from here, but it looked like it might be *The Hobbit*—was clutched against his chest.

Even as a toddler, Clay had been quiet and shy. But ever since Source had taken him under her wing, as she put it, the little boy had become downright withdrawn. He barely spoke to anyone. And of course, anytime Joy tried to talk with him, much less get him alone, she was chastised by Source.

Joy set her jaw, clenching her teeth so hard they hurt. Source acted like she was Clay's mother. Of course, she claimed she *was* Goddess, which made her all their mothers.

For just a moment, her little boy looked up, and their eyes met across the room. He'd gotten much of his coloring from his father, but those blue eyes were all Joy's. And those little blue eyes widened, the whites showing all around, as though pleading with her. Joy's stomach sank.

"Children." Source's resonant voice broke the silence and the moment between Joy and Clay.

The blond woman was gorgeous, Joy had to give her that. With her flowing hair, long white robes, and icy blue eyes, she was certainly captivating. Her voice was deeper than you'd expect and only added to her mystique.

She spread her palms. "I have received a new revelation from our elders, from the ascendants."

A collective murmur swept through the room as members turned to each other in excitement. Source waited for the commotion to die down.

"I shall detail it in time, but for now, I will tell you this. We must prepare for a grand ceremony in two months' time. A ceremony that will help to usher in the Reckoning."

Gasps sounded around the room, and Joy stood upright, pushing away from the pole she'd been leaning against. A grand ceremony? Is that what she'd overheard Source speaking about this morning through the vents in the bathroom? Did this have to do with what Source had said about the boy?

The hairs rose on the back of Joy's neck.

"Tonight, rest and rejoice. Soon, soon I will reveal more of the elders' grand plan." Source concluded the announcement, and the dozens of members devolved into excited conversations, gathering around Source, professing their devotion.

Joy stayed back, a strange stirring within her.

While she had never much cared for her parents, finding them overbearing and stifling, she had never much cared for herself, either. Time after time, she had found herself in dangerous situations, hurt, taken advantage of, betrayed by people she'd once called friends.

What did it really matter? She wasn't anyone important anyway.

But now she felt a burning in her core. A sense of purpose. A sense of conviction.

Was this maternal instinct, she wondered. Because suddenly, she felt it imperative to find out what they meant to do in this grand ceremony and if it involved her son.

With her heart racing, Joy inched toward the stairs. Her gaze ricocheted around the room, but no one looked her way. Perhaps, in some ways, her isolation from the others was a blessing, because no one paid her any attention as she slowly crept up the staircase, watching constantly to see if someone would notice. It was as if she were invisible.

Once she reached the top of the stairs, she darted across the landing and slipped into Source's room, easing the door mostly closed behind her. She stood there a moment, surveying the space. She'd only been allowed up here a few times. It had been at least a year since her last visit. This was where Source and her inner circle spent most of their time. This was where Source kept Clay, away from her.

Like much of the rest of the mothership, white Christmas lights hung in strings all across the ceiling and wove through the posts of the bed frame. Colorful curtains covered the windows. The bed itself was a big pile of purple, teal, and gold blankets, and pillows and cushions of every size and shape.

She darted to the right toward a long row of low bookcases that lined the entire wall. She stopped short when she noticed the small bedroll just beside the nightstand, wedged in between the king-size bed and the bookcase.

Just a small pillowcase, speckled with stars and spaceships, and a matching sleeping bag. This was Clay's bed; this was where her son slept.

Source always kept him close, even through the night. Books lined the bottom shelf next to the little boy's sleeping bag. They were all fantasy novels, from *The Return of the King* to *Harry Potter* to *A Wrinkle in Time*.

At least Source allowed him that escape. It was clearly the only part of his personality he was allowed to express. Joy cast a nervous glance at the door, then continued scanning the bookshelves. Every inch of the rest of them were stuffed with wire-bound notebooks. She pulled one out at random and skimmed through the pages of cramped handwriting.

9 a.m. Source is snoring. She says that she never sleeps, only astral travels. She says that when she's snoring, it's actually an indication that she's speaking with the elders.

Joy rolled her eyes. *Either that, or she has sleep apnea.* She flipped to the next page and found a detailed account of Source's bowel movements, including hand-drawn illustrations. *Ugh.* Crinkling her nose in disgust, she closed the notebook and shoved it back into its place on the shelf.

These were Rainbow's detailed journals of every single one of Source's revelations, visions, every sentence she uttered, plus every bowel movement, apparently. Where would her most recent notebook be? Joy ran her fingers over the wire-bound spines of the notebooks, skimming.

As she moved from left to right, she noticed a single notebook sitting on top of the bookcase and snatched it up. She pressed her back against the wall, keeping one eye on the door, and flipped it open. She noted the date at the top of one of the pages. It was from earlier in November. This must be the current month's journal.

Joy flipped to the back, to the last page of writing with trembling hands. It was a violation for her to be in Source's room without invitation. Source considered herself sacred, as did the others. This sacredness extended to her space and possessions.

Rainbow and Source were the only people authorized to look through these notebooks, which were considered divine records.

Joy flipped to the last page and scanned Rainbow's cramped handwriting. She passed a 10:07 sneeze, a detailed account of Source's lunch of chili and cornbread with exactly one tablespoon of honey, and then found what she was looking for.

She covered her mouth to stifle the cry that wanted to escape her lips. Joy let out a choked sob. She read on, her trembling finger following the line of the paper.

"Oh my god," Joy muttered out loud.

"What are you doing?"

She jumped at the high-pitched voice, startled, and looked up from the journal.

Laura stood just inside the door, her big doe eyes wide. She already constantly looked surprised, but now she looked downright shocked, her mouth agape. "What are you doing up here?"

Joy slammed the notebook shut.

"You're not allowed to be here. Don't touch that." Laura rushed forward and snatched the notebook from Joy's hands with a strength that surprised her. Laura had always been thin, but her time at the compound had turned her downright skeletal. And yet here she was, practically vibrating with anger. She shoved Joy back, and she stumbled, nearly falling over.

"This is Source's sacred space. You are not allowed to read this."

"S-sorry," Joy sputtered, before she darted past her, out onto the landing, and ran down the stairs.

CHAPTER 9

Achoo!

I glance over at Nathan, shooting him a dubious look, and plant my cold, wet feet. Shadow's sniffing up ahead, winding between tree trunks.

We've been searching for the remains for over two hours, and we're losing the light. The sun's not setting quite yet, but the overhead clouds have turned dark and ominous. We've had no luck yet. I'm cold, tired, and starving.

I know Nathan's got to be feeling the same way. Yet he hasn't complained once. He sniffles, rubs his nose with the back of his hand, which is just as wet as the rest of him, then sneezes again. The rain's coming down in earnest now. We've both donned the ponchos Nathan had packed in his bag.

The rain sounds loud, pattering against the plastic around my ears.

"Nathan?" He doesn't hear me at first. "Nathan," I say louder. He turns and raises his brows in question.

I give him a wan smile. "You've been sneezing for the past ten minutes."

He sniffles. "Sorry about that." His voice is hoarse and

scratchy, and his nose glows bright red. Red rims his bright blue eyes as well, and I cock my head.

"You're sick."

He coughs, a deep raspy cough from deep in his chest, and shakes his head. "No, I'm not. It's allergies."

I bark out a laugh. "This isn't allergies. We've been out in the cold in a torrential downpour for hours. Come on." I tip my head back the way we've come. "Let's head back to the car and regroup."

He shakes his head. "No, Eden, I'm fine." He continues on, eyes glued to the ground, searching for evidence, but I hurry forward and grab his arm.

He sneezes again and then turns towards me.

"Come on, Nathan. You're catching a cold. Let's head back." He opens his mouth as if to protest, then sniffles and hangs his head in defeat.

"I'm sorry, Eden. I know how important this is to you. I don't want to be the one slowing you down."

I can't believe he'd think that way. I squeeze his hand. It's just as cold as mine.

"You're not slowing me down. You're the only one who believed in me enough to come out here. But we all need a break. Even Shadow." We both glance at my German Shepherd, whose ears perk up at his name. "Come on, boy." I pat my thigh. "Let's head back to the car."

We retrace our steps, searching a new section of the grid on the way so the trip isn't wasted. We rejoin the trail and from there walk the short way back to the police SUV.

I insist Nathan climb into the driver's seat and let Shadow hop into the back. I slide into the passenger side, my boots making a muddy mess of the floorboards.

I pull back the plastic of my poncho, as does Nathan, and he turns the ignition, cranking the heat up to high. Once the car warms up, it's going to feel like heaven in here. Maybe I'll even start to feel my fingertips again.

He starts to shift the car into Drive, but I place a hand on his forearm, stalling him.

"What's up?" He blinks at me with his red-rimmed eyes. "I thought you wanted to call it for the day."

It's just after three thirty, rainy, and we're losing light quickly. It might be reasonable to head in and regroup to make another pass tomorrow. But I shake my head. "I think *you* need to go home. I can't stop yet."

He takes his hands off the wheel. We're sitting alone in the parking lot. "I'm not leaving you out here all by yourself."

I reach into the back seat and ruffle my dog's wet fur. "I won't be alone. I've got Shadow."

He shakes his head. "It's not safe. It's gonna be dark soon and it's against protocol."

He's set his messenger bag on the console between us, and I pull it closer to me, flipping the flap open. I rummage around inside and pull out a heavy flashlight, clicking it on. "I'll have light." I hold it under my chin for a moment, making a scary face.

He smirks but shakes his head. "I don't feel good about this." He coughs into the crook of his arm and sniffles. "Eden, this woman's remains have been out here for goodness knows how long. One more night isn't gonna make a difference."

I give my only friend on the force a smile as the rain pings down against the metal of the car roof. "I know it won't make a difference to *her*, but it will to me. This might be my only chance to prove myself." Nathan gives me a reluctant nod.

"Besides, I do hate the idea of her being out here all alone." I grimace at the misty forest. "She deserves justice, and while I'm not sure how much I deserve a chance at making detective, I know I'm sure as shit a better candidate than Bulldog."

Nathan snorts out a laugh. "You've got me there."

I nibble my lip, mulling this all over. "But, you're right. It wouldn't be safe to search the wilderness without any way to get in touch. How about a compromise?"

My friend gives me a curious look.

"Do you feel well enough to rest in the car for a couple of hours?"

He snorts. "Where it's dry, warm, and has heated seats? Yeah, I'd be just fine. Why?"

I splay my palms. "I propose that Shadow and I head back out and keep searching, while you wait here and get some rest. I'll check in every hour and I'll only be at it until 6, when we'd normally clock out anyway. If I don't check in, you'll know to send help, and I'll tell you exactly which quadrants I'll be searching so, in the event I get injured, you'll know exactly where to send rescuers."

He frowns, but I can tell he's considering my idea. "I'd feel better if we could reliably communicate."

I grin. "I thought of that, too." I reach into the back seat and retrieve our portable signal repeater. We packed a bunch of gear before leaving the station, and though at the time Nathan and I had no plans on splitting up, I'm glad I had the hunch to bring it. "I'll stick this up in a tree right before I leave the trail, so its roughly halfway between us and it should help us keep in radio contact."

Nathan lets out a resigned sigh. "Fine. You win." He glares, though a grin tugs at the corner of his mouth. "Just don't kill yourself trying to climb some tree."

I chuckle and press a hand to my heart. "Scout's honor. Now…want to eat? I'm starving."

Nathan, who can normally wolf down an excessive amount of food and stay magically trim in spite of it, cringes as I pull two thermoses from a bag in the back seat. "No thanks." He sniffles. "I don't have an appetite and probably couldn't taste it anyway."

I set his in the cup holder anyway, in case he changes his

mind. Then reach back again and pull out a Tupperware container that Shadow is suddenly very interested in.

I pop the lid off. It's full of kibble, with Shadow's favorite chicken topper drizzled over the dry nuggets. It actually smells kind of good, like chicken stew. I hand it back, setting it on the seat beside him, and Shadow immediately starts chowing down.

Nathan raises his brows. "Wow. He was hungry."

I chuckle and twist my thermos open. We swung by my house on our way to the trail to grab Shadow's raincoat. When Grandma heard what we were up to, she insisted we also take some chicken noodle soup she'd just finished cooking and a meal for Shadow. At the time I'd been impatient to get out searching, but now I'm incredibly grateful for my Grandma's foresight.

I pour some steaming soup into the thermos top, using it as a cup. Nathan leans back in the seat as he watches me slurp down the delicious soup. "You really think you're going to find her today?"

I don't answer for a moment. I'm too busy enjoying the warm salty broth, the chicken chunks, the noodles, peas, and carrots. My fingers are slowly starting to gain feeling again. Honestly, I haven't tasted anything this good in ages. I savor it for a moment longer, then lower the soup from my lips to answer.

"Honestly, I'm not sure. But I know if I quit now, it's all I'll be able to think about until we hit the trail again tomorrow morning." I give him a dubious look. He's pale, red nosed, and looks exhausted. "If you're feeling better by then, of course." I give my friend a concerned look.

We hang out for another fifteen minutes or so, and by the time Shadow and I climb back out of the SUV, I'm feeling recharged. I'm warm, I've got a full belly, and I'm more determined to find this woman than ever. Nathan waves, then holds up his radio and points at it, reminding me to keep in touch. I nod, grinning at my friend, then head back to the trail. It's a good idea to be cautious and follow protocol as closely as we can, but to be honest, I think he's overly concerned about me. I hike all the time--I've got this. I sling the heavy messenger bag across my shoulders, pull out the flashlight, and take up Shadow's long lead.

Just before I leave the trail to start searching the next quadrant, which Nathan and I agreed to, I set my phone alarm to go off in fifty minutes. I'll check in with Nathan then, either by radio or it should give me enough time to scramble back to the parking lot if I need to do it in person. I then choose a young spruce tree, scramble up a couple of low branches and wedge the repeater as high up as I can reasonably reach. Height helps the repeater work better, especially in terrain as unforgiving as this, so the meager boost I'm giving it probably won't make much difference. But it's better than nothing, and not like I can climb one of the tall, smooth trunked pines towering all around us. It'll have to do.

With that, Shadow and I head back into the dark forest. The light's almost completely gone, and with no one on the trail, or in the forest, it's both beautiful and spooky.

An owl hoots in the near distance, and the rain pours down steadily against my poncho.

Shadow and I continue searching for the next hour. We find nothing. I stumble and fall a few times. My left ankle hurts, but not so bad that I think I've really done any damage. I manage to get a weak radio signal and check in with Nathan, telling him we're hitting the next quadrant and I'll talk with him in an hour.

Though we press on, I start to wonder if we should turn back. I'm soaking wet. My feet are cold. And now it's not only raining, but lightning. A bolt streaks across the sky, and several breaths later, thunder booms overhead. It's so loud and terrifying that I drop down, cowering, covering my head. I stay there, trembling, as another light flashes in the distance, followed by another booming burst of thunder. It's not safe to be in the forest during a lightning storm, but it looks to be several miles away. We're probably safe where we're at, in terms of the lightning, but even if I had to book it, I couldn't.

I can't move. Shadow's suddenly by my side with his furry wet head nuzzled under my chin. I manage to lower my arms from covering my head enough to give him a hug. We stay like that, crouched in the dirt, thunder shattering the sky overhead. I'm shaking badly and yet I can't force my muscles to move. I can't stand. I can't get control over myself.

It's just like New Year's Eve. It's just like the fireworks.

All I'm feeling is pure panic, pure terror. I'm back to being fourteen years old, with bullets whizzing right by my head as Hope and I escape.

I like to think I've left that life behind me, but still it haunts me. In moments like this, that's clearer than ever. Will I ever be free of what those people did to me? Of what my father did to me?

I stay frozen, shaking, holding on to Shadow for dear life, until the rain becomes less of a solid sheet. The thunder recedes, and the lightning stops, leaving us in quiet, drizzly darkness.

Finally, I'm able to swallow, murmur my thanks into Shadow's fur, and push myself to my feet. I'm just grateful no one besides Shadow was here to witness that embarrassing display.

I know it's trauma, and I know it's not my fault. But I hate that Bulldog and some of the other officers witnessed me that way on New Year's Eve. They'll never let me live it down. And the fact that it's happened again, just weeks later, twists my stomach with worry. Am I losing it? Am I still that broken little girl running across that stretch of open desert? Besides, if anyone knew I'd had another incident before my six month check in with the doctor, I'd be pulled from active duty. Shame makes my stomach clench and tears prickle at the corners of my eyes.

I shake my head, squeezing my eyes shut against the traumatic memories. I take some deep breaths and open my eyes. I point the flashlight ahead of me on the trail, determined to continue on. I check my phone's clock. We still have about forty minutes until it's time to head back to Nathan and clock off. I might as well make the most of them.

Shadow trots ahead a few feet, but looks back at me, clearly worried about my state of mind. I don't blame him. I square my shoulders, sling the messenger bag around behind me, and walk on, shoving thoughts of everything besides finding that woman aside.

We march on for a bit more, and suddenly Shadow's ears perk up.

His nose wiggles, and he puts it to the ground, his tail wagging.

I snap to attention as he zigzags across the forest floor, moving quicker now. I stumble as I chase after him, nearly tripping over a root. I manage to catch myself, though my feet are numb. But these are Shadow's signals that let me know he's on to something.

"What have you found, boy?" I shine the light ahead, following my dog as quickly as I can. "What did you find?" Could he be picking up Jenna's trail... or the scent of the body? After more than 24 hours and heavy rains, it'd be difficult, but not unheard of.

Up ahead there's a slope. My heart pounds as I shine the light up the wet earth. The hill is covered in fallen logs and giant ferns. I scramble after Shadow, who's winding his way up.

I climb, my feet sliding under me, and dig my hands into

the earth, clutching at large stones and long roots. Dirt embeds itself under my fingernails, but I don't care. I can tell Shadow's found something. This could be it.

I'm climbing, reeling in his long lead, until suddenly, I stagger to my feet on level land. There's a natural sort of shelf, halfway up the slope… just as the hiker, Jenna Morales, described. Shadow stands stock still with his nose glued to the ground.

I pant, trying to catch my breath as I stumble up beside my dog. I sweep my flashlight over the ground, and there she is. I gasp and step back, then steel myself to look again.

The flashlight beam skitters across blue hands bound together at the chest and a tangle of blond hair between the feet. The body is piled with stones. A moment later the smell hits me, and I turn away with a gag, burying my nose in my wet sleeve.

I don't need Shadow's impressive nose to recognize the smell of death.

I'm awake now. The adrenaline has me nearly buzzing. "Good job, boy." I drop down beside Shadow and wrap him in a tight hug, my eyes welling with tears. "We did it, buddy." I kiss him right between his eyes. "You are brilliant." He smiles back at me, panting, and I give him one more hug and a handful of treats from the pouch attached to my belt, before I lurch to my feet.

I reach into the messenger bag and pull out one of the yellow evidence flags. I plant it next to the remains. I check, but as has been the case most of the day and night, find my GPS not working. The radio can't get a signal; neither can my cell phone.

"We'll have to do this the long way." Shadow and I retrace our steps, leaving a trail of yellow flags so we'll be able to find the body again.

We hike our way back to the trail and out to the parking lot where Nathan waits in the SUV. We jog the rest of the way and Shadow leaps into the backseat, before I fling myself into the passenger's side. Nathan grins, his eyes watery and nose red. "I'm so glad you're okay. Did you guys get caught in that storm?"

I nod, breathless. "Nathan." I beam at my friend. "We did it," I gasp. "We found the remains."

CHAPTER 10

"Mercer, go home."

I sniff and jerk upright, blinking Chief Jamison into focus. My head's heavy with exhaustion.

"Respectfully, sir, I'd prefer to stay." I adjust how I'm sitting on the hard rock. "Just until we can examine the crime scene."

Jamison shakes his head as if to say, "Whatever, your choice," and shoves his hands into the pockets of his deep blue raincoat with the Nightfall Police Department crest emblazoned on the breast.

Detective Hanks, Shadow, the chief, and I are huddled a little ways away from the crime scene as Red, the night lieutenant, has been working for the past couple of hours to secure the perimeter and establish a safe route to and from. Our department is small enough that we don't have dedicated CSI techs, so regular officers will have to do.

Last night, I ended up working overtime. Once backup arrived, Nathan headed home to sleep off his cold, but I stayed on to guide Red and the night shift officers back out to the crime scene. Red made the call that it was too dark and the terrain too dangerous to do a thorough examination until the next day, but we still set up portable lights and left a couple of officers out there to guard the site.

I barely got a couple of hours of sleep but insisted on coming back out here first thing in the morning. Now we're just waiting on Red's team to finish cordoning off the area around the crime scene and making sure that everyone uses a safe path so that we're not trampling or contaminating evidence. Once that's established, we'll be allowed through to more thoroughly examine the remains. Even though I keep nodding off where I sit and I'm sure that Shadow wants to climb back into bed just as badly as I do, I can't bear to leave until I get a better look at the scene.

The gray sky is just beginning to gently lighten. Rain's still coming down, but it's just a light drizzle. Nothing like last night's thunderstorm.

And though my hands and feet are cold and numb and my head aches with exhaustion, I also feel light and proud. Shadow and I did it. We found the woman's remains.

We've proven ourselves... or at least, we've taken an important first step in earning respect as competent, respectable officers.

"Red, you got an update?" Hanks waves him down.

The tall night lieutenant strides toward us from between towering pines and curling green ferns. He's probably in his early forties. I worked under him when I started on the force and pulled the night shift for the first couple of years. He's always treated me fairly and seems like a decent cop.

"We've set up a tent and better lit up the crime scene. Trail's been established."

"Good." Detective Hanks nods. "I want someone taking photographs and everyone else combing the forest for at least half a mile in all directions."

"Understood." Red nods.

"That mean you're ready for us?" Hanks continues.

Red turns. "Follow me. Just be careful to stick to the path."

I rise, eager, and Shadow, who's been snoozing at my feet, stretches and then gets to his feet as well.

I trail behind the chief and Detective Hanks as we follow Red deeper into the forest. The path has been denoted by a border of yellow flags, much like the ones I used to mark my own path last night.

We soon reach the slope and scramble up the least steep part, the dark earth soft under our feet. My heart's pounding as I stagger up to that small, level shelf where the woman is buried under a pile of stones. A large white tent is now erected over the crime scene. It shields the remains from the elements, and a couple of stadium lights on stands illuminate the area starkly. The generator powering the lights hums loudly, and I crinkle my nose at the strong smell of gasoline.

Red steps aside and gestures for us to continue. Another young officer moves about the scene, taking pictures, the flash from his camera lighting up the area over and over again, like a strobe light.

I stop beside Detective Hanks, standing shoulder to shoulder with him and Chief Jamison on his other side. The three of us gather under the plastic tent and gaze down at the grisly sight below.

Chief Jamison speaks first. "Hanks, you're the one who came up with this… deal. Mercer found the body, so she'll be the one to assist you on this case."

I glance hopefully up at the detective beside me, but he just grunts and folds his arms across his chest, shifting on his feet. He clearly isn't thrilled about the idea, but hopefully I can win him over.

He sucks in a deep breath and then lets out a sigh, his sharp eyes glued to the body.

"All right, Mercer, tell me what you see."

I glance over at the detective again, surprised that I'm being consulted for my opinion. Maybe he means to critique me, but even that would be akin to coaching, and I'll take it. I start at the top of the body. Even though I shudder and my throat grows tight, I steel my nerves and force myself to keep looking. A good detective doesn't look away from the evidence. She studies it.

"Looks to be female, youngish, blond." My stomach turns. "Her head has been removed and placed between her feet."

My gaze travels from the severed neck down. "Someone, or some*ones*, has placed her body in a natural hollow and then covered it with stones." I glance around the forest floor, noting many other similar rocks. "They seem to have been gathered from nearby."

I glance at Hanks, but he gives me no reaction, either positive or critical, so I clear my throat and continue my initial impressions.

"Her hands are bound as if she's praying. They've been wrapped with a small necklace, maybe, that has an odd symbol as a pendant." I frown, tilting my head for a different perspective on the necklace. I get the impression of the outline of an eye with a vertical line straight through the center. "Between the beheading, the odd position of the hands, the strange symbol, and the stones, we might be looking at some kind of ritual burial or killing here."

I force myself to look down from her red sweater to her jeans, all the way to the tangled mat of blond hair surrounding the severed head, which rests between her feet.

"Disturbing," Chief Jamison mutters. "Why cut off her head and put it… there?"

Detective Hanks grunts. "Maybe the ME will know something about that." He gestures towards the tangled blond hair. "What do you notice about the head, Mercer?"

I gulp. "Beside the obvious…" I crouch down for a closer look, though every one of my instincts is screaming at me to run. I bring the back of my hand to my nose to block some of the stench. A peek at the face between strands of hair and the rocks piled on top makes me wince. "Looks like pink crystals have been placed over her eyes. She's partially decomposed, her skin peeling away from the bone. Her lips are curled back from her teeth." I look away and stand quickly, eager to avoid the body. "Again, to me, this suggests some kind of ritual burial here."

This case keeps getting stranger by the minute.

I crinkle my nose at the smell, and my stomach turns. I can't help but be grateful that I don't have much in it. Otherwise, the contents might have already been spilled all over the forest floor. "I don't know if this is common. These are the first, er, remains I have seen, but there seems to be a bluish tint to her gums and skin." I gesture at my own mouth.

Detective Hanks nods and points at the woman's hands, which are bound in a prayer position over her chest. "Her hands as well."

Chief Jamison swipes a hand down his face. "Absolutely bizarre."

Detective Hanks lets out a humorless laugh. "Damn strangest thing I've ever seen." He clears his throat. "I've already called up to the ME in Warrenton. As soon as we get the scene cleared and transport her remains up there, the doc has promised to make the autopsy top priority. Which means..." He turns to me. "We'll be heading out first thing tomorrow morning. Be at the station ready to go at 6:00 a.m. You're a minute late, I leave without you."

I gulp and nod. "Yes, sir."

Chief Jamison glances over the detective's head at me. "You've seen it now, Mercer. Go home. Get yourself some sleep and take the rest of the day off. You've earned it."

"Yes, sir," I say again, relieved to leave the woman's bizarre remains. I nod to each of the men and then head back with Shadow trailing along beside me, careful to stick to the established trail.

On my way back, I run into Officer Tanaka, who holds out

a paper cup of steaming coffee to me. It's straight black, not the fancy stuff I usually like, but at this point I'd have gratefully chugged straight rocket fuel if it had given me a boost. I give him a grateful smile. "Thank you."

The typically stoic man nods. "The chief just radioed and asked me to give you a ride home."

"Thank you." I follow him back to the Pine Crest Trail, dreaming of sleep. At this point, I can barely see straight, so I probably shouldn't drive. Tomorrow we'll begin the investigation. But for now, I can be proud of what we've done. I grin down at Shadow who trots along beside me and lean over to ruffle his fur. "Thanks, buddy. I couldn't have done this without you."

CHAPTER 11

EIGHT WEEKS AGO

Officer Dobre yawned and blinked his bleary eyes, which drifted to the wall clock across from his desk. Nearly 3:00 a.m.—four hours to go. His eyes drifted lower to the windows in the lobby. It was pitch-black outside, and all he could see was his own reflection and that of the lobby, bathed in the stark fluorescent lights.

He scrubbed his cheek and stared down at the towering stack of paperwork in front of him. He let out a heavy sigh. The paperwork seemed never-ending. He jotted down some notes, flipped the page, and moved on to the next form. More than half of these weren't even his. Chief Novak treated him like his personal assistant.

Then again, if it wasn't for the paperwork, he'd have almost nothing to do on the night shift. Not much happened in Elk Ridge after 6:00 p.m. Then again, not much happened in Elk Ridge before then, either. Dobre supposed he should just be glad he had a job at all in a town this small. In fact, the police station was nothing more than a few rooms consisting of Novak's office, the lobby where Dobre set up his permanent desk, and a holding cell, which nearly always sat empty.

They shared the building with the post office, community center, and council chambers. Elk Ridge was about as small as you could get and still be considered a town.

The officer lowered his head, resigned to hours of more paperwork and trying to stay awake, when the bell over the door tinkled and a woman stumbled in.

"Hello, ma'am." The words died on his lips as he took in the strange woman's appearance. Her wild eyes darted around the room, as though she was being chased. Her long hair hung in tangled braids over her shoulders, and her blond fringe brushed over her blue eyes, which were bloodshot.

She stumbled up to him, slamming her palms on the counter. Up close, she was younger than he'd guessed. Her thin frame and overly tanned skin had aged her. "I need your help."

Dobre's eyes drifted to the door. Was someone chasing her?

Almost subconsciously, his hand drifted to the firearm at his hip. "What's the problem, ma'am?"

"They're gonna hurt my son." She bared her teeth, her gums an odd shade, almost blue. "I think they're gonna kill him."

Officer Dobre blinked, wondering for a moment if he had drifted asleep and this was some strange dream. But no, here she was standing across from him, worried someone was going to hurt her kid. His eyes drifted to the picture of his own family sitting on the desk facing him.

This woman who'd wandered in off the street in the middle of the night was ringing alarm bells for him, but his stomach clenched with sympathy. Were his own children in danger, he'd be panicked too. He came around the counter with a yellow legal pad and pen in hand and gestured for the woman to sit.

She hesitated a moment, her chest heaving, eyes on him like she might run out the door, but he sat first and gently patted the plastic seat beside him. "Please, ma'am, I'd like to help. I need you to tell me what's going on." She pressed her lips into a tight line but gave him a slight nod and lowered herself onto the seat beside him, her spine bolt upright as if she might break away at any moment.

"What's your name?"

She licked her lips. "They call me Gaia, but my name's Joy Ackerman, and my son's name is Clay Ackerman. They call him Chosen One."

He held up a hand as the words tumbled from her lips. "Hold on now, hold on. Who's they?"

"The group." She tipped her head toward the windows, which now reflected the two of them sitting alone in the quiet lobby. "The Ascendant Light Fellowship."

That rang another alarm bell in Officer Dobre's mind. "You, you're part of that, uh, commune, that lives out there in the forest?"

She nodded, then frowned and shook her head. "I was. Not anymore, I guess." She let out a half mad laugh. "I'm telling you, they're planning to kill my son. They think he's the chosen one or some shit. Source, the leader, she's out of her mind. I need your help."

"Okay. Okay. Hold on now," Officer Dobre said, his tone as soothing as possible. "This is serious business. Let me give my chief a call, okay?" He licked his lips and rose, gesturing for her to stay seated. She folded her bony hands together in her lap and squeezed them so tightly that they turned blotchy red and white. She was practically vibrating in her chair, wringing her hands and looking around like a cornered animal.

Officer Dobre moved down the hall to the back and called the chief from the phone on his desk instead of using the one out in the lobby. He eased the door mostly closed behind him, but not all the way, so he could keep an eye on this woman, Joy.

With reluctance, he punched in the chief's number and braced himself as he waited. The phone rang once, twice, thrice.

"What the hell do you want?" Chief Novak barked on the other end of the line. He heard some mumbled words from a woman in the background, no doubt Novak's wife.

Dobre cleared his throat. "I know, Chief, I know, but you said to call if there was any trouble with that group, the one out there in the forest?"

Novak went quiet for so long that Dobre wondered if he'd lost him. "Chief?"

"Okay," he gruffly replied. "I'll be there in ten minutes." He hung up on him, and Dobre was left staring at the phone before placing it on the receiver.

Nothing about this felt right. When Novak had asked Dobre to alert him about that group, it hadn't felt right either, but Dobre had eased his own worries by rationalizing it away. They were an odd group of people. Probably prudent of Novak to keep a keen eye on them.

But this woman wasn't here because she was making trouble. She was here because the group was making trouble for her.

And while the chief ranked above Dobre in the chain of command and he was beholden to follow his orders, Dobre didn't particularly like the man himself. He worried what Novak would make of this poor woman. She seemed half out of her mind, yes, but there was something in the earnestness of her gaze that made Dobre feel compelled to help her.

He poured her a cup of coffee and returned to the seat next to her. Dobre asked Joy Ackerman questions for the next several minutes as she sipped from the steaming cardboard cup, all about that group she'd been with and what made her think they were going to hurt her son.

"I overheard some kind of conversation this morning," she explained, the words coming out in a rush. "I didn't know what it meant, but then I went and read Rainbow's journals. And in one, it said Source had downloaded some kind of vision or decree from the elders and that my son--"

"Hold on, back up," Dobre muttered as he struggled to keep up, taking notes. "Who's Rainbow? What is this about journals and downloads?"

She was about to explain when the revving of an engine cut her off, followed by a loud screech, which made them both look up. Chief Novak's truck skidded to a stop, parked sideways in front of the station. The headlights clicked off.

Dobre gave a rueful smile at a memory from last year, when Novak had first bought the truck. Dobre's wife had commented that it seemed like the chief might be compensating for something. The truck was ludicrously enormous, jacked so high the man needed a stepladder to climb up into it. It didn't help that Novak drove as though traffic laws didn't apply to him.

A moment later, Novak threw open the door and stomped into the lobby, which caused Joy to leap to her feet, her eyes wide with alarm.

"Now what's this all about?" Chief Novak barked. The man wasn't much older than Dobre himself, probably in his midforties, but was already balding and had a large gut. It hung over his plaid pajama pants, which he'd stuffed into a pair of cowboy boots. Novak had thrown on the top half of his blue uniform, complete with the badge pinned at the chest, which he'd then topped with a heavy jacket.

Dobre hurried to his feet, trying to smooth things over. "Chief Novak, this is Joy Ackerman. She's the one I called you about. Belongs to that group; or rather, she did." He turned to

Joy, trying to ease her panic. "This is my boss, Chief Novak. He's come to help."

Novak planted his hands on his hips and stared Joy up and down, picking at something in his teeth with his tongue. "You one of those wackos from out in the compound?"

Dobre's eyes flew open with surprise. "Now, Chief." He started forward, shocked that the man would speak to someone that way, much less a mother concerned about her son's well-being.

But Novak just held up a hand, stopping Dobre in his tracks. "Oh, save it, Dobre. She's probably high out of her mind. You know what they get up to out there in that forest? Nothing good, I'll tell you that." He turned to the scared woman. "Now get." He jerked his thumb toward the door behind him. "I want you out of here. You just go back to where you came from and no trouble will come of this, got it?"

The woman's chest heaved, and her wild eyes darted between the chief and Dobre.

This felt very wrong to Dobre. He caught Novak's eye. "Sir, if she really is high out of her mind, we should hold her then, right? She could be a danger to herself or someone else."

Novak rolled his eyes. "Bullshit. She'll sleep it off and be fine, but she don't belong here. Get out. Get out, I said."

Joy Ackerman licked her thin lips and turned to Officer Dobre. "Could—could I call someone first?"

Dobre looked to the chief for direction.

Novak considered a moment and then nodded. "Sure."

"Come around." Dobre guided Joy around his desk and pulled the phone forward for her. She picked up the receiver, her thin, almost skeletal hand hovering over the buttons for a moment, then punched in a number with an 805 area code. That was California, Dobre was pretty sure.

He stepped back a few feet, giving her a little space, while

Novak watched, tapping his toe, impatiently. Joy stood there as the phone rang, and rang, and rang. Finally, she slammed the receiver down and shrieked, "Fuck."

"Now that's no kind of language for a lady. Out with you." Novak stepped back, yanking the door open and pointing her out into the cold, dark night.

Dobre's eyes widened in horror. "Chief, we really oughta make sure she—"

Novak shot him a look that could kill. "You say one more word, I'm writing you up for insubordination." He turned back to the blond woman. "I told you to get out."

She balled her skinny hands into fists and bared her teeth at the two of them. "They got to you. They paid you to look the other way, didn't they?"

The words cut into Dobre. Either this woman was rambling, in which case she needed help, or she had a point. Why else was the chief so intent on brushing her concerns under the rug? Then again, Novak was known for his laziness, and maybe he was right. She might be high or just out of her mind.

Chief Novak looked barely perturbed, more bored than anything. "Get out." With one more wild look, the woman spun, hugging her red sweater around her, and marched back out into the cold. Dobre looked after her, noting that the parking lot stood empty aside from Chief Novak's giant black truck.

How had she gotten here? Did she have a ride? But before he could wonder for long, Chief Novak stood in his way.

"Now, I did not appreciate you questioning my authority a moment ago." He glared up at Dobre. "But I do appreciate the call. You did the right thing there, son."

Son? Again, Novak couldn't be more than five years older than Dobre himself.

The chief clapped him on the shoulder. "You ever see her or any one of those nut jobs again, you give me a call. Doesn't matter if it's day or night, you hear?" He stopped at the door on his way out. "But you do not question me, especially in front of civilians."

He waited until Dobre nodded. "Yes, Chief."

"Good." And with that, Novak stepped back out into the darkness. The woman, Joy Ackerman, was already long gone.

CHAPTER 12

I wake with a start and a gasp, startling Shadow. He lifts his head, his pointy ears perked up, and he stares at me. I flop back down onto the pillow and cover my face with my hands.

It takes a few moments for my breathing to slow, the dark visions of my nightmare already fading away. I can't exactly remember what I've been dreaming, but it must be some variation of the same nightmares I've been having for years, ever since Hope and I escaped.

I let out a heavy sigh as my heartbeat gradually slows, and I cringe at the cold wetness chilling the crooks of my elbows and underarms. Apparently, I've worked up quite a sweat. *Ick*.

I pat around on the side table for my phone and check the time. It's a few minutes after five. My alarm is going to go off soon, anyway, so I get up.

After a quick shower, I jog downstairs, already dressed in my neat blue uniform, and blink in surprise as I step into the kitchen. All the lights are on, glowing a comforting golden yellow, and the whole room smells wonderful, like toasted butter and sweet maple syrup.

I flash my eyes at Hope, whose pink hair is piled high into a messy bun on top of her head. "What are you doing up?"

She gives me a sleepy smile that soon turns into a yawn. She's wearing her pajamas, an oversized tee with a picture of Edward from *Twilight* on it, and slippers. Grandma Gloria looks put together as always in her long cardigan, button-up shirt, and stretchy slacks. She bustles around the kitchen island, and as I near, I see her flipping pancakes.

Instead of wolfing down his own food per usual, Shadow stands nearby, his eyes laser-focused on those golden brown discs on the griddle. I grin as I give Grandma a hug. "What's all this?"

Hope wraps me in a tight embrace next. "We wanted to make you a special breakfast."

Grandma nods, and a strand of silver hair slips forward from behind her ear. "Indeed, to celebrate you finding that poor woman's remains."

Heat flushes my face, and I look away. "You guys didn't have to do this."

"We know." Hope grins. "But we're kind of the best like that."

I roll my eyes and chuckle.

"Grab yourself a plate." Grandma points behind her. "There are some pancakes staying warm in the oven.

She didn't have to tell me twice. As I dish myself up breakfast, I glance at my dog. "Why does Shadow think he's going to get some pancakes?"

Hope glances up and away in an attempt to look innocent, but Grandma busts her. "*Someone* may have accidentally on purpose been dropping pieces of them."

Hope shrugs, a mischievous grin pulling at the corners of her lips. "What? I can't help it if I'm clumsy."

I snicker. "Right."

As much as it embarrasses me, it also feels good to have my grandma and sister being so supportive. Shadow and I worked so hard the other night, and I'm both excited and nervous to ride along with Detective Hanks today. After I stuff my face with as many buttery, syrupy pancakes as I can handle, and possibly sneak Shadow a few bites, we head out into the dark night, me all bundled up in my puffer jacket and Shadow sporting his official police harness. I stop at my usual spot to dump out my travel mug.

I make it to the cafe with just barely enough time to grab coffee (no scone this morning, as I'm still stuffed from pancakes) and even pick up a cappuccino for Detective Hanks. I have no idea what he drinks, but I figure an offering of coffee is never one anyone turns down. We make it inside the station just as Detective Hanks bustles into the lobby, a set of keys in his hand, shrugging into his long wool coat.

He looks me up and down, his bushy brows knitted together. "You just made it. Barely. Let's go." He stomps past me as I meet Linda's gaze.

She gives me double thumbs-up and mouths, "Good luck."

Detective Hanks ducks out the door.

"Thanks, Linda." I give her a wink. "I have a feeling I'm going to need it."

Shadow and I follow the detective outside and hop into his sedan. Our department is small, but Detective Hanks has been given his own departmental car. He makes a face at Shadow as he lowers his haunches in the back seat but says nothing as he backs up and pulls out onto Highway 101.

Shadow, no doubt sensing my nerves and picking up on the awkward silence in the car, lowers his head onto my shoulder, always ready to give me comfort. I give him a quick pat, then gesture at the to-go cup in the cup holder. "I, uh, didn't know what you drink, but I got you a cappuccino from the Daily Grind."

Detective Hanks sniffs, casting the drink a dubious side-eye. "Cappuccino." His tone drips with disgust. "I drink my coffee black."

Like your soul, I want to say, but I bite my lip to keep it to myself. Why do some people think drinking black coffee is a sign of moral superiority? Like, what's wrong with adding some cream and sugar to make it delicious? Whatever. I lean back in my seat and sip from my mocha as we cruise along, heading north to Warrenton.

It's only about a twenty-minute drive. But even in the dark, it's a beautiful one. The vast void of the sea stretches out to our left, swallowing all light, while here and there along the coastline, the little lights of towns and homes perched in the hills sparkle in the night. The sky is just beginning to lighten when we pull up to the sheriff's station in Warrenton.

Compared to ours, it's enormous. Though the town of Warrenton is tiny, the sheriff is based here, and the station functions as a hub for several of the little towns like ours scattered along the northern Oregon coast.

When we park, Detective Hanks turns to face me, suddenly talkative. "Now listen, Mercer, you need to observe and let me take the lead. Got it?"

Part of me wants to protest that that had been the plan anyway, but I give him a solemn nod. "Got it."

We march into the station. Administrators, officers, and other personnel greet Hanks with waves and polite greetings. He comes up here every week for the detectives' meeting, so he must be as familiar with the Warrenton station as our own.

He leads the way to the bank of elevators and hits the down button. When we step inside, he presses the button for the morgue. We drop down a couple of stories, and the elevator doors open to sterile white halls lit by flickering fluorescents. I shiver, the air noticeably colder.

The chill stings my nose, and I shove my fingers into my coat pockets as Shadow and I follow Detective Hanks down the hallway and then to the right. An officer sits behind a desk with a computer, reading a novel. He glances up at our footsteps, bookmarks his page, and sets the novel aside. He looks up at us with eyebrows raised expectantly.

"Detective Hanks and Officer Mercer to speak with ME Harper."

"Right." The officer nods. "She's expecting you."

We step forward, but he shoots an arm out. "Wait, you're not going to be able to take the dog back with you. Sanitation protocols."

I sigh, not liking to leave Shadow alone in this creepy place, but I can't really protest. "Can I leave him here with you?"

The officer nods, grinning at Shadow, who is already wagging his tail. "Yeah, I'll keep an eye on him. Come here, buddy." I hand over his leash, and the officer scratches behind Shadow's ears.

"Come on, Mercer." Detective Hanks is already a few feet ahead of me. With one last look at Shadow, I follow. Okay, so maybe Shadow is going to be totally fine without me. Maybe my worries lie more in how *I'm* going to fare without my dog. I've never been in a morgue before, and I'm not sure what to expect. My breathing becomes shallower, the cold biting at my skin.

Hanks knocks at a door with a window, and a woman inside looks up. She wears a white lab coat, her dark curly hair piled on top of her head in a pretty bun. She smiles, her teeth white against her dark skin, and motions for us to enter.

Detective Hanks holds the door for me and then follows me inside. We stand across from her on the other side of a metal slab where a body lies draped under a sheet.

Detective Hanks greets the woman like an old friend. "Hey, Beth."

Her eyes sparkle behind her large stylish glasses. "Hey, Gordon."

I blink in surprise. I've never heard *anyone* call him Gordon before.

"Who's your friend?"

Hanks clears his throat as if he disagrees with her assessment of me being a *friend*. "This is Officer Eden Mercer." He gestures between us. "Mercer, meet Dr. Beth Harper, medical examiner. She's the best in the state."

I try not to look at the body under the sheet as I extend a hand to the lithe, athletic-looking woman. "Pleasure to meet you, Dr. Harper."

She takes my hand in her own, which is covered in a blue latex glove. "You too." She smiles warmly. "Call me Beth."

"Okay." I nod. "Feel free to call me Eden."

"All right, you two. You want to hear about your victim?" She peels off her gloves, tosses them in a metal-lidded trash can, and then replaces them with new ones.

"Absolutely," Detective Hanks says. With a lump in my throat, I sidle up beside him and force myself to look down at what used to be a living person below the sheet.

I'm doing my best to focus, but this place has me on edge. It isn't just the body under the sheet either. It's the strong stinging scent of disinfectant with just a hint of decomposing flesh underneath it. It's the shiny silver metal instruments on the cart beside Dr. Harper, their sharp blades glinting. It's the hum of the refrigeration units, nearly drowning out her words, and the bank of drawers all along the wall that no doubt hold even more dead bodies.

I mentally shake myself and tune back in to what Beth is telling us.

"That's my best estimation."

Hanks shifts on his feet beside me, widening his stance. He crosses his arms, frowning. "Dead six to eight weeks? That's a big window, Beth."

She splays her latex-gloved hands. "It's the best I can do

for now." She pulls the sheet back, exposing the woman's severed head, neck, and collarbones.

I flinch, my stomach turning at the marbled blue veins beneath the pale blue skin, which curls at the rough edges of where her head was separated from her neck.

"You see," Beth continues, seemingly oblivious to my discomfort, though Detective Hanks is shooting me concerned looks. "It's the fact that she was outdoors, exposed to the elements. On one hand, I'd be tempted to say it was longer than six to eight weeks, because the cold has slowed down decomposition. On the other hand," Beth goes on, "the forest where she was found has seen a lot of moisture. We've had a lot of rain, and that's going to increase the decomposition process. So, balancing the two, again, we've got that window of six to eight weeks."

Detective Hanks grumbles something under his breath and huffs. "Fine. What else have you got?"

"She was shot, which is the cause of death." She pulls the sheet lower, exposing the bullet wound, nearly right in the center of the woman's chest. I hadn't expected that. It'd been hidden by the stones piled on top of her body.

"Judging by samples taken at the crime scene, it appears she was killed there."

Detective Hanks nods. "We found the bullet embedded in a tree near the body."

I look over at him; that's news to me.

The doctor nods. "The head was removed after she was killed."

"Thank God," Hanks mutters. I can't help but second his sentiment. The alternative is too horrifying to seriously contemplate.

Beth gestures at the space between the head and the neck. "Looks like it was removed with an eight-to-ten-inch serrated blade. I'm guessing something like a hunting knife."

"If she was already dead, why remove the head?" Detective Hanks wonders aloud.

Beth nods. "Intriguing indeed." Her amber eyes dance behind her glasses. Despite the dark nature of what she does, she's clearly passionate about her work. "If it was only the head, I wouldn't know to say for sure, but considering she was also found with rose quartz crystals placed over her eyes and that unique symbol placed over the hands which had been arranged in a prayer position, I'm thinking this points to a ritual burial. The head placed between the feet reminds me of a custom from the 1700s in the Northeastern United States."

She shifts on her feet. "There was something of a vampire scare, and so to prevent the dead from rising, people would bury their deceased in various ways, one being with the head removed and placed between the feet because they thought it kept vampires from coming back to life."

Detective Hanks scowls at her as though he hasn't understood a word of what she's said.

"That's fascinating," I mutter. "Do you know of any cases in the Pacific Northwest where that's happened?"

She grins at me. "Nope, this is definitely the first."

"First for all of us," Hanks mutters. "What else can you tell us about her?"

"She's female, obviously. I'm guessing between twenty-five to thirty years of age." She gestures down the body as she pulls the sheet further back. "She's showing signs of malnourishment."

The woman's ribs clearly protrude beneath her skin.

Hanks frowns. "Malnourishment? Was she being held somewhere? Starved?"

Dr. Beth shakes her head. "No signs of restraints." She gestures at the smooth skin around the woman's wrists and ankles. "She was also found with no ID or any personal possessions on her, aside from what I'm guessing is a necklace. That odd symbol on that leather thong was wrapped around her hands, binding them into the prayer position. If this is a ritual burial, that's obviously something of great import to whoever killed her."

Dr. Beth makes her way down the body, stopping at the feet. "The bottoms of her feet are quite tough, suggesting to me that she went barefoot outside a lot."

Even though Detective Hanks has told me to leave all the talking to him, I can't help myself. "What about this blue tint to her skin? Is that normal for a corpse?"

"Nice observation." Beth nods.

Detective Hanks seems completely unimpressed.

"I've wondered that myself. Now typically, we might see a blue tint to the skin where it made contact with the earth. That's something that can happen. In this case, we would expect it solely on her backside or possibly around the sides of her body where she was lowered into that shallow embankment. However, that's not the case. When we see a blue tint to the gums, nails, and skin in this way, it's called argyria."

"Ar-what?" Detective Hanks follows up.

"Argyria. Basically, it's silver poisoning."

"How does someone get silver poisoning?" I muse.

"Typically two ways," Beth explains. "They might work with silver, so possibly a silver miner."

Detective Hanks sniffs. "I guess we'll check and see if there are any working silver mines in the area."

Beth nods. "Or they might work with silver if they're a jeweler, for example."

"What's the other way?" Detective Hanks asks.

"Sometimes people take colloidal silver as a supplement. It's kind of a new age thing, not backed by the FDA, notably." Beth shrugs. "If someone took too much of it, or it was too high of a concentration, it could lead to argyria over time. In any case, this condition is really rare."

"Odd," I mutter.

"The other thing you should know," she gestures at the nails, "is that we've found tissue underneath her nails. She fought back against her attacker."

The detective raises his brows, his eyes fixed intently on the doctor. "Any hits?"

She shakes her head. "The lab's running it to see if it matches any DNA in our database. I'll let you know if we get a match, obviously, but nothing yet."

"Thanks, Beth. Appreciate you rushing this through."

"Are you kidding?" She grins. "This is fascinating. I haven't seen a body this interesting in years."

We thank Beth for her time and expertise and head toward the door. "We've got a detectives' meeting to get to," Hanks explains.

"Great. Well, it was nice to meet you, Eden," she calls after us. "Don't let this grump push you around too much."

I smile back at her, and she leans on her toes to holler after Hanks, "You be nice now. I like this one."

Hanks merely grumbles something under his breath in reply.

CHAPTER 13

After leaving the morgue, and with Shadow once again by my side, we take the elevator back upstairs. Detective Hanks navigates through the maze of hallways before stepping into a large conference room. Shadow and I follow him inside, and I'm grateful to be out of that claustrophobic, astringent-smelling basement. The conference room, like the rest of the sheriff's station here in Warrenton, is much larger and more modern than ours.

Instead of aged wooden floors, gray carpet muffles my footsteps. Giant whiteboards cover two of the walls, while windows span the other two, which are currently shaded by drawn blinds.

Three other men already sit chatting around one end of the long table.

As we enter, they look up, their eyes darting from Hanks to me and Shadow, which makes heat rush to my cheeks. I've never been very good at being the center of attention. Ever since I was a kid, I've preferred to blend more into the background. But as Nathan likes to remind me, if I want new opportunities, I have to be open to new experiences.

Which apparently includes having lots of curious eyes on

me. The three men around the table stand as Detective Hanks raises his hand in greeting. "Hey, fellas."

The men greet him back.

The tallest and oldest-looking of the men, a handsome fellow with dark skin and short, curly silver hair, grins at me. "And who do we have here?"

"Gentlemen, this is Officer Eden Mercer. She's, uh, *assisting* me on this Jane Doe case. Mercer, this is Detective Alex Ramirez from Cannon Beach." I reach across the table to shake hands with the young man with slick black hair. It's shiny and sharply cut. He sports stylish glasses and an expensive-looking suit and tie.

"Ramirez is our tech expert," Detective Hanks explains. Next, he introduces me to the tall older man. "This is Detective Malcolm Johnson from Seaside."

He takes my hand in both of his large ones and gives me a warm smile. "You must be tough if you're putting up with this one." He tips his head toward Hanks, who scowls back at him.

"Johnson is our resident old fart," Hanks grumbles.

My eyes widen with surprise, but Detective Johnson just plants his hands on his hips and stares Hanks down. "That's big talk coming from you!" He brushes his hands down the sides of his head. "Silver fox is how I hear it more often."

Ramirez grins.

"If we're talking old farts," Johnson continues, "I'd think you'd be referring to yourself, Hanks." He jerks a thumb at me. "Looks like your chief finally realized you were too senile to do the job on your own." Though his tone is playful, I can tell the comment rankles Hanks, who's made it quite clear he has no interest in anyone assisting him, much less me.

His neck above his shirt collar turns red, the flush spreading up to his cheeks. He sets his jaw and does his best to ignore the grinning Detective Johnson. He turns to the last man. "And this is Detective Dean Wilder, from up in Astoria."

As I reach across the table to shake hands with the man, our eyes meet. He looks to be a few years older than me, maybe in his early thirties, medium tall with a muscular build, judging by the way he fills out his suit. His eyes widen as they linger on my face, and my cheeks flush even hotter.

I blink and look away, though his hand stays wrapped around mine just a moment longer than is strictly polite.

Nervous, I clasp my hands behind my back and keep my eyes down on the shiny wood table, which is littered with papers and manila file folders as well as a couple of laptops. A shiny new silver one sits open in front of Detective Ramirez.

Detective Johnson flashes his bright smile, bends forward, and pats his thighs. "And who's this?" Shadow trots right over, wagging his bushy tail. Johnson crouches down beside him and pats Shadow's neck.

I open my mouth to answer, but Hanks cuts me off. "That's Shadow, Mercer's K-9."

I close my mouth and simply nod my agreement. The man is clearly doing his best to keep me from speaking. Hanks and I take our seats at the table while Shadow stays glued to Detective Johnson's side, shamelessly nosing his hand for more pets. They discuss a couple of task forces the detectives all work jointly on. I do my best to follow, though I'm not familiar with any of the cases and they don't bother to clue me in.

One is a house fire that burned down a large chunk of a ranch outside Seaside they're investigating for possible arson, while Ramirez explains the work he's been doing to help build some kind of database that would help track missing and possibly trafficked children.

Although I don't follow a lot of it, nervous excitement bubbles in my stomach. This is the exact type of work I want to do someday, hopefully sooner than later. I just have to do a good job on this case, which I suppose starts with proving to

Detective Hanks that I can be an asset instead of a pest, which is currently the way he's treating me.

After fifteen minutes of discussion, they circle around to our case.

Detective Hanks fills them in on what we know and glosses over the fact that Shadow and I found the remains. It's not like I'm looking for praise and glory, just some acknowledgement that I'm not a dead weight Chief Jamison has strapped around his ankle.

"Anyways," Hanks explains, "clearly we've got to start by identifying the victim, then go from there."

"She didn't have ID on her?" Wilder clarifies.

Hanks shakes his head. "The sketch artist here is working on a mock-up of what she might have looked like when alive, based on the remains. That's about all we've got to go from so far."

Detective Johnson nods, still scratching between Shadow's ears. "Once you get that, fax it over to us." He gestures at the circle of them with his pencil. "We'll keep an eye out. Spread the word."

Hanks nods. "I'd also like to request your help searching through the missing persons database for anyone who might match the victim's general description."

The men take notes as Hanks describes our Jane Doe. "Blond, blue eyes, ME says between the ages of twenty-five and thirty, most likely. Caucasian. She's got this odd blue tint to her skin. Beth thought maybe she could have worked in a silver mine or possibly be some kind of jeweler."

I pipe up. "Or she might be someone into new age supplements."

Detective Hanks scowls at me, his bushy brows knitting together. "Sure," he growls, "but that's not something we can search the database for."

I lick my lips and sink back in my seat. I hadn't meant to contradict him. I just thought it might be relevant. In any case,

I vow to keep my mouth shut for the rest of the meeting to avoid any more dirty looks from the detective.

After a few more matters to discuss and some pleasantries, the detectives end the meeting and we say our goodbyes. Detective Johnson winks at me. "Nice to meet you, Officer Mercer. Don't let Hanks jerk you around. He's got a shriveled, toughened exterior, kind of like an old prune, but he's got a good heart inside."

I have to suck on my lips to stifle a laugh at the image that generates in my mind, but Detective Hanks marches out of the room without sparing Johnson another glance. Ramirez chuckles, but Detective Wilder, who appears to be possibly as serious as Detective Hanks, though not as grumpy, seems lost in the paperwork in front of him.

Still, as I wave goodbye, the handsome Wilder looks up for a moment, and his dark eyes lock on my face. I have to call several times to Shadow to pull him away from Detective Johnson. But once I get a hold of him, we jog to catch up with Detective Hanks, who hasn't bothered to wait for us.

He marches, chest puffed, toward the exit. We're nearly pushing through the doors into the gray midmorning light when someone calling Detective Hanks's name stops us.

We turn. A young man in a white button-up and tie waves at us as he jogs down the hall past other office workers and uniformed officers. He carries a manila folder tucked under his arm.

He comes to a stop in front of us, taking a beat to catch his breath. "The artist finished the sketch." He holds the manila folder out, and Hanks eagerly takes it. He flips it open, and I glance over his shoulder, though he angles it in a way that makes it more difficult for me to see.

I bite my lip, shoving down my annoyance. I understand he's set in his ways, sure. But does he have to be such a jerk to me? It seems like he's going out of his way to be rude.

Still, the drawing catches my attention. The pencil sketch

depicts a young woman's face and upper torso. Long blond hair plaited into twin braids hang over her narrow shoulders. Her eyes are large and blue, and freckles pepper her nose and cheeks. In the drawing, she looks painfully thin, with her cheekbones protruding from underneath her skin and her jawline sharp.

Detective Hanks flips the manila folder shut, making me jerk back, and thanks the man who chased after us. As we march across the parking lot out to the detective's sedan, he extends the folder toward me without even making eye contact.

I hesitate a moment, unsure what he wants, but take it from him.

"Fax it out to the other stations." He climbs into the driver's seat and slams the door shut behind him. I stand outside the car for a moment, my lips parted in shock.

I huff and open the back door, helping Shadow leap up inside. I close the door behind him and mutter to myself, "Sure, that's an administrative job, but I can *nicely* ask Linda or Joan to do it." I grind my teeth and slump into the passenger seat beside Hanks.

CHAPTER 14

We arrive back at the Nightfall Police Station twenty minutes later. It's shaping up to be a foggy, misty, dreary winter day. Most folks grumble about weather like this, but I secretly enjoy it. I grew up in the scorching desert of northern Arizona. When my grandpa rescued Hope and me and drove us three states north to his and Grandma's home on the Oregon coast, it felt like a reprieve.

Instead of sunburns and car door handles that could fry an egg, I got lush green forests and the calming sound of the waves. I woke up to soft gray light and misty mornings instead of bright sunlight that made me wince. Everything up here was soft and foggy, all shades of gray and soft greens. Instead of hard-packed dirt, tulips and daffodils sprang wild from the rich, dark earth without anyone even having to plant them. They just grew between the cracks of sidewalks.

It seemed like a paradise up here, and after over ten years of it, I still love it.

Detective Hanks marches into the station with Shadow and me hustling to keep up. There are a few folks milling around in the lobby, so I don't linger long but merely hand over the artist's sketch to Joan and ask her to please fax it out to local stations. "Tell them we're looking for an ID on the Jane Doe."

She winks. "You got it." Then leans closer. "You have fun up there in Warrenton?"

How to answer that question? I open my mouth, then shoot a look at Hanks, who has already stomped his way back into the bullpen, and Joan giggles. She waves me off. "That tells me everything I need to know."

I chuckle, thank her again, and Shadow and I head back to my desk. Shadow curls up in his bed, and I settle into my chair, planning to check my emails and voicemails. No sooner have I logged into my computer than Detective Hanks hollers at me from his office to come join him. I sigh. Could he not have asked me *before* I sat down?

I get to my feet. Shadow lifts his head, but I hold a hand out. "You can stay, boy. I'll be right back." He lowers his head, and I stride into Detective Hanks's office. Only Hanks and Chief Jamison have their own offices, though we do have a spare one that currently sits empty and is used as storage. "Should I close the door?"

Hanks waves me off. "Nah, this will only take a moment. I'm gonna get to work searching the missing persons database, and I expect you to do the same."

Earlier, up in Warrenton, we'd divided up the state. The northern half went to Detectives Ramirez, Johnson, and Wilder to search, which left the whole southern half of Oregon to Hanks and me. "I want you to take southeast," he directs. "I'll take southwest." He gives me a skeptical look. "You do know how to use the database, don't you?"

I nod and then immediately am flooded with fear. Should I not have said that? Truth be told, I haven't had any official need to use the database in my several years on the job. Unofficially, I definitely comb through it every week.

Luckily, Detective Hanks doesn't ask any follow-up questions, or that might have been the end of my time assisting him. "Go ahead, get to work." His eyes are already glued to his computer screen, and he dismisses me without another glance. I bow my head and step back out into the bullpen.

Retaking my seat next to Shadow, I give him a quick scratch on the rump, then hop onto my computer. For hours and hours, I search the missing persons database, breaking only for a quick turkey sandwich lunch I eat at my desk, and then keep searching. The light outside the windows grows dimmer and then dark.

The fluorescents overhead glow all the brighter and give me a headache. I lean my cheek into my hand and continue clicking through. There are lots of maybes; hundreds, in fact. Missing women who might match our Jane Doe's description.

Most of them were reported missing a lot longer than six to eight weeks ago, though. Months and years longer. That doesn't automatically rule them out, but still, nothing obvious is jumping out at me.

Bored and frustrated, I glance around the bullpen. Hanks is still in his office, as is Jamison. It's getting late, and I suspect he'll be heading home soon. A few other uniformed officers mill about, but nobody pays me any attention.

The hairs rise on the back of my neck as I try a new search —one for the last name Warner. The surname I was given at birth. As the little wheel on the screen spins and I wait for the database to do its thinking, Bulldog slams a hand on my desk. I yelp and jump, then hurry to click out of the database to my desktop.

Even though he stands on the other side of my desk, where he can't see what I was doing, my heart pounds in my chest. As an officer, you're not supposed to use the database for anything outside an official capacity. Yet I find myself every so often searching for my missing family members. My mother, my brothers and sisters and cousins who are still in the cult.

The guilt threatens to destroy me some days. Survivor's guilt, a counselor had once told me when I was young. When we'd first come to live with my grandparents, they'd made sure to send Hope and me to a therapist down in Cannon Beach.

I knew it was expensive, and they sacrificed to get Hope and me the help we needed. Part of me knew I couldn't have saved them all. Part of me knew even if I had offered them the chance to escape with me, most of them would have turned me down… or more likely, turned me in to my father and the other elders.

If I'd tried to help them all, chances were I'd never have helped myself or Hope, and we'd still be stuck in Canaan Springs. Married. Mothers to dozens of children. Oppressed. And that was the *best*-case scenario.

I have a strong hunch it's more likely I'd be dead.

And despite all the therapy and all the counseling from Hope and Grandma Gloria and Grandpa assuring me that I was just a child, that I wasn't responsible for the others… that guilt persists. It settles in my stomach, like silt sinking to the bottom of the ocean. And it just piles up there. Deeper. Murky.

As much trouble as I'd be in with the chief if I got caught searching for my family, Hope and Grandma would take it even worse. They wouldn't be angry, really, but disappointed, worried, deeply concerned for my mental health. So I lie.

I stopped telling them years ago that I'm still looking for Mom and for our brothers and sisters. I don't tell them about the searches I sneak through the database. I don't tell them about the forums and the search engine alerts I have set up for any mention of them or the group. Hope is my younger sister. She doesn't know what it's like to be the oldest. To have helped raise your siblings and then left them all behind to live a life you couldn't bear to live yourself.

I swallow, my throat tight.

"Mercer! You there, Mercer?" I shake myself and look up at Bulldog's fleshy, scowling face. "Earth to Mercer. There she is." He squints his beady little eyes, and I glare up at him before darting a quick glance at my computer, just to make doubly sure I clicked off the database.

"What do you want, Bulldog?"

He shrugs, plants both hands on my desk, and leans forward, leering over me. I crinkle my nose at his bad breath. "You're gonna mess up. You're gonna mess up bad, and soon. And when you do, Mercer, I'm right here to replace you." He shrugs and straightens, folding his arms across his massive chest. "So I don't want anything. I just have to sit back, wait, and let you get in your own way."

My nostrils flare, and I clench my fists under my desk, but keep very still. Shadow must have picked up on the subtle cues of my anger, because he rises and stands beside me, planting his massive head on the desk and looking up at Bulldog. His hackles are raised, and his tail is straight and stiff behind him.

Bulldog gives the dog a wary look, then scoffs and moves on. I watch him go for a long moment, my heart pounding in my chest, both at the panic of almost being caught and with anger. Shadow nudges me, and I tip my head against his for a moment, giving him a hug.

"Thanks, buddy," I murmur into his fur. I click back over to the database and get back to work searching for Jane Doe, vowing not to look up my family again. Until this case is over, at the very least, I can't afford to miss my shot at detective by getting caught using station resources for personal reasons.

Eventually, the day shift officers filter out and head home, including Chief Jamison, and the night shift clocks in. I glance up across the bullpen and note that Detective Hanks is still at his desk. *Interesting.* He might be a jerk to me, but apparently he's a hardworking jerk.

He gets up, heads to the break room, and then moseys

past my desk, a mug of freshly brewed coffee in his hand. He pauses and scowls down at me. The wrinkled brow, narrowed eyes, and set jaw seem to be his permanent expression. "Staying late?"

I nod and lean back in my chair, gesturing at the screen. "Just combing through the database, like you said."

He sniffs, then takes a sip of his coffee, the steam curling around his face. "Yeah, me too, Mercer. Wife wants me to get home, but there's work to do."

I raise my brows, surprised he's sharing any personal details with me. "Do you..." I search for the right words. "*Not* want to go home to your wife?"

He snorts. "Please, Mercer. I love my wife. But being a detective? This isn't just a job. It's a vocation, you know? To do it well, you've got to be deeply devoted." He sighs and shakes his head. "It's hard to be pulled in two directions."

I nod, tapping my fingers against my desk, confused as to why Detective Hanks is suddenly chit-chatting with me. He swallows a gulp of coffee. "It's a good thing you're not dating anyone. You don't have to worry about that."

My jaw drops as I look up at him. "Excuse me? How do you know?"

His dark eyes widen, all innocence. He presses his lips together, looks me up and down, then shrugs. "I assumed."

I gasp. "What the heck?"

With another shrug, the detective spins away and strolls back to his office, leaving me gawking at his back. Sorry, but what the hell? How did *he* know I wasn't dating anyone? I huff and stare at my computer screen without really seeing the data on it. As if he knows my personal life. I could get a boyfriend if I wanted one. I fold my arms across my chest. But I don't want one.

Do I? Why does my mind drift to Detective Dean Wilder and the zip of energy I felt when his warm hand closed around mine earlier? I suck in a breath and shake off the feeling. Great, now Hanks is getting in my head.

Red, the night lieutenant, stands up from his desk and points at another uniformed officer, a young guy by the name of Simmons. "We got a fender bender at the intersection of Main and Skyler. I'm gonna need you to head out." The young officer nods and rises from his desk, keys in hand, then heads out the door.

Red shakes his head, muttering to himself. "Damn tourists. Gonna get worse once they start flooding in for that eclipse party this weekend."

I nod, though he hasn't really been speaking to me or anyone else in particular, and get back to work searching the database.

CHAPTER 15

Officer Dobre glanced at the wall clock across from his lobby desk and sighed. He'd already worked fourteen hours with no end in sight. Chief Novak asked him to stay late to cover for him until he could come in.

"Are you even listening to me?"

The tiny old woman, whose loose skin was creepy beneath her muumuu and housecoat, was glaring up at him with her hands on her hips. Officer Dobre nodded. "Yes, ma'am. Of course I'm listening." He held up his yellow legal pad and pen, with which he'd been taking notes, as evidence.

She scowled and patted at the permed white curls atop her head, "Well, I want to press charges against Howard for eating that cherry pie I made for the church bake sale." She shook her finger at the legal pad. "Write that down."

If he wasn't so tired, he'd laugh. Instead, Officer Dobre licked his lips and did his best to adopt a sympathetic tone. "Mrs. Scudder, it is very understandable that you'd be upset with your husband over such an action. However, I'm not sure this warrants police intervention."

She stomped her foot. "By God, it does." She jutted her chin out.

Officer Dobre summoned every ounce of diplomacy he could muster for the cranky old woman. She was a frequent visitor to the police station for all manner of minor incidents. "We would actually consider this a domestic matter."

"Domestic, my ass," the old woman scoffed in her wavering voice. "That man stole my property and ate it."

Officer Dobre set his jaw but was spared from having to answer Mrs. Scudder immediately by the sound of the fax machine printing behind him. He held up a finger. "Please hold on just a moment, Mrs. Scudder. I need to check on something." In truth, whatever it was could probably wait, but Dobre needed a moment to himself.

He was a patient man but had been pulling double shifts and overtime for months, as Chief Novak seemed to constantly need vacation time and mental health days to go fishing. He was worn out, and tired of not seeing his family and young children. But what could he do? Job options in Elk Ridge were limited.

So he bought himself a few moments to summon the strength to deal with Mrs. Scudder. Most likely, she just wanted someone to air her grievances to. But if he wasn't careful, he could escalate things until he actually needed to take a drive out to her home and speak to Mr. Scudder himself. And that was the last thing he felt like doing.

He turned, walked to the fax machine, and pulled up the page that had just finished printing, the paper still warm under his fingertips. As he stared at an artist's rendering of a woman, his breath caught.

It was as though he'd fallen and had all the air knocked out of him. He knew this woman. He covered his mouth with one hand, the paper shaking in his trembling fingers. He had to blink a few times to get his brain to make sense of the words he was reading. This had just been sent out by the Nightfall Police Station.

They were looking for an ID on a Jane Doe whose remains

were found in the woods outside Nightfall. His stomach twisted with a wave of guilt and fear.

He knew this woman. He spoke with her.

Could he be the reason she was dead?

"Officer? Officer!" Mrs. Scudder's shrill voice jolted him out of his stupor.

He held a hand up to her, instructing, "Just a minute," and rushed down the hall as she yelled after him. He ignored her cries, threw open the chief's office, and dialed from the back phone so as not to be overheard. The phone rang a few times before Chief Novak picked up.

"Now what, Dobre? We're in the middle of breakfast. Don't you know that—"

"Chief, we have a problem."

CHAPTER 16

The next morning, I roll out of bed, feeling half dead. I must look it, too, because when I drag myself into the kitchen, Grandma looks up and makes a face. "You okay, dear?" she asks uncertainly.

I grunt something in reply. I'm so tired from working late at the station and only getting a few hours of sleep that I'm even tempted to drink some of Grandma's coffee sludge. I hesitate with my travel mug at my lips before I pull myself together. *No. I'm not that desperate.*

Soon, Shadow and I are out the door, performing our normal ritual of dumping out Grandma's coffee, stopping by the Daily Grind for our respective treats, and then heading into the station.

Once I've had a few bites of scone and a few sips of coffee, my head feels a little less heavy. I still have to squint against the fluorescent lights, though. I wouldn't feel half as bad if my efforts had paid off. But Hanks and I had stayed until midnight searching the missing persons database without any luck. With nothing to show for my sleepless night, I'm hardly feeling motivated this morning. Still, I remind myself this is an opportunity I've been working years for, and there's a woman who died out in the woods who deserves justice.

I've barely logged on to my computer when Detective Hanks bustles out of his office with a briefcase tucked under his arm. I hadn't even realized he was in yet. I blink in surprise as he heads for the lobby. It looks like he's planning to just leave without even speaking a word to me. I leap to my feet. "Hanks."

He stops dead and slowly spins, clearly reluctant to address me.

I raise my brows. "Uh, should I come with you?"

"Nah." He waves me off. "I, uh…" He scratches the back of his neck. "I've got an errand to run." He turns to leave.

"Wait!"

He huffs and hangs back, even though he's clearly impatient to go.

"I, uh—was hoping we could brainstorm next moves for the case. While you're gone, what should I work on?"

He splays his hands. "Listen, Mercer, just do whatever you'd, uh, normally do. I'll be back in a few hours. We can talk then."

I frown at his back as he nearly runs out of the station. What errand could he possibly have to do this early in the morning and in the middle of an active case, too? I shake my head and plop back down in my seat. Shadow lowers his head with a heavy sigh. "I know, buddy. It was a late night for both of us."

I turn to my computer. What did Hanks mean by "just do what you normally do"? Normally, I'd have some kind of assignment, patrol, or my beat, but I've been assigned to assist him on the case.

I could double-check through the missing persons database, which sounds about as fun as pulling teeth right now. I click through to my email. "I guess I'll start there."

A grin tugs at the corner of my lips and my heart picks up

its pace when I spot a message from Detective Dean Wilder sitting in my inbox. I catch myself and glance around the bullpen, just in case anyone sees me grinning to myself. It's like I'm afraid they know what I might be thinking. And what am I thinking?

I mean, he's just a detective I met briefly. It's not like we're even going to be working together. I shake it off. Probably just the caffeine pumping through my veins that's causing my heart to speed up. I open his email.

Eden, great to meet you yesterday.

I slap my hand over my mouth when I realize I'm grinning like an idiot. I look around the bullpen and make sure Bulldog didn't notice. That's just what I need—one more thing for him to tease me about.

Unfortunately, that first line is where my pleasure stops. Detective Wilder's email goes on to explain that he apologizes, but he's had no luck with the missing persons database, or rather too much luck. Our description of our victim is so general, that he's found lots of hits that *might* be possibilities, but nothing concrete.

I sigh. That's what we've run into, also. It doesn't mean our Jane Doe isn't in there; it's just we don't have enough information on her to say for sure.

I go through the rest of my inbox fairly quickly and soon find myself bored. "Now what am I supposed to do?"

My bestie on the force, Nathan Brooks, strolls out of the locker room with that lopsided grin on his face that makes both of his dimples pop.

He pulls a chair over and sits beside me. "So"—his eyes light up—"how's the case going?"

I shrug and gesture at my face. I know I've got bags under my eyes and I'm paler than usual. "Can't you tell how good it's going?"

He winces. "What's up?"

I explain the ME's findings from yesterday and the

meeting with the detectives from the other cities. I leave out the part about how cute Dean Wilder is. I then recap my night spent at the station poring over missing persons reports with Detective Hanks.

I sigh. "You'd think that working late alongside the man would earn me a modicum of respect, right? But no. Hanks just breezed right past me fifteen minutes ago, saying he has errands to run and that I should just do, quote, 'whatever I normally do.'"

Nathan tips his head to the side, frowning. "Seriously?" I nod and take a sip of my mocha. "When's he gonna be back?"

I shrug. "He said a few hours."

Nathan strokes a hand across his chin. "Well, what do you think your next move should be?"

I scoff. "Oh, since I'm an expert on murder cases now?"

He levels me a look.

"Sorry, I'm sleep deprived."

"Come on, be serious. You're smart, Eden. Give yourself some credit. There's a reason you're assisting Hanks. Pretend this was your case—what would you do next?"

I suck in a breath, thinking over what we know. "Well, we need to identify the victim, and we've had no luck with the missing persons database."

He nods. "Okay..."

"We know she was buried in a ritual fashion... so I suppose I could look into fringe religious organizations in the area?"

He grins. "That's a good start. What else do you know?"

"We know she's blue." I give him a wry grin. "I shouldn't make light, but it's just so strange." I blink, really thinking it over. "But yeah, actually, the ME said there were a few different ways the victim could have developed argyria, that blue tint to the skin."

"There you go." Nathan claps me on the shoulder, grinning broadly. "You're off to a good start. I've got to head out on patrol, but you got this, Mercer." He pumps his fist, and I hold my own up in solidarity.

"Thanks, Brooks."

He waves and is out. I drum my fingers on the desk and pull up my internet browser.

Beth said one of the ways the victim could have developed argyria is through working in a silver mine. I search for active silver mines in the area and quickly discover there aren't any.

I jot "silver mine" down on a pad of paper beside me and cross it off. Next, I write down "jeweler." Maybe a jeweler could tell me a little bit more about argyria and possibly give me some insight into that strange necklace wrapped around our victim's hands.

I look up jewelers in Nightfall, and while one's located really close by on Main Street, they're unfortunately not open today. I huff, frustrated, but get to thinking. I could look for other jewelry shops in nearby towns, or I know the community college has some classes on jewelry making. Hope's taken some art classes there just for fun.

I pull up Nightfall Community College's list of faculty and search the arts department, where I find Zelda Irving. She teaches the various ceramics and jewelry classes. I give her office a call at the listed number, but it goes to voicemail, so I leave my information. I could leave it there, but I'm impatient.

I pull up the class schedule and see that she has Intro to Ceramics starting in about an hour—meaning I know exactly where to find Ms. Irving.

Twenty minutes later, Shadow and I pull up outside Nightfall Community College. It's a small campus of mismatched buildings. Some of the brick ones are quite old, from the forties, with some concrete monstrosities added in the seventies, and then another newer building, all glass windows, that was added maybe five years ago. It doesn't take me long to locate the art department. I knock before stepping into the ceramics classroom with Shadow glued to my side.

An older woman, probably in her sixties with dyed blond hair, stands to the side. She sports a long white tunic with black leggings underneath, a chunky, artsy necklace topping off her stylish ensemble.

"Hello." She looks me up and down, her gaze lingering on my badge and Shadow at my side. "You don't look like you're here for class."

The room smells swampy, like clay, and something faintly reminiscent of paint fumes. I wonder if that's the glazes. Pottery wheels sit on the left-hand wall with tables arranged in a U shape, taking up most of the room. In the back, shelves are filled with vases, mugs, plates, and various small sculptures.

"I'm Officer Mercer. Are you Zelda Irving?"

She hesitates, then nods. "Am I under arrest?" She chuckles, though I pick up on some uneasiness.

I raise a palm. "No one's in any trouble. I just was hoping to ask you some questions regarding jewelry making. You do teach those classes, don't you?"

Zelda grins. "I do, indeed. Looking to change careers?"

I laugh. "No. Just looking for some information regarding a case I'm working on."

"Ah! Walk with me, won't you?" She holds a cardboard box tucked under one arm, and I follow her over to the shelves along the back. She moves along the racks, placing glazed pieces of pottery onto the shelves.

"I'm wondering about argyria."

"Ar-what?" she says, her faint brows raised.

"Argyria. It's a, uh, result of silver poisoning that can lead to a blue tint to the skin, nails, gums—that sort of thing."

She continues placing the pottery pieces on the shelves.

"One cause of that condition can be working with silver as a jeweler. Have you ever experienced anything like that?"

She scoffs. "Never. I think one would have to be touching *a lot* of silver to make that happen."

I nod. It seemed a fairly rare condition. "Do you know anything about it?"

She shakes her head, her long blond hair swishing over her shoulders. "No, can't say that I do. I've been a hobbyist jeweler for decades now, but it's not something I've ever experienced myself, and neither have any of my students, as far as I know."

I make a thoughtful noise. This isn't shaping up to be all that helpful. Deciding to try a different tack, I fish a photo out of my pocket and hand it over to Zelda. It's a picture of the necklace that was wrapped around our victim's hands, with the strange symbol hanging from the thin leather band. It's almost like a cross, but instead of the horizontal line, it's sort of a cat eye shape.

"Does this look familiar to you at all?"

Zelda shifts the box to her hip and studies the photo for a moment, then shakes her head. "No, can't say that it does." Her gaze flicks to my face. "Is this what your blue-tinted jeweler was working on?"

I shrug. "Does that symbol mean anything to you?"

Again, she shakes her head. "No, sorry." She stares at the photo a moment longer. "I *can* tell you that this is the work of a hobbyist jeweler. It's certainly not professional quality work here. Looks like one of my beginning-level students might have made this."

I nod. Interesting. "And this blue tint of the skin—I know you don't have any experience with it, but is reasonable to assume it would be something more prevalent in a hobbyist jeweler over a professional? The teacher presses her lips together and nods thoughtfully. "I think that's a fair conclusion. Even though a professional might work more often with silver, they'd doubtless be better prepared and know how to protect themselves."

"Alright, thank you so much. I'll get out of your way." As Shadow and I leave, a few college students filter in, shooting Shadow curious looks.

Once we hop back in the SUV, I sit behind the wheel without turning on the car and sigh. "That was a bit of a dead end." I suppose we did learn that the necklace was likely made by a hobbyist jeweler.

However, if our victim was the one who made it, or someone she knew made it for her, it only makes my job harder. It would be a lot easier to look for a professional jeweler who has a website and a store than for somebody who just makes necklaces with strange symbols on the side.

So, what next?

CHAPTER 17

I drum my fingers on the steering wheel, and I'm so lost in thought that I startle when Shadow places his big head on my shoulder with a whine. I jump and then chuckle self-consciously, ruffling his fur. "I'm sorry, buddy."

He's been patient with me. We're still sitting outside Nightfall Community College as I ponder our next move. I check my phone. I still have no texts from Detective Hanks, which means no direction as to my next step.

I sigh. For now, it looks like the jewelry angle is a dead end. But there's still one more cause of argyria that I can investigate: colloidal silver. I recall Dr. Beth said something about it being a new age type supplement.

I use my phone to search the internet for the kind of stores that might carry it. Pretty soon, I land on a page for Sage and Crystal Mercantile, located on the eastern outskirts of Nightfall.

I scroll through their online inventory, noting all manner of supplements, homeopathic cures, and tinctures, including colloidal silver. "Jackpot." I put the SUV in reverse and glance back at Shadow. "Hold tight, buddy."

My app guides us to the quaint little store in less than

twenty minutes. I hop out with Shadow, noting just a couple of other cars in the small parking lot. The place is quaint, set in what used to be an old house that they converted into a store. "Sage and Crystal Mercantile" is painted in pretty white script across the big front window, and when we walk inside, high-pitched chimes tinkle overhead.

I choke, immediately hit with the strong scent of patchouli. Squinting through burning eyes, I note the incense smoking on the countertop nearby. That explains it. The main area of the shop isn't too big, probably comprising what used to be the old home's living room and a bedroom or two, with all the walls knocked down so that it's just one big space. Tiny bottles of vitamins, supplements, and various other odds and ends line several rows of shelves.

A thin middle-aged woman with a long black braid down her back spares me a quick glance as she peruses a bookshelf, a wicker shopping basket slung over her arm. The books include titles about gardening, crystals, tarot, and various handicrafts.

Hope has a little bit of a hippie streak in her, and honestly, it's the kind of place she might enjoy. I make a mental note to tell her about it.

"Welcome in!"

A short older woman with long wiry gray hair smiles at me from behind the checkout counter. She's got a loosely knitted purple shawl slung over one shoulder, and her neck, wrists, and fingers are bedecked in bohemian jewelry featuring large stones and crystals.

She smiles at Shadow, then looks back up at me and notes my inquisitive expression. She raises her brows. "Can I help you?"

I give her a friendly smile. "I sure hope so." I stand across from her and place my hands on the counter. "I was hoping you could tell me a little bit more about a supplement I believe you carry: colloidal silver."

"Ah, yes." She nods and tucks a kinky curl behind her ear. "Are you looking to buy some?"

She starts to come around the side of the counter, gesturing toward one of the rows of shelves, but I wave her off. "No, no thanks. Just hoping to learn a bit more about it for a case."

"Oh." She looks interested. So does the other lady, the customer with the black braid. I note her attempting to look nonchalant as she inches closer, obviously eavesdropping, though she's pretending to read the book in her hands.

I lower my voice to keep our conversation as private as possible. "Do you know anything about developing argyria from colloidal silver? It's a kind of blue tint the body can take on."

She flits her eyes to the ceiling and nods. "Oh yeah, definitely something to watch out for. I've seen it happen to a few of my customers. Sometimes people think if a little is good, then a lot must be fantastic." She shakes her head and leans forward, lowering her voice as though she's letting me in on a secret. "Not so much."

I nod.

"So to develop argyria, someone would just be taking too much colloidal silver?"

"Uh-huh." She tips her head to one side. "Or the colloidal silver itself might be too high of a concentration and lead to silver poisoning that way."

"And how do people go about taking colloidal silver? Or do doctors prescribe it, or...?" I trail off, and she picks up for me.

"No, no. Truth be told, it's not really FDA approved, but then again, most vitamins and supplements aren't. It appeals to people who aren't afraid to take their health into their own hands. I suppose naturopaths might recommend it at times, but no, it doesn't require a prescription."

I nod. "Do you, uh, sell a lot of it?"

She shrugs. "Yes. Somewhat. It's not as common as people coming in for vitamin A, for instance, or arnica gel for a bruise. But yeah, it moves."

"Some of these customers you've seen develop it—are these people you've seen recently?"

She squints and tips her head from side to side.

"I'm looking specifically for a woman, young, probably twenty-five to thirty years old, long blond hair, probably quite thin."

The woman looks off as if searching back through her memory, then shakes her head. "No, nobody like that. The only ones I remember were a couple of older gentlemen and then a woman a little older than me."

"Thank you." I hold my hand out, and she gives me a firm handshake.

"Mara. I'm the owner of Sage and Crystal Mercantile."

"Thanks, Mara. Officer Mercer."

I reach into my pocket and hand her one of my cards. "If you think of anything else, please give me a call."

I'm about to leave when I hesitate, noting the collection of handmade jewelry on the glass shelves under the counter. Mara catches me looking and explains, "From some local artists. Do you want to try anything on?"

"No, but um…" I fish around in my pocket and unfold the printed photo of the necklace we found on our Jane Doe. I hand it over to her as the black braid lady continues to pretend not to listen, though she's so close, she's now within feet of the shop owner.

"What's this?"

"A necklace, I think." I tap the symbol. "Have you ever carried anything like that or know who might have made it? Does it look familiar?" I'm expecting a no, but instead, Mara gasps.

"Actually, yeah."

My breath catches. "Really?"

She sucks in her breath over her teeth and squints as though thinking hard. "Yes, I know I've seen this symbol before." She taps the photo. "But it wasn't in jewelry. Actually," she brightens, "now that you mention it, it was a brand of colloidal silver. That was their logo."

I raise my brows in surprise. "Their logo?" That's about the last thing I expected this symbol to represent.

"Mm-hmm. Hold on just a sec." She pulls open a drawer below the cash register and fishes around. Seems like this is her junk drawer. She pulls out handfuls of pens and pencils, rubber bands, and paper clips. Finally, she grabs a stack of business cards and thumbs through it. "Ah, here it is." She holds up a white business card and shakes it before handing it over to me.

My jaw drops when I take a look at it. Sure enough, there's the exact same symbol on our victim's necklace, right there on the card.

And next to the symbol is the company name: The Ascendant Light Fellowship.

I flip the card over, and I'm even more shocked to discover a website, a link for a YouTube channel, and even a PO box in Elk Ridge, Oregon. It's a town only about an hour from us.

I hold up the card and gape at Mara. "You're saying this company tried to sell you their brand of colloidal silver?"

"Mm-hmm." She huffs, crossing her arms over her chest. "Indeed they did. But no way would I carry such shoddy stuff."

I raise my brows. "Was it bad quality?"

She scoffs. "That's an understatement." Mara gestures at the card. "It was way too potent, highly concentrated, and inconsistent from bottle to bottle. These people had no business making colloidal silver, much less selling it."

"Wow. Thank you. Do you mind if I take this?"

She shakes her head and gestures with both hands as if

pushing it on me. "No, no, no, please. There's no way I'm ever doing business with them."

Another question comes to mind. "Did you meet with them personally?"

She nods. "Uh-huh. This fellow came in with a box of bottles for me to sample. Strange guy. Talked and acted real slick, like a lawyer or some kind of Wall Street dude. But he was dressed like, well, like me, like a hippie. Long black hair, lots of jewelry, flip-flops, torn jeans." She shakes her head. "It was strange."

"Thank you. Thank you so much, Mara. You have no idea, but this is a huge help."

I look up and catch the customer staring, her cheeks red, and she looks away, but I'm too excited to care. I thank Mara again, and then Shadow and I hurry out to the SUV. Once in the driver's seat, I stare at the business card in my hand.

"I can't believe it. We have a lead—a real lead."

CHAPTER 18

7 WEEKS AGO

Clay re-read the same page for the third time without actually processing the words. He looked up from *The Fellowship of the Ring* and slowly closed it. This was his third read-through—*The Lord of the Rings* was his favorite series, and normally he could get lost in its pages, transported to another world entirely. It was why he loved his fantasy books; they were the only escape he had. But for the past week or so, he'd been distracted—too worried to get lost in the pages and tune out reality.

Zephyr, who stretched out on the giant bed beside Source, muttered something low in her ear, and Source giggled. Clay sat criss-cross on the space-patterned sleeping bag and sleep mat that made up his bed. That small area, along with a portion of the bookshelves to his left which were dedicated to his fantasy books, made up his little corner of the cabin. It was the only space he could call his own, even though that was a stretch considering it was still Source's room and she could always keep an eye on him.

Orion, Source's right-hand man, paced on the other side of

the bed. Sitting across from Clay, Rainbow perched on an armchair, scribbling in her spiral-bound notebook. She did that all day and a lot of the night, noting every little thing that Source said, did, and thought about. She even stayed there and watched Source while she slept, sometimes.

Clay smirked to himself. Source pretended she never slept. That instead, when she appeared to sleep, she was actually astral traveling, whatever that meant. She said her spirit traversed the energy realms, or something. Most of the adults on the compound seemed to buy it, but Clay didn't. Who snored while they were astral traveling?

Clay summoned his courage to ask the question that had been eating at him every day for the last week, growing stronger and more urgent. He cleared his throat. "Where's my mom?"

Orion froze, raising a dark brow, but Source and Zephyr kept murmuring and whispering to each other as if they hadn't even heard him. Maybe they hadn't. Clay rose to his feet, setting the book aside.

Zephyr lay there shirtless, his long, stringy hair draped over his shoulders, sipping from a flask, while Source lounged on a pile of pillows beside him in a sky-blue robe that matched her electric blue eyes. She had a cigarette between her fingers and a glass of amber liquid and ice cubes in the other. They'd been drinking all afternoon. Clay hated when they drank. Source only smiled or giggled when she was drunk, which oddly seemed to make her more dangerous. It was like her filter was gone, and she'd say the most cutting, brutal insults, or dole out the cruelest punishments. But maybe that lack of a filter would make her spill the truth.

Clay stared at Source, his tone firmer this time. "Where is my mom?"

A slight movement drew his gaze to Rainbow. She used to be called Laura. He faintly remembered meeting her for the first time when they drove up here to Oregon with his mom.

He was really little then, and she'd seemed nice. But after they got here, his mom and Laura didn't seem as friendly anymore.

Rainbow cleared her throat and unfolded her legs, flashing Clay a smile. He thought she looked nervous, though, her eyes darting between him and Source on the bed. "Now, Chosen One," she said in her high-pitched voice, which dripped with honey. "You know that Source is your mother." Her smile grew strained as she stared at him, as if willing Clay to accept her answer. "She's the spirit mother to all of us."

But Clay shook his head. "No. My *real* mom."

Rainbow grew pale, her eyes widening. She had big brown eyes, and Clay could see the whites all around them before she dropped her gaze. Clay spun to face Source, whose legs were stretched out over the comforter, her feet entangled with Zephyr's. "I haven't seen her for days. I usually see her around. Where is she?"

Source peeled her gaze away from her sort-of boyfriend and looked Clay up and down, her expression bored. Smoke trailed from her cigarette, spiraling up toward the peaked ceiling of her second-story room.

Finally, she shrugged. "She left."

Clay frowned. "Where did she go? When is she coming back?"

A cruel smile twitched at the corner of Source's mouth as her glowing blue eyes bored into him. "She's never coming back, Chosen One. Your mother left you." She lifted a thin shoulder. "Doesn't sound very motherly if you ask me."

Hot anger flushed up Clay's chest, and he spun, irritated. As Rainbow scribbled down everything he and Source had said in her stupid spiral-bound notebook, he clenched his hands tightly into fists and glared back at Source and her stupid boyfriend who was pawing at her. "She wouldn't do that." Would she?

Source sniffed, that mean smile still on her face. "Well, she did."

Tears stung at his eyes. Had his Mom really just left him here? He didn't want to believe it, but maybe she had. He barely got to see her anymore, anyway, but why wouldn't she have taken him with her? "You're lying," Clay sniffled.

The room got very quiet. Zephyr, Orion and Rainbow held stock still as Source pushed herself up to sit tall and leveled Clay with an intense look. He'd never dared speak to her like that before. In fact, he'd never seen *anyone* speak to her like that. He tried to keep his chest puffed up, though the tears tracked down his cheeks.

"No, Chosen One," Source purred, her tone too gentle. "No, I *never* lie. I'm Source, your divine spirit mother." She spread her hands wide, her silky robe draping from her thin arms. "I only speak the truth." She cocked her head, examining him. "You know, Chosen One, I believe you need to be purified before our upcoming ceremony."

Clay's stomach twisted with fear. What did she mean by *purified*? And why did this ceremony fill him with such terror? Now that he thought about it, Source had announced her new revelation about this big ritual on the very same night he'd last seen his mother. She'd been running out of the cabin when he'd spotted her, and his mom had looked scared.

Clay sensed something bad was going to happen.

"Rainbow," Source ordered without taking her eyes off Clay, "fetch the colloidal silver."

"Yes, Source." Rainbow leapt out of the chair, placing her notebook on her seat, and dashed past Clay and Source to the nightstand, which stood easily within Source's reach. Rainbow picked up a large amber bottle that was half full with clear liquid and carried it two steps to Clay. Source easily could have done it herself, but she liked to show off her power by ordering other people around.

"Now, take your medicine, Chosen One."

The little boy clenched his teeth together and shook his head. "No."

Source blinked her bloodshot eyes, unbothered. "Chosen One, one way or another, you *are* going to take your medicine."

Clay didn't want to drink the stuff. He'd been made to do it several times and hated the metallic taste. Plus, it always made his stomach hurt after. The other grown-ups seemed to love it, but he couldn't understand why.

He shook his head again, his chin quivering. "Why don't you take your own medicine?" He jerked his chin at the glass of whiskey in her hand.

Rainbow recoiled as if Clay had struck their leader. Source's pale, slightly blue-tinted face flushed bright red. She bared her teeth, revealing blue-tinted gums. "This *is* my medicine, Chosen One. You have no idea what it's like being a conduit for the divine, for the elders, for the salvation of all humanity."

Zephyr stroked her back as if to calm her down while shaking his head in disappointment at Clay. Even Orion shot him a stern look. A vein bulged in Source's forehead. As Zephyr murmured calming words, the loaded gun the man kept on the nightstand beside him didn't escape Clay's notice.

"Now I'm not going to say it again," Source hissed, spit flying from her mouth. "Take your medicine. Or I'll make you."

Clay held his breath, debating. He knew Source would make him take it, and he doubted that would be the more pleasant option. "Fine." He huffed, snatching the amber bottle and a spoon away from Rainbow, who still seemed unable to meet his eyes. She knew something about his mom. He could tell. And he was angry at her for not telling him.

With shaking hands, he poured himself a spoonful of the colloidal silver and gulped it down, crinkling his nose in disgust. It left a tangy metal aftertaste in his mouth. He handed the bottle to Rainbow, but Source shook her head. "More."

Gritting his teeth, Clay poured himself another spoonful and slurped it down.

"More."

He knew what this was. This was Source showing off her power again. When would it be enough? He didn't know. But he was afraid of the alternative punishment if he stopped. He kept drinking spoonfuls of colloidal silver, losing count, until he'd downed nearly a quarter of the bottle. His stomach turned and the liquid threatened to come right back up again.

Finally, Source smiled, though there was no joy in it. "The elders have just told me you've had enough. You're well on your way to cleansing yourself for our lunar eclipse ceremony, Chosen One. Well done."

Nauseous and slightly dizzy, he handed the bottle and spoon back to Rainbow, who replaced them on the nightstand next to Source and then returned to her chair and notebook.

"Oh, and Rainbow," Source added, "the elders are telling me that to help purify Clay, he needs to skip dinner tonight." She leveled the little boy with a threatening stare. "We'll have to see about breakfast and lunch tomorrow, too. Perhaps his purification will put him in a good enough state that he'll be allowed to eat again. But we'll see."

"Yes, Source, of course." Rainbow bowed before dashing out of the room to let Terra know. Terra was the older lady in charge of all the household duties that kept the compound running. She coordinated everyone's chores and mealtimes.

While Clay wasn't too happy to miss dinner, he did have a secret stash of snacks hidden behind the books in his bookshelf. As if Source could read his lack of disappointment, she leaned over the edge of the bed and grabbed the boy's face in her bony fingertips, squeezing it hard, her nails digging into his cheeks.

"If I ever sense that your spirit is in rebellion again, or you dare to speak to me in such a manner, I'll take all of your books away." A smile stretched across her face. "You remember what happened to your teddy bear, don't you?"

Clay felt like he was going to throw up. He nodded, though he could barely move, held tight in her grasp.

"Good."

She let go of his face and smacked his cheek a couple of times, hard enough that it stung. Clay sat back down, feeling the spots on his cheeks where her nails had left little crescent-shaped indentations. He knew not to ask about his mother again, and he also had a sinking feeling that she was indeed gone. He knew he didn't have the full story, but something in his gut told him she wasn't coming back.

CHAPTER 19

I sit idling in the police SUV outside Sage and Crystal Mercantile, staring at the business card the owner gave me. A chill runs down my spine at that symbol—the cat eye with the line straight down the center. I can see it in my mind's eye, placed over our victim's rigid blue hands, bound together in the prayer position.

The Ascendant Light Fellowship tried to sell the mercantile their brand of colloidal silver. Overuse of the supplement is a potential cause of argyria, which our Jane Doe suffered from. It all fits. Our victim has to be tied to this group, and we stand a good chance of at least identifying her, if not even catching her killer among them.

Still, for all the excitement at this break in the case, a sense of heavy dread settles in my stomach. I've been sitting in the car, watching the YouTube channel linked on the back of the business card. I hadn't known what to expect, but skimming through several videos, I notice they seem to follow a similar formula.

One or two people, members of the Ascendant Light Fellowship, sit criss-cross on pillows or floor poofs in front of a hanging backdrop, sometimes tie-dyed, sometimes a brightly painted wall crisscrossed with Christmas lights. They talk directly to the camera, professing their group's beliefs and convincing the viewer to join them, or to show their support by buying products from their website—like colloidal silver, various crystals, or even online blessings.

There seems to be a rotation of several different hosts for the videos. Some men, some women, but all quite thin, almost malnourished. Many have long wild hair and bohemian clothes. They talk of Source being a divine being, a woman with a direct tie to the elders, and describe various revelations she's had bestowed upon her by spiritual beings. They claim that this Source, with a capital *S*, will be their salvation and the salvation of all mankind.

I stare at the business card in my hands and try to breathe, despite the feeling of dread creeping over me. It's pretty clear we're dealing with a cult. And I've had enough of cults to last a lifetime.

Hope and I grew up in the Zion House, a fundamentalist Christian sect convinced the apocalypse was near. Our childhood was horrific. And while this cult seems to be more of the new age variety, I know all too well the abuse of power and coercive control that cult leaders force upon their followers. If our Jane Doe was a part of this Ascendant Light Fellowship, we're not just looking into her murder; we're opening up a whole can of worms.

Shadow turns in the back seat, trying to get more comfortable, and it snaps me out of my ruminations. Staring at this business card won't change anything. It's time to clue in Hanks. I grab my phone and punch his number in on the speed dial. It rings several times before going to voicemail.

Damn it. I leave him a curt message. "Detective Hanks, it's Mercer. Call me back."

I hang up and huff, slumping back in the seat. What is this mysterious errand Hanks had to run? Why isn't he picking up his phone? Maybe he's come back to the station. I call there next, and Joan picks up after a couple of rings.

"Nightfall PD, this is Joan. How can I help you?"

"Hey, Joan, it's Eden," I say.

Her warm, melodic voice has a slight Mexican accent, though her family moved to Oregon when she was a girl. Joan and Linda, the two admins, are besties and frankly, the backbone of the station. They handle all the recordkeeping, organization, and keep everybody straight. Lucky for me, they've both taken me under their wings, and I view them as kind of second mothers.

"Um, is Hanks there? I'm trying to get a hold of him, but his phone just goes straight to voicemail."

There's a long pause on the other end. I can hear the beep of machinery, another phone ringing in the background, and muffled conversations.

"Joan?"

"Oh, Eden, I'm not supposed to say." She lowers her voice to whisper. "But he's in Seaside."

"Seaside?" I scoff. "Why?"

Another pause. "He, uh, took the bullet from your crime scene down there to ballistics for analysis."

My jaw drops. "Without me?"

"Look"—she's still whispering—"he dropped it off and shot me a text that while he's waiting for the report to come back, he'll be at the Seaside PD shooting range. But you didn't hear it from me."

I set my jaw. "Thanks, Joan. You're the best."

"Good luck, Eden. I've gotta go."

As soon as she hangs up, I throw the car into Drive. "Hang on, Shadow," I say, clenching the steering wheel and peeling out onto the highway. "We're heading down to Seaside."

CHAPTER 20

I make good time, pulling up in front of the Seaside Police Department firing range less than twenty minutes after my call with Joan. Still, it's been plenty of time to ruminate over Detective Hanks's infuriating behavior. The chief told him I was assisting on this case.

Why would he ditch me to go speak with ballistics, especially when I was the one who just discovered a key piece of evidence and a huge break in the case? Which he'd know about if he'd frickin' pick up his phone.

I deserve to be a part of this case. I found the body. And I found the business card linking our Jane Doe to the Ascendant Light Fellowship. The grumpy old dude has done nothing but jerk me around, be rude, and leave me out.

I park and yank the keys out of the ignition. That stops now.

I hop out of the car, slam the door, and open up the back for Shadow to hop out. I grab his leash and march into the shooting range.

I'm familiar with the large, dark building. Officers are required to put in a certain number of hours every month practicing, and Seaside is the place to go.

I recognize the officer manning the armory table at the front, though not by name, and raise a hand in greeting.

Bulletproof glass windows look onto the actual firing range, which sits nearly empty aside from Hanks, who holds his standard-issue handgun, firing at a target fifteen yards away from him.

"Hi." I don't wait for the officer to respond. "I need to go in there and speak to Detective Hanks. Can you please keep an eye on my K-9, Shadow?"

"Uh, sure." The officer gestures at a pile of ear protection and safety glasses. "Do you need any bullets or—?"

"Nope." I shove the enormous earmuffs over my head, put on the glasses, and stomp into the range, leaving Shadow and the armory behind.

I march to the middle, and Hanks doesn't look away from his target until I stand right next to him, arms folded across my chest, glaring.

He does a double take, then lowers his weapon and frowns at me. He is clearly shocked and displeased to see me there.

I tap at my earmuffs, then thumb back toward the lobby, mouthing, "We need to talk." He hesitates a moment, then, ignoring me completely, raises his gun and fires off a few more rounds at the target. My jaw drops. What a jerk. I clench my fists and march back outside.

I fold my arms and glare at Hanks's back as he continues to fire at the target. Nostrils flared, I will myself to take deeper breaths until my anger fades to annoyance. As the senior officer, I suppose it's his prerogative to run this errand on his own, but I wish he'd give me a shot. Being underestimated gets old.

I shift my weight and let out a heavy sigh. It doesn't look like Hanks is stopping anytime soon, and I'm already here. Might as well log some practice time.

I walk over to the armory and Shadow wags his tail.

"Sorry, buddy, not done, yet." I turn to the officer. "I changed my mind. Could I get a box of bullets please?"

"What are you using?" I unclip my handgun from the holster and hold it out to him.

He examines the Glock 22, then reaches onto the shelves behind him and slides me a box of bullets across the table. "Thanks." I spin on my heel and stroll back into the range, grabbing a paper target on my way in. I take the lane right beside Hanks. He looks up and rolls his eyes, but I just ignore him.

I clip my paper target up, hit the button, and send it zooming down to the end of the range, twenty-five yards away. It's far. But I take my job and skills seriously and have lots of practice under my belt.

I double-check my clip, adjust my stance, hold the weapon in both hands, and raise it. I take some deep breaths, steadying my hands.

Then I fire off fifteen rounds, grinning when I finish. The thing about me that most officers don't know is that I'm a crack shot.

It's not like I grew up shooting or anything. It's just one of those things I've taken to immediately. When I finish, I set the weapon down, turn on the safety, and then reload. As I do, I glance over and note Hanks isn't shooting anymore, just watching me with a curious expression on his face. I'm slightly amused that now he's interested in what I'm up to. I gesture for him to go ahead and shoot next, but he shakes his head and indicates for me to continue.

Fine. I adjust my stance, lift my weapon, and fire again until I'm out of bullets. I hit the button on the side of the dividers, and my target zooms back toward me. Hanks steps up and does the same for his own target.

We stop them side by side. While Hanks has managed a couple of headshots and several in the center of the chest, the others have missed the outline of the man altogether.

However, my shots are so tightly clumped together in the center of the head they almost could have been one hole.

We stand there several moments in silence before Hanks turns to me and lowers his ear protection. I do the same. He presses his lips together and nods. "Not bad."

I chuckle. Was being a good shot really all it took to get his attention?

He sighs, planting his hands on his hips. "Come on, kid. I know a good place for fish and chips. My treat."

CHAPTER 21

I bite into a delicious piece of fried rockfish—perfectly seasoned, crispy on the outside, with a juicy tender inside.

Hanks speaks around his own mouthful of fish. "Pete knows how to do it right."

We sit outside on the back patio of Pete's Fish and Chips. It's a Seaside staple. During the summer, getting one of these tables overlooking the beach and the ocean beyond is nearly impossible. The place is always at capacity, known not only for its delicious food, though the menu is small, but also for its amazing views. But in January on a cold, blustery day? We've got the back patio to ourselves.

In the distance, towering rock formations jut out of the sea, with more seagulls circling above them. Closer up, Shadow tears across the beach, leaping over pieces of driftwood and chasing away errant seagulls. I chuckle as he nearly gets one. Technically, I probably shouldn't be letting him romp around like this, especially when he's on duty. But though he's remarkably well trained and well behaved, he's still a three-year-old, basically a puppy at heart, and he doesn't get enough opportunities to let loose.

Since the beach is nearly empty, I don't think it's harming anyone. The waves churn, violent and rough, thrashing at the base of the rock outcroppings.

I stuff a few hot fries in my mouth, chew and swallow, then drum on my white mug. Luckily, Pete serves coffee, too. Hanks and I are still bundled up in our heavy coats, but I'm not sure I could take the cold without the hot beverage.

"So..."

I swallow my bite of fries and glance over at Hanks.

A red flush creeps up his neck, and he drops his gaze. "I, uh." He clears his throat, then lifts his dark eyes to mine. "I'm sorry for ditching you."

I raise my brows in surprise. Those aren't words I was expecting to hear from the grizzled detective. He wraps his hands around his own coffee mug and pulls it toward him. "Just used to working alone, you know?"

"Thanks." I nod as I chew on another bite of fries.

Shadow's got the zoomies and tears down to the waterline, going in up to his belly. I groan. "Great, now I'm gonna have to give him a bath."

Hanks grins. He always seems to have a peppering of stubble on his cheeks and jaw. "How did you find me down here, anyway?"

I shrug. "Good detective work, I guess."

He barks out a laugh and tips his head to one side. "You're determined, I'll give you that." He takes another bite of fish and chews on it. "Some might say annoyingly so."

I fold my arms and shoot him a look. "And what do you say?"

He swallows. "I say... you're not a bad shot."

I grin and lean back in my seat. "A better shot than you."

He rolls his eyes. "I just didn't want to make you feel bad."

"Right."

We enjoy a moment of silence, the most companionable one we've shared, watching Shadow have the time of his life.

"No offense," Hanks continues, licking his lips.

I brace myself.

"But I was under the impression you were scared of gunshots."

I don't look at him. "Because of what happened on New Year's Eve?"

He doesn't answer.

I take a deep breath and sigh. I don't like talking about my childhood or my past, but if Hanks and I are going to be working together, I suppose it makes sense to open up a bit. The people closest to me—Nathan, Hope, Grandma—are always encouraging me to talk about myself more, to be less reserved. When you've grown up like I have, I think it's understandable to keep things to yourself, but still, I suspect they're right. I'm not close to anyone at the station except for Nathan, Joan, and Linda, but it'd be nice to have more friends on the force. Or if not a friend, at least an ally.

I take a sip of coffee, the warm liquid sliding down my throat and warming me from the inside. I cup my hands around the mug, letting the heat sink into my fingertips. "I'm not afraid of gunshots," I explain, my voice quiet.

Hanks shifts, leaning closer to better pick up my words over the sound of the waves and the wind.

"Have you heard about how I grew up?" I let my gaze drift over to his elbow and shoulder, not meeting his eyes.

He shrugs. "May have heard a couple of rumors, but I'd rather you tell me."

I nod, steeling myself to talk about something so difficult, so personal. I have a hard time knowing what to share and when. I generally feel like I'm oversharing when I talk about myself, especially my past. I decide to just dive right in.

"My sister Hope and I grew up in the Zion House religious group in Canaan Springs. It's in northern Arizona, right on the border with Utah." I swallow against the tight lump in my throat. "They're basically a cult. They believe the apocalypse is near and that they're the chosen people who'll be saved. They practice polygamy, communal living, and"—I make air quotes—"benevolent dictatorship."

Hanks snorts, and I nod my agreement with his derision.

"The Zion House believes in a chosen speaker, who happens to always be an old white man." I watch my dog tearing around at the waterline. "The speaker has a direct connection to God, they say. And the speaker decides who marries who, among other things."

I fight to keep my breathing even. "Apparently, God told the speaker that there were a lot of underage girls who should be married to old men."

Hanks makes a disgusted noise in the back of his throat.

"The speaker also happened to be my father."

Hanks drags his hand across his mouth but doesn't interrupt.

I press on. "I was fourteen when God told my father that I should be married to my creepy uncle."

"No," Hanks groans.

"Oh, yeah." Saying this with a glib tone is the only way I can get through it. If I really think about it, really dwell on it, I'll be lost in that hole of depression and anguish that swallowed me whole for so many years. I turn away from that hole, from those feelings, and press on with my story, hoping to wrap it up quickly.

"I just... I couldn't do it. The thing is, the entire town was monitored. Six thousand people, isolated from the outside world, from heathens, as they were called. We had no TV, no news, no books."

"Jesus." Hanks shakes his head.

"So when I decided to run away, I didn't know what I was running to. I suspected death, but I came to terms with that. Death was better than the fate that awaited me. I'd seen what happened to my mom, to friends, to cousins. I just couldn't." I lick my lips. "I decided to run away Sunday morning. That was when everyone would be at church. I pretended to be sick and stayed at home, but Hope figured out what I was up to. She's two years younger than me, and we were best friends even back then."

"You weren't gonna take her?"

I look up at Hanks's bushy brows pinched together. I shake my head, mixed feelings of guilt and fear twisting in my stomach, as though I'm reliving those moments.

"We weren't allowed to talk about these kinds of things, even in private, even among each other. I didn't know how she felt and, frankly, I didn't know how to take care of myself, much less a younger sister. I couldn't be responsible for her. But she didn't give me the choice. She pretended to be sick too and insisted I take her with me."

I suck in a deep breath, trying not to be swallowed by the trauma of that morning. "I knew how dangerous it was going to be. I didn't know what would happen to me or to her. And my dad liked Hope. He never liked me. I thought she'd probably get better treatment. Maybe she'd get married to a young guy, someone she actually liked. But Hope begged to come with me. So we ran out across the desert." I lift a palm. "I'd spent weeks planning my escape route. We had chores. Digging up cactus to clear the land was one of them. During that time, I'd found spots where the cameras didn't reach. And so that morning, we took off across the desert. We headed for the mountains."

I clutch my coffee mug like it's a lifeline, digging my fingers into the porcelain. "We'd almost made it when…" I look down and shudder, reliving the moment a bullet had whizzed just past my hair. "They fired at us. Hope and I dropped to our stomachs and looked back. It was our dad and a couple of guys with long-range rifles. I think they were warning shots, though they almost hit us. Dad had a bullhorn. He ordered us to come back then and our penances would be more lenient. Instead, we crawled across the desert all the way to the mountains."

Hanks just stared, his mouth set in a grim line. I knew that look. The one that told me I'd overshared and traumatized my listener.

I took a deep shuddering breath, figuring I might as well finish my story.

"We made it to the other side. Found some cops who listened to us. We called our grandparents up here in Oregon. My mom hadn't been raised in the cult, so these were her parents. And my grandpa came down, picked us up, and took us up to Nightfall. We've been there ever since." I took a deep breath, settling into the more pleasant part of my history. "They adopted us, and Hope and I changed our last names to Mercer.

"So," I pick up a fry, "I'm not afraid of gunshots. But when I'm out in the open and I hear them, or fireworks, or thunder —some loud booming noise—the sounds of those shots whizzing right past my head come rushing back to me. I get triggered. And on New Year's Eve, not only were the fireworks going overhead, but some dumb teenagers fired bottle rockets down the street and nearly took me out."

I set the french fry down, my stomach twisting. I no longer had an appetite. I pushed the basket of fish and chips away. "I'm not proud of what happened. I'm a cop. I should be better than that, but I couldn't help it. I just... reacted and hunkered down like I was under attack."

I clear my throat, struggling to keep my tone light. Shame and embarrassment flood through me, making me unable to meet Hank's gaze or judge his reaction. "New Year's Eve was not my finest moment, but I'm working on it. I've been to more counseling sessions than I can count." I shrug. "I'm better than I was. A lot better. But I obviously still have some issues I have to work out."

Hanks doesn't say anything for several moments. The wind whips my hair.

As Shadow zips past a couple walking hand in hand down the coast, Hanks angles himself toward me and opens his mouth, about to say something, when his phone rings. He glances at the caller ID, then answers it, holding a finger up to me. "Hanks here." He listens for a moment. "Okay. Okay. Yeah, just email me the report. Thanks."

He hangs up. "Ballistics came back on the bullet. It's from a Glock 17 9mm semiautomatic."

I sigh. "So, super common. Probably hundreds of people in Oregon, maybe more, own those."

He nods. "Yep. But listen, kid, when you're working a case, a lot of times it's not one piece of information that gives you a break. It's a lot of little pieces of information that add up to a bigger picture."

I grin. "Actually, that reminds me." I pull the business card for the Ascendant Light Fellowship out of my pocket, put it on the table, and slide it over to him.

He looks at it a moment before his eyes get wide. He taps the symbol on the card. "That's the, uh—"

"Yep, the symbol on that necklace our Jane Doe had wrapped around her hands."

He flips it over and notes the PO box address, just as I had done. "This is in Elk Ridge."

I point. "See the address for the YouTube channel too? I skimmed through some of their videos. Looks like we might be dealing with a cult." I fill him in on the other details I discovered.

"Damn." He taps the card against his hand and gives me a long look, really taking me in. "Well done, kid. Well done."

I give him a tentative grin. Why does praise from the old detective feel so good? He still hasn't directly addressed the history lesson I gave him about myself, but maybe that's not his way. And in any case, I'd rather he just treat me normally and with respect than show me pity or get awkward and avoid me, like others had in the past.

He clears his throat and pats the table, pushing to his feet. "We should get back to the station and look into this."

I raise a brow. "We?"

Hanks smirks. "Yeah, *we*. You're assisting on the case, aren't ya?"

I smile.

He starts across the sand back to the car. "You, me, your wet mutt. Let's go."

CHAPTER 22

Clay crouched down behind the flat tire of a rotting teardrop trailer. Making himself small, he sidestepped until he could peek around it. It'd been a month, or two maybe, since Source announced her latest revelation about the great ceremony they were going to have during the lunar eclipse. It'd also been about two months since his mother went missing. Since she'd stared at him like she was terrified and then run out the door of the mothership.

He didn't know where she'd gone, and he hadn't heard from her since.

He rarely found himself anywhere besides his bed on the floor in Source's room or glued to the leader's side. Still, even from his limited perspective, he'd noticed an uptick in activity. It seemed the compound was always busy with people running back and forth. The chopping of wood and the crash of trees being felled outside started early each morning, and there had been more trips into town. But anytime Clay showed his face, people dropped their voices to whispers and looked at him askance. Or, worse, they rushed up to him, lavishing him with praise, putting their hands all over his shoulders and head, as if his "holiness" could rub off on them.

He didn't feel particularly holy, but Source had deemed him the Chosen One. He often wondered—chosen for what? And now he had nothing but questions. Where was his mother? What was all that frantic activity about? What was this great ceremony Source had been teasing?

Clay was dying to know. After everyone gathered in the mothership that evening for dinner, Source started drinking and smoking and lying all over Zephyr. While Phoenix played the guitar and sang in his gravelly off-tune voice, and others danced, Clay found himself with an opportunity to sneak away.

He glanced back toward the cabin with the lights shining in the windows and the soft strums of the guitar filtering into the quiet night. He turned and looked the other way, toward the clearing behind the buildings. It was too dark to see much, so he crept forward to get a better look.

There was *something* out there in the clearing—a dark looming shadow.

Clay glanced around, then dashed forward, running as fast as his legs could carry him, until he ducked behind some rusting old barrels. Sprint by sprint he got closer, until there was nothing left to hide behind.

With one last glance back toward the glowing yurts and bright cabin, he stood tall and walked into the clearing. He was nearly right up on the big shadow when he was finally able to make it out. He frowned at the giant pile of wood. Big logs, chopped wood, mounds of kindling, all stacked up tall —nearly as tall as the cabin.

Clay stood there in the open, puzzled. What was it all for?

He didn't know what he'd been expecting. Maybe it was reading all those fantasy books going to his head, but he thought they might be building some kind of contraption? A trebuchet, maybe. Or a giant torture device.

He certainly hadn't been expecting something as mundane as a giant pile of wood.

As he stood there puzzling over his discovery, a twig snapped behind him, and he whirled.

"There you are."

Clay stumbled back as River, the only other child on the compound, darted out of the shadows and pulled Clay into a headlock.

"Ow." Clay pried at his arm, but the boy was a couple of years older and much stronger than him. River was allowed to go outside—to run, to play, to get strong, while Clay was kept inside, weak, and small.

"You're not supposed to be out here," River chided him, tightening his grip, nearly choking Clay in the process.

"Cut it out!" Clay coughed, scratching at the boy's arms.

River let him go but gave him a hard shove from behind, which sent Clay tumbling forward, falling on his hands and knees. His palms stung, and as he climbed to his feet, he brushed embedded pebbles out of his hands. "Ow."

"Don't be a big baby."

River grabbed him by the collar of his coat and dragged him back toward the big cabin. "What were you even doing out here?"

At first Clay didn't answer. He just stumbled along, trying to stay on his feet as River pulled him forward. But maybe River will tell him what's going on. "I was just trying to see what everybody's up to. Nobody will tell me anything."

River smirked. They were closer to the buildings now, past the barrels and the yurt his mother used to live in. Clay had no idea where she'd gone. There was enough light now to see River's features. There was a cruel glint in his eyes and a malicious curl to his lips as he grinned at Clay. "Let's just say, I hope you like barbecue."

Clay had no idea what to make of that, but he didn't have

much time to think about it. River dragged him up the stairs of the big cabin and pushed him through the door.

All the adults were busy drinking, laughing, dancing, playing music, but Source noticed as soon as Clay stumbled inside. She looked up from where she lounged on one of the couches, her head resting in Zephyr's lap. She propped herself up on her elbow. Her eyes were bloodshot, and she held a glass of whiskey in her hand.

She was drunk, which made her dangerous. Clay's legs trembled. He knew he was in trouble now.

Her blue eyes locked onto River, who shoved Clay forward again. Clay nearly fell but managed to catch himself. "He was out in the clearing."

More of the adults quieted and looked his way as Source rose to her feet. She wore one of her long flowing robes that made her look like an angel, though she couldn't be further from one.

"Now, Chosen One," she purred as she folded forward at her hips so that her eyes were level with his.

Clay couldn't meet her gaze.

"You know you're not supposed to go outside alone. Don't make me worry about you." She grabbed his cheek and pinched it so hard that tears sprung to his eyes.

"Sorry," he muttered.

"Are you all right, dear?" Terra, the older woman who reminded Clay of his grandma, or at least his faint memories of her, rushed forward along with a few other men and women, who all fussed over him.

"Chosen One, are you all right?"

"You're not supposed to be out there in the dark by yourself."

"Were you scared?"

Source waved them all away. "He's fine." She said it with a smile on her face, but her jaw was tight.

After she shooed the concerned adults away, Source

lowered her lips until she was speaking in a whisper right against Clay's ear, which made him shudder. "You love all the attention, don't you?"

Clay froze.

"You love taking it from me."

He had no idea what she meant. Source was always the center of everything. The only reason he got any attention from the adults was because she dubbed him the Chosen One. Was she jealous of him?

Source planted a hand on his shoulder and dug her fingernails into his skin. "Well, Chosen One, you'll soon be the star. No one will be able to look away from you."

She gave him one more painful pinch of the cheek before swaying her way back to the couch and flopping down in Zephyr's lap. He handed her a cigarette, and she fell easily back into her role as the divine mother of all, laughing and smiling, looking like a blond goddess.

Tears sprung to Clay's eyes and he rushed upstairs to collapse in his corner. He let the hot tears flow down his cheeks as he hugged his knees up against him. Sometimes Clay thought he was the only one who saw that other side of Source. The side that wasn't angelic or divine.

But why was he the only one who saw it? Was he the one in the wrong? Was he crazy? And what was that pile of wood in the clearing all about?

CHAPTER 23

"Blessings. Blessings." The two women in the video bow their heads, their hands held in the prayer position at their chests.

Hanks taps the keyboard of his computer, pausing the video. "That's the last one, posted two days ago."

"Got it," I say, standing beside the wall where we've been arranging all our information about the Ascendant Light Fellowship. Hanks and I have been watching the cult's YouTube videos for hours, and we're using one of the walls in his office as our evidence board. We've screenshotted the cult's videos going back months and printed out pictures of each of the members who make an appearance, then tacked them to the wall.

I squint at the paused image on Hanks's screen. "So that's Rainbow." I tap an image on the wall of a thin woman who looks to be in her late twenties, with dark brown, shoulder-length hair and wide, big brown eyes.

All the videos are starting to run together in my mind since we've been at this for hours. But Rainbow sticks out to me—she seems nervous and meek.

"And Athena," Hanks says, gesturing at the older woman beside her on screen.

I slide to the right, finding the photo of the older, gray-haired woman already on the wall. "Got her."

I back away from the wall, and my colleague spins in his chair to face it, alongside me. "So in summary, we've identified Source." I gesture at the beautiful blond woman with intense blue eyes who seems to be their leader. "Rainbow, Phoenix, Athena, Zephyr, Terra, and Luna."

My colleague leans back in his chair, his arms folded over his chest, and nods. "We have no clue who else might be there, though. These are just the ones who've appeared on screen."

I nod my agreement. The two women in the latest video are sitting on floor pillows, filming in front of some kind of hanging tapestry background covered in colorful tie-dye. That's how all the videos are filmed. Sometimes they sit at a table that I guess to be in a kitchen. But their setup always features some sort of hanging backdrop, so we can't see much of their surroundings. My gut tells me there are probably many more followers off screen.

In this latest video, Athena and Rainbow went on and on about some great ceremony they have planned for a couple of nights from now, during the lunar eclipse.

Hanks drums his fingers on his desk. "What do you think this ceremony of theirs is all about?"

I shrug. "Could just be their own version of a lunar eclipse party. You know, incorporating some of their beliefs into it, giving the natural event their own significance."

The detective sucks in a deep breath, his brows knitted together. "Could be. So what do we know?" he muses. "What do we know?"

"We believe they're filming from a house," I say, glancing at all the photos tacked to his wall. "But it's hard to tell. There are at least seven members of the Ascendant Light Fellowship, but those are only the ones we've seen on screen, and they make reference to quite a few others."

I step closer to a piece of paper where I'd been jotting down the tenets of their philosophy in Sharpie. Although a lot of their words are gibberish, we've done our best to outline what we've gathered of their beliefs.

"One," I recap for the detective. "Source is a divine being and the mother of them all. Two, everyone is to worship Source. Three, they seem to value nature. Four, it seems to be their goal to indoctrinate the entire world, as far as we can tell, into their belief system, and in order to raise the money and resources they need to do that, they sell colloidal silver, crystals, soap, and remote healings. Five, their symbol supposedly represents the third eye, with the vertical line through the center symbolizing Source's direct connection to the elders and other divine beings."

My colleague scrubs his hand over his stubbled chin. "We've seen several of them wearing similar necklaces to the one we found on our Jane Doe." He sighs. "Which strongly suggests that she was either a member of this Ascendant Light Fellowship or one of their victims."

I fold my arms. "If she was one of their members, why wouldn't they have reported her missing?"

My colleague splays his hands. "Groups like this don't tend to be the most trusting of the government. Could be innocuous, but my money is that one, or all, of them killed her."

I think about the way in which the killer arranged her body and stifle a shudder. The memory of that body buried under the stones, the head between the ankles—those weren't images I was going to get out of my head anytime soon.

We stand there staring at the evidence arranged on the wall, puzzling over it for a few minutes in silence. Finally, I turn to Hanks. "Any news from the judge?"

He spins to face his computer and clicks over to his email,

scanning the inbox. "Nothing yet. I expect we'll get it first thing in the morning, though."

He'd rushed through a warrant to get information from the USPS on that PO box out in Elk Ridge. Hopefully, the address of the group's headquarters will be on file with them.

Nathan pops his head into Hanks's office, knocking on the open doorjamb. He nods at the detective, then grins at me. "Hey, Eden."

I frown, shocked to see him. "Nathan, what are you doing here so late?"

He shrugs and steps into the office. "We've got tons of tourists flooding into town already for the lunar eclipse party this weekend. The chief has quite a few of us pulling overtime to help with traffic, parking, tickets, keeping the order. You know how it can get down on the beach."

I nod. Most of the time, it's peaceful and quiet. But when we have big influxes of tourists, sometimes the beach bonfires can get out of control, especially when there's drinking and other substances involved.

Nathan grins, showing off his dimples. "Just got off duty, though. A bunch of us are heading over to the pub. You wanna come?"

I don't hesitate. "No, thanks. Have fun, though." Nathan pats the doorjamb and then ducks out. I notice a few other officers filing out of the station, grabbing their coats.

"You should go sometimes." Hanks raises his brows at me. "Builds camaraderie."

I smirk. "You never go out."

He scoffs. "I'm old. Don't you have somewhere more fun to be on a Friday night?"

I plant a hand on my hip. "First of all, I'm assisting with a murder case. But also, no."

My colleague's gaze drifts to the framed picture of him and his wife on his desk. They're out on a lake somewhere, fishing poles in hand. "Let me give you some advice. Don't let this job be your whole life, kid. Trust me. Not everyone's as accepting as my wife. You don't want to get twenty years in, look around, and find your life empty."

CHAPTER 24

Clay slowly pushed himself up to sitting. It was cold and dark. He'd been pretending to be asleep for hours, waiting for Source to finally come to bed, then waiting for her snoring to grow loud and steady. Luckily, she came to bed alone and was in a deep sleep now. It was his time to act.

Shaking with a mix of nerves and cold, Clay slowly and carefully moved around in his bed on the floor. Tucked under his pillow was a small bundle of the only possessions he'd be bringing with him: *The Fellowship of the Rings* and a small amount of food he'd been able to hide away—an apple that was probably past its prime but still edible, a piece of bread, and a few crackers. He'd tied it all up in one of his few shirts.

He got to his hands and knees and crawled off his bed toward the door. Slow as he went, a floorboard creaked under his knee, and he froze, listening. Source continued her steady snoring. Barely daring to breathe, Clay crawled toward the door and slowly rose to his feet.

Usually, his coat was kept on a hook on the back of the door. He took a risk earlier and stood on a chair, pulled it down, and draped it over the armchair next to the fireplace.

Before Source came to bed, he counted on her being too drunk to notice, and the risk paid off. Otherwise, he would have been too short to reach his jacket, and without it, he probably wouldn't last long out there in the cold night.

He slipped his arms into the puffer jacket and, still in his socks, picked up his bundle and slowly turned the cold metal doorknob. He eased the door open, wincing at the creak of the hinges.

Source snorted, mumbled something in her sleep, and then rolled onto her side. Clay's heart thundered in his chest, his heartbeat pulsing in his ears. He held his breath, waiting until the snoring became steady again. He waited even longer before easing the door a few more inches open and slipping out.

Once on the landing, it began to feel real to him. He eased the door closed behind him, then crouched down and crept up to the banister. He peeked down onto the great room below. Embers still burned in the fireplace, casting the large space in dim light. He blinked, letting his eyes adjust, then scanned the dark shadows for any adults. It was late enough that it looked like everyone had gone back to their rooms or trailers or yurts. Sofas and beanbag chairs cluttered the downstairs, but he didn't spot any people.

His heart hammered as he slowly crept down the stairs, one at a time, easing his weight onto them to avoid creaking.

Earlier in the day, he'd made a decision. He was leaving. He would look for his mom, or go back to his grandma, but no matter where he ended up, it'd be better than living with Source. Clay eased down another step, and as he got closer to the ground floor, overheard voices. A deep voice. And a couple of higher ones. Some laughter. *Shoot.* There were still some adults in the kitchen. This would make things more difficult, but maybe if he ducked behind the furniture, he could make it out the front door without them noticing.

Clay eased off the final step onto the cold wooden floorboards. He crouched down and backtracked to hide behind one of the couches. He listened for a bit. The adults were speaking too softly for him to make out any words, but he heard their voices. A man and two women, at least.

Hugging his little bundle of belongings tight to his chest, Clay crept toward the front door until nothing but a last dash stood between him and the outside world. No furniture to hide behind. And he had to pass in front of the opening to the kitchen.

He could do it, though. Even though his heart pounded and his legs trembled with fear, he told himself he could do it. Somewhere in the shadows near the door, his small shoes sat piled up next to the big shoes of the adults.

He just had to find them, get out the door, put them on, and then he could make a run for it. If he could just get out unseen, it would be hours before anyone noticed he was gone, and he'd have a head start.

Slowly, slowly, staying low to the ground, Clay crawled to the front door.

He rummaged around in the piles of shoes when a light flicked on to his left. He raised his hand instinctively, shielding his eyes and blinking away the spots.

"Hey, what are you doing up?"

He recognized Zephyr's deep voice and spat out the first lie that came to mind. "I had to go to the bathroom."

Clay grabbed his shoes, finding them at the last moment, and ran all the way across the big room to the bathroom on the ground floor, slamming the door behind him and locking it.

"Hey, kid," the man called after him. "Kid, what are you doing?"

Clay shoved his feet into his shoes. His hands trembled as he fumbled with the laces, finally managing to tie them.

Zephyr banged on the door. "Hey, kid, open up."

A woman asked, "What's going on?"

"What's Chosen One doing out of bed?" another woman questioned.

Clay bit down hard on his lip, looking around the bathroom, panicked. If he was discovered now, with his shoes and his jacket and his little bundle of belongings, they'd figure out that he was running away. There was nowhere in the bathroom to hide his things. But there was a small window high up the wall.

To Clay, it seemed his only choice was to continue on. He climbed up onto the toilet seat, then the tank. From there, he managed to unlatch the window and slide it open. Cold night air flooded in.

"Hey, open up, kid!" Zephyr banged on the door, his tone less perplexed now and more demanding.

Clay tossed his little bundle out the window first, then stood on his tiptoes and managed to pull himself up. Once his torso was out the window, he tumbled out, falling hard onto the ground below. "Oof!" He lay there, the wind knocked out of him, trying to breathe again. He couldn't move.

The dogs started barking. *Oh, no.* Clay loved animals, but these compound dogs were practically feral and lived entirely outside. There were four or five of them, all big and unfriendly, and Source used them as guard dogs. If they kept up like this, they'd wake up the whole compound.

Clay managed to scoop up his bundle, stagger to his feet, and break into a run toward the tree line. If he could make it into the forest, he could at least hide. They'd come looking for him, sure, but he was little, and the forest had infinite hiding places. He just had to get there.

He glanced back. Silhouettes of a man and some women rounded the side of the big cabin.

"There he is!" one of the women screamed.

Although icy fear flooded through him, Clay pushed himself to run faster. His lungs burned but he pushed on, his legs pumping as hard as they could.

He wanted to look back, but he wouldn't do it. He knew it would just scare him. He knew they were chasing after him. He just had to make it to the trees.

The dark shadow of the forest loomed closer and closer. There was safety in the darkness. But just as Clay began to think he was going to make it, he was thrown to the ground. Again, the wind was knocked out of him. A heavy weight landed on top of him.

"Gotcha, kid." It was Zephyr. Clay scrabbled to his hands and knees, still making a run for the forest, but the much stronger man grasped him by the back of his jacket. He spun Clay around and got in his face. "What were you thinking?"

Clay didn't answer. He'd had one chance at escape, and he blew it. Still struggling to catch his breath, tears poured down Clay's face.

The man shook his head in disgust, then straightened and dragged Clay back toward the big house. "Come on, Chosen One." There was a hint of mocking in his voice. "Source is going to have some words for you."

CHAPTER 25

Hanks parks his sedan in front of Elk Ridge's post office. We both lean forward, squinting at the old building through the windshield.

"It's…" I trail off, looking for the right descriptor. "Historic."

Hanks snorts. "That's generous. Place is on its last leg." He turns off the ignition, and we hop out of the car. I fetch Shadow out of the back, and we walk up to the tiny building.

I consider Nightfall a small town, and many of our buildings, including our post office, police station, and city hall are housed in quaint, old buildings, full of brick, real wood, and a certain charm. Our main street bustles with boutiques, shops, and cafes, and a hotel sits at either end.

Unlike Nightfall, Elk Ridge consists of one short strip through the middle of what apparently constitutes their downtown. Boards barricade half of the shop windows, and instead of quaint boutiques, I spot an ammunition store, a check-cashing place, a pawnshop, and a couple of bars I'd be afraid to step into after dark.

A bell tinkles over the door as we step into the post office.

I follow Hanks, with Shadow strolling along at my side, past a bank of brass PO boxes up to the counter.

Dark scuffs mar the linoleum floor, and fluorescents flicker overhead. The dirty windows let in a murky brown light. There's a female postal worker engaged in helping a middle-aged man ship a dozen parcels. She barely spares us a glance. We stand in front of the other worker, a portly older guy with a white goatee and a lanyard around his neck with an ID that tells us his name is Gary.

He sits perched on a stool and fiddles around in the drawer in front of him, ignoring us for long enough that Hanks and I exchange amused looks before the detective loudly clears his throat. Gary looks up with a bored expression that says he's clearly aware of our presence and simply doesn't care.

Hanks pulls out his wallet and flashes his badge. "I'm Detective Hanks from Nightfall PD." He gestures at me. "And this is Officer Mercer." He slides the very official-looking warrant we picked up from the court this morning across the counter. "We've got a warrant to get information on an Elk Ridge PO box."

Gary slowly peels his eyes from Hank's face to the signed warrant in front of him. He pats his pockets and his head until he finds the reading glasses hanging from his neck and carefully places them on his nose. He then examines the warrant with the speed and urgency of someone perusing the local newspaper on a Sunday morning with a cup of coffee.

Hanks is scowling within seconds, and even I'm losing my patience by the time Gary lowers the warrant, takes off his reading glasses, and gives us a nod. "All right, give me just a moment, please." He slides off his stool and lumbers through swinging doors into the back.

Hanks turns around and leans his back against the counter, pinching the bridge of his nose. "For fuck's sake."

I chuckle, keeping my voice down as the other worker scans packages. "This seems like a sleepy town."

Hanks snorts. "More like comatose." He shakes his head. "Seems like an odd place for a cult to set up."

I think back to Canaan Springs, where I'd grown up. It'd been a remote blip out in the middle of the desert, well isolated from the nearest town. I shake my head. "Nah. Cults like to keep to themselves. They don't like a lot of outside interference. The more remote, the better."

Hanks tips his head, acknowledging my point. About fifteen minutes later, Gary shuffles back up front with a handwritten note. He slides the paper across the counter and Hanks snatches it up, holding it so I can see as well.

In Gary's chicken scratch script is written *17573 South Maddox Road, Elk Ridge*.

Hanks holds up the paper. "This the address tied to that PO box?"

Gary nods as he slides onto his stool. "Yup." He looks at each of us. "You two got business with that group of weirdos out there?"

Hanks and I exchange looks. Sounds like we have the right address. Hanks presses his lips together. "Possibly."

"Well—" Gary lets out a humorless laugh. "—good luck."

Hanks leans forward, his elbows on the counter, and adjusts his tweed jacket. "What do you know about them?"

"Eh." Gary tips his head to one side. "Like to keep to themselves. They come in every few days, pick up their mail, don't say much."

Hanks narrows his eyes. "Same person or different people each time?"

The postal worker looks off as though racking his brain. "Eh, they rotate through, but maybe two or three of them taking turns. One of them seems a little more normal than the others. Says hello, goodbye, the normal stuff." He shakes his head. "The others, though, smell terrible. Half the time they don't even wear shoes."

Hanks pats the counter and holds up the piece of paper in his other hand. "Thanks for this, Gary."

Gary holds up a hand. "Course, Officers." We bid him goodbye and step back outside.

We're about an hour inland, and it's colder than in Nightfall, which benefits from the ocean keeping the temperature a little more mild. I shiver even in my big coat, and my breath fogs in the morning air.

A light drizzle falls, and even here on Main Street, the place smells like pine and fresh earth. Elk Ridge is rural, nestled deep in the forest. "Well, what next? Are we going to head out there?"

Hanks looks up and down the nearly empty Main Street. "Yeah. But first we'll check in with the local PD." He shoves his hands in the pockets of his jeans. "They can give us an idea of who we're dealing with. Plus, we'll give them a courtesy heads-up that we're investigating in their jurisdiction."

"Sounds good." Luckily for us, the police station is literally next door in the same building as the post office.

CHAPTER 26

Officer Dobre yawned, nearly nodding off at his desk. He glanced at the picture of his young family, framed beside his elbow. He should have gone home over an hour and a half ago, but when Chief Novak came in, he asked him to stay later to do some more paperwork that rightfully should have been Novak's. Dobre heard his wife's voice in his head, telling him he should set stronger boundaries with the chief.

But she didn't know what he was like—his temper, the threat of violence that always seemed to lace his words. Besides, Dobre needed this job to support his family. And keeping his job depended on staying in Novak's good graces. He'd just finish up this paperwork and get home. He missed the chance to make his kids breakfast and send them off to school like he normally did, but hopefully he could be there to pick them up after school.

His eyes were down when the door chimed, and he inwardly groaned. *Great.* Some new complaint to deal with before he could clock off. Stifling a sigh, he looked up and tried for a pleasant smile that immediately faded when he took in the small group gathered in the lobby.

A pretty, blond young woman in uniform blues just like his own stood there with her K-9 on a leather leash. He was a big, handsome-looking German Shepherd. Beside her, an older man with gray stubble in a tweed blazer and jeans fixed his sharp gaze on Dobre.

His stomach twisted in a nervous knot as he forced himself to ask, "Welcome to Elk Ridge PD. How can I help you?"

The trio stepped forward, and the older man pressed a hand to his chest. "I'm Detective Hanks from Nightfall PD. This is Officer Mercer and her K-9, Shadow." Dobre gave each a polite nod, then a genuine smile for the dog, who wagged his tail a couple of times.

The detective raised his thick eyebrows. "Is your chief in?"

Dobre's heart sank the moment he heard "Nightfall PD." He knew what this was about. He and Novak had already discussed this scenario, but Dobre felt uneasy. He cleared his throat, which was quickly closing up. "Um, yeah. Let me just go and, uh, get him."

To his surprise, Chief Novak came strolling down the hall before he could go fetch him. Novak gave the Nightfall cops a broad smile and shook hands with each of them. "Chief Novak, at your service. Now, how can I help you folks?"

Dobre blinked, shocked. He had been expecting Novak to be hostile, angry at cops from Nightfall infringing on Elk Ridge territory. Instead, he was acting downright chummy.

"Well, we appreciate your assistance." The detective smiled. "We're investigating a case that might have us looking into some folks on the outskirts of Elk Ridge, and we're hoping you could give us some information about the Ascendant Light Fellowship. Plus," he lifts a palm, "we wanted to give you the professional courtesy of a heads-up that we'll be in your area."

"Well, that's downright decent of you," Chief Novak said with a broad smile. "Yeah, I know that group you're talking about." He waved it off. "Just some kooky folk living on their own, way out there in the forest."

The detective nodded, and the young officer kept her eyes glued to Novak's face as though studying him. "So they don't cause you much trouble?" the detective asked.

"Oh no." Novak rocked on his heels. "A few of them come into town every now and then for groceries, supplies, get their mail, that sort of thing." He laughed. "But they mostly just keep to themselves."

"How many would you say there are?" Detective Hanks asked.

Novak looked off into space. "Well, hard to say. But maybe fifty, sixty of them? How come? They in some sort of trouble?"

The younger officer stepped in. "We're looking into a Jane Doe we have reason to believe might be associated with that group." She pulled a piece of paper out of her pocket and unfolded it, holding it up for Novak and then Dobre to see.

Dobre felt like he might throw up. He was lightheaded and suddenly grateful he was still sitting, for fear of fainting.

"Do you recognize her?" the officer asked Chief Novak first.

Of course they recognized her. When the fax had first come in, Novak forbid Dobre from contacting the Nightfall PD. He denied the drawing was the same woman who had come into the station that night a couple of months ago. But now that the detective mentioned her connection to that culty group, surely Novak couldn't deny it was the same person they'd spoken with.

But Novak made a show of studying the artist's rendering of the blond woman with braids, then shook his head. "Can't say I do. If she's part of that group, she must not be one of the ones that come through town."

Dobre gaped at his chief, shocked that he was maintaining his denial.

Hanks made a thoughtful noise, and the young officer turned to Dobre. "Do you recognize her?"

Dobre's mouth went dry. He tried to swallow, but his throat was so tight, he could barely manage it. "I, uh, um. Hm...," he stammered, then caught Novak glaring hard at him.

Novak already made it clear what he expected from Dobre. The officer's eyes briefly flicked to the framed picture of his family, reminding him of the need to keep earning money, to keep putting food in their mouths. He cleared his throat and managed to mumble, "No, no I don't."

Both the detective and the uniformed officer stared at him, letting the silence stretch on. A trickle of sweat tickled at Dobre's hairline, and he hastily wiped it away.

"Well." Detective Hanks eventually broke the silence. "We faxed out this image to all the local stations a few days ago. You fellas didn't get this?"

Dobre looked to Novak for help. He already felt terrible about lying and was sure he had a terrible poker face. Novak pressed his lips together and shook his head. "Apologies, but can't say that we did." He chuckled. "We're a small station, as you can see, just the two of us. Easy for things like that to get lost in the shuffle."

A disbelieving smile stretched across the detective's face. "Right, of course."

Maybe it was just in Dobre's head, but the tone of his voice clearly suggested he didn't believe them. More sweat trickled down the back of his neck.

"Well, thanks for your help, fellas. We'll be in touch if anything comes of this."

To Dobre's relief, the cops and their dog headed back out the door. The detective popped his head back in, and Novak, who'd let his chummy smile slip, plastered it back on his face. "Forget something?"

"No, just wanted to say it's quite the truck out there. That belong to either of you?" He gestured at Novak's ridiculously large, lifted truck parked in front of the station.

Novak smiled, genuinely prideful. "That'd be mine."

Detective Hanks nodded as he looked from the truck out the window back to Chief Novak. "Must pay well to be Chief of Elk Ridge, hm?"

His words hung in the air between them. Dobre could practically feel Chief Novak bristling, but he managed to keep that grin on his face, though his eyes were hard. "Much obliged."

With a little wave, Detective Hanks stepped back out the door, and it swung shut behind them. Chief Novak's face was rapidly turning a deep shade of red as he planted his hands on his hips, breathing heavily through his nose. He waited until the Nightfall cops pulled out in their sedan and headed off down Main Street toward that odd compound they were asking about.

"How dare they," Chief Novak hissed through gritted teeth. "How dare they!" He slammed a fist against the wall. "We have this under control."

Dobre's stomach churned with an uneasy mixture of fear and guilt. He hated that he lied. Not only morally, but because legally he was obstructing an investigation by not telling them what he knew. He was tempted to raise his concerns with the chief but hesitated. Novak's temper was notorious. In a state like this, the man could easily turn violent.

Still, Dobre mustered the courage to speak up. "Shouldn't we have told them that the woman came into the station?"

"No." Chief Novak swiped a hand through the air. "Like I already told ya, it wasn't her. It wasn't. You got that through your thick skull? We have nothing to tell them." He raises his brows. "Understood?"

Dobre was too scared to answer, so he merely managed to nod.

"Good." Novak stomped down the short hallway to his office, where he picked up the phone. He could only hear the chief's side of the conversation, but it was enough to make his blood run cold.

"Hey. It's Novak. Yeah, we had two Nightfall cops just in here sniffing around. Heads-up, they're headed your way."

CHAPTER 27

We bump along the dirt and gravel road. It's uneven, full of divots and potholes. All the recent rain hasn't helped the poor condition of it.

"You sure this is the right way?" Hanks peers through the windshield.

I nod, consulting the map on my phone. "I think so." I punched in the address we got from the Elk Ridge USPS before we left Main Street. Despite the chilly, drizzly day, Hanks has rolled the back window down for Shadow, and he has his enormous head sticking out, a giant grin on his doggy face. The wind ruffles his fur, though we're crawling along at a snail's pace. At least the rain means we're not kicking up a bunch of dust and dirt.

I glance back at my goofy dog. We passed a rundown farmhouse with several broken-down cars in the yard about ten minutes back but haven't seen another home since. I look back down at the map on my phone. Maybe we did get lost after we left Elk Ridge. My app estimated it would take us about twenty-five minutes to reach the Ascendant Light Fellowship's compound. I retrace our steps in my mind. From Main Street, we'd turned down a two-lane highway, and then from there off onto this dirt road. And now, we find ourselves winding back through the dense forest.

"I see something." Hanks points through the windshield, and I lean forward, squinting. A break in the dense line of trees lining the dirt road suggests we might be nearing private property. Hanks slows as the tree line drops away, revealing acres of cleared land.

We roll past a tall metal fence, and Hanks turns into the pullout, only to stop short as we nearly run into a closed metal cattle gate. "This it?"

I nod, checking the map. "Looks like it."

I'm too busy checking out the buildings in the distance to notice the man sitting on a camp chair right next to the gate until he rises and walks up to it.

"The hell is this?" Hanks mutters. "Come on." He turns off the ignition, pockets the keys, and we hop out of the car. I open the door for Shadow and grab his leash.

The three of us walk shoulder to shoulder up to the gate, where the man now leans with his elbows on one of the bars, a pleasant smile on his face. He's got long, shiny dark hair pulled back into a low ponytail. He's dressed casually, but his white button-up shirt, worn open at the neck, and dark jeans are well cut, almost as if they've been tailored to fit him. His rain slicker looks new too, as do the pointed cowboy boots peeping out from under his pants. He looks oddly put together considering the rural setting.

Behind him, down a long dirt road, sits a grouping of buildings. In the center stands a tall wood cabin with peeling paint and one window boarded up. Encircling the cabin is a mishmash of trailers on blocks, yurts, and little shack-like buildings with rusting barrels, rotting wooden pallets, and various other debris sprinkled between. A few cars and a truck are parked in front of the cabin, though I can't tell from this distance if they're in working order or not.

We walk up to the well-dressed man, who lifts a hand in greeting. "Can I help you, officers?"

His voice is low, smooth. He smiles broadly at us, his teeth oddly white and straight. While he might be living here now, he doesn't look like he comes from a place like this. If I'd seen him on the street, I'd have guessed him to be a well-groomed businessman. Then again, the long hair and the overly tanned skin do hint at a more hippie-ish, outdoors lifestyle.

I let Hanks take the lead. He introduces us, and then asks the man his name.

"I'm Orion."

Hanks waits a beat, then sniffs. "You got a last name, Orion?"

"Orion is the name Source gave me. Source is the leader of our—"

Hanks cuts him off by holding up a hand. "We're familiar. You're with the Ascendant Light Fellowship, correct?"

Orion's smile deepens. "That's right."

"We're looking for someone. You recognize her?" Hanks gestures at me, and I hold up the artist's rendering of our Jane Doe.

The drawing features the symbol, which I know is the logo they use on their business cards. But Orion merely shakes his head. "Sorry, no, but I'm bad with faces." He splays his hands.

Bullshit. I'd put down money that he's lying. "Have any of your people gone missing?"

He doesn't hesitate. "No, ma'am."

Hanks gestures with his chin toward the grouping of buildings behind Orion. "Think we could come in and ask around, see if anyone else recognizes her?"

"I'm afraid not." Orion's brows draw together as he gives us an apologetic smile. "It would disturb Source."

Hanks folds his arms and steps his feet wider. "Well, we wouldn't want that, now would we?"

Orion keeps the smile plastered on his face, pretending not to pick up on Hank's sarcasm.

I try to go the nice cop route. "We understand. We don't want to disturb anyone." I lift my palms. "Maybe we could just take a look around?"

Orion presses his lips together tightly and shakes his head. "Sorry."

I set my jaw, frustrated. This man is stonewalling us.

A red flush creeps up Hanks's neck, and his nostrils flare with anger. "Maybe we'll just come back with a warrant then."

Orion, his expression as pleasant as ever, smiles. "Maybe you will. Have a good day, officers."

He turns, picks up the camp chair he'd been sitting on, folds it, and then starts down the long dirt road towards the buildings. He keeps his back to us, not turning once, and takes his time.

"Fucker," Hanks mutters. "Come on, kid."

We climb back into the car, and Hanks slams the door. He backs up and peels out onto the dirt road. As we bump along, heading back toward Nightfall, Hanks clenches his fingers around the steering wheel. Rain patters the metal roof, and the windshield wipers swish rhythmically as the weather worsens. "I don't like this. I don't like this at all."

I scoff. "Me neither."

"And I don't like that Chief Novak," Hanks adds as he sets his jaw. "He's hiding something."

I nod my agreement.

"And that son of a bitch back there is just holding us up."

I stare out the window, the trunks of the pines flashing past, and fight to slow my breathing.

Hanks softens his tone. "You're quiet, kid. What's up?"

I can't help but grin a little that the detective is already picking up on my little mannerisms and moods, despite us only working together for a couple of days. I shrug. "Just being around that place reminds me of where I grew up, you know?" I shake my head. "I know there are people behind those gates being brainwashed."

I angle myself toward him. "Those gates aren't just keeping us out, but also them in. They're hiding secrets." I sigh. "In Canaan Springs, where I grew up, they had cameras on every corner. The leaders monitored us 24-7, restricting who could come and go. If the Ascendant Light Fellowship is anything like Zion House, there are people suffering in there."

There's a moment of silence as we bump along the uneven dirt road. "Patience, kid."

I glance over, and Hanks gives me a bracing look. "We'll nail him. We just need more proof." He narrows his eyes. "Or a new tactic."

CHAPTER 28

I laugh around a bite of Grandma Gloria's famous homemade lasagna, nearly choking, as Hope finishes her story.

"So I turn the lady away," my sister explains, "because I did a strand test on her and told her that if she tried to go any more blond, her hair was going to fall out, right? You'd think that would discourage someone." Hope takes a sip of wine.

Grandma gestures for her to continue, impatient. "Well, what happened? Did her hair fall out?"

Shadow lies curled up at my feet. He's already gotten a few bites of ricotta and meatball that I "accidentally" dropped.

Hope sets her glass of wine down. "Well, I'm kind of a nosy bitch."

I chuckle.

"So I find her Instagram." Hope leans forward. "Three days later, she found somebody out in the sticks who'd do it for her. And she's posting about, you guessed it, all of her hair falling out. All of it. I mean, okay, it didn't exactly fall out, but it broke off pretty close to the roots. So now she looks like some deranged Barbie doll who had all her hair cut off by some kid. It's sticking out at all kinds of weird angles."

I bring a napkin to my lips and try hard not to spit my food out from laughter. I should know better than to try to eat when Hope's telling a story. She always cracks me up.

"And guess who comes crawling back looking for me to somehow fix her hair?" My sister throws her hands up. "Guess what, lady? I can't magically glue your hair back together."

"Extensions?" Grandma Gloria suggests.

Hope shakes her head. "Nah. I need more than a couple of inches to work with. Plus, whatever's left on her head looked damaged beyond repair. I told her she should try just shaving it all off before blocking her."

"Hope," Grandma Gloria chides her. "The poor lady's going through it."

Hope sniffs, swirling her red wine in the glass. "Normally, I'd agree with you, Grandma. But after I told her I couldn't bleach her hair, she went online and left me one-star reviews everywhere she could think of."

Grandma Gloria bristles, sitting up straight. "Well, in that case, she deserves it." She narrows her eyes. "Nobody goes after my girls."

I can't help but laugh. Grandma is a spiritual woman and professes love and kindness towards all, with her actions following through on her words. But if anybody crosses her family, she's the first one ready to brawl for us.

We finish up our weekly family dinner and I help Hope and Grandma do dishes before heading up to my room to do a little more work. After visiting the Ascendant Light compound, Hanks and I headed back to the station and tried to work the case for a few more hours before giving up for the night.

I'm not planning to work the case necessarily, but I have a

little bit of my own work to do. Work I don't want Grandma or Hope to know about.

"I'm going to head up to my room for a bit," I call as I jog up the stairs with Shadow bounding ahead of me.

I close my door, grab my laptop, and get comfy in bed, with Shadow curled up beside me, his big head resting on my shin.

I love my room. It always feels so cozy. I've got the lights dimmed, with only some white twinkle lights wrapped around my headboard and a salt lamp casting warm light. I open my laptop and go to a bookmarked page.

It's a subreddit, a forum of sorts for friends and family members of Zion House members. It's not a very big or active subreddit, but I check it every day, hoping for any word about where the rest of my family might be.

After Hope and I escaped the cult, we called my grandpa, who drove down from Oregon to save us. Once he got there, he laid into the local police enough to finally mobilize them into taking some action against the religious fanatics who'd raised me. Unfortunately, somebody had tipped them off, and that, plus the several days' delay between our escape and the police making their move, meant that Zion House had enough time to pack up and vanish.

When the police went in to raid Canaan Springs, they found it empty. A ghost town. Everyone had literally just packed up their possessions and left what they couldn't carry.

I shudder. I've only been back that one time. It'd been surreal.

I wonder what's become of the town now, if it still sits empty, frozen in time. The couches, the pictures on the walls —as if waiting for everyone to come back any day now.

I still wonder about the family and the friends I'd left behind. Where are they now? They could be somewhere nearby. Somewhere in Oregon. Or they could be on the other side of the country. I have no idea. I scroll the posts, skimming for any news of their whereabouts, but don't spot anything promising.

A knock sounds at the door and makes me jump. Hope pokes her head in, and I quickly slam my laptop shut. She notices, of course, and gives me a little frown. "You, uh, okay in here?"

I nod. "Oh, yeah." I hug a pillow to my chest. "What's up?" I keep a neutral look plastered on my face, willing my sister to drop it.

She lingers a moment longer, observing me. "I'm gonna make some tea. You want any?"

"I'm good. Thanks, though."

She gives me one last curious look before stepping back out and closing the door behind her. I let out the breath I'd been holding.

Hope and Grandma wouldn't like it if they knew that I was still on the hunt for Zion House and the rest of our family, but I just can't let it go. I used to be pretty obsessed with it. It was one of the reasons for my counseling sessions years ago. I felt guilty keeping a secret from them, but at the same time, it was my family, and I felt I had a right to search for them. Plus, what Hope and Grandma didn't know wouldn't hurt them.

While I don't gain any promising news about my own family's cult, I do have the idea to check for a subreddit for the Ascendant Light Fellowship. Maybe friends and family members, parents, sisters, and brothers have formed their own forum to share information and commiserate. I hunt around and pretty quickly find one.

Sweet. I click into it and scroll through the posts. Most are from worried parents or children of cult members, lamenting that they haven't heard from their loved ones in ages.

Unlike my family, though, who I haven't heard from or seen in over ten years, the Ascendant Light Fellowship posts videos on YouTube. Some of the victims' loved ones report seeing their children or friends in some of them.

What a bizarre feeling, to be able to see and hear your loved one, and yet know they are unreachable.

I skim all the most recent posts but don't learn anything about the group that I don't already know. Still, maybe one of these posters could recognize our Jane Doe and be able to identify her.

I send a private message to the moderator of the group, introducing myself as a police officer and explaining that I'm working a case that involves the Ascendant Light Fellowship. I ask if she'd be willing to speak with me.

Now, I have nothing to do but wait. I watch some movie on streaming, partly paying attention while I play a game on my phone. I've been working long days, and it doesn't take long before my eyelids grow heavy. I decide it's time to hit the hay. I apologize to Shadow for disturbing him as I do my best to climb out of bed without jostling the furry boy. He still huffs at me, despite my best efforts.

I pad down the hall, brush my teeth and wash my face. Once I'm ready for bed, I climb under the sheets. A notification on my laptop catches my eye before I close the screen. "Huh." I pull open the message and note that the group's moderator has already responded. And she's available now. She's sent her Zoom ID and asked me to call her.

I sit up in bed, quickly click over to the video calling service, and dial her. The dim light in my room isn't ideal for a video call, but it'll have to do. It rings a few times before the woman joins the call, and suddenly I'm looking at her through the video feed.

"Officer Mercer?" the middle-aged woman asks.

I nod. "Yes. Thanks so much for agreeing to speak with me." The woman has soft brown eyes and shoulder-length brown hair.

She's pretty, though there's a sadness in her eyes, and I

suspect if it weren't for the stress of her family situation aging her, she'd look much younger. I chide myself as I note my own image on the screen. It's late, and I'm not really looking my freshest, either.

She's sitting at her kitchen table, with a fridge and stove behind her. Food containers sit out on the counter. "I'm Sharon, one of the moderators of the group. I was excited to hear there's a case about the Ascendant Light Fellowship?"

I hold up a palm, quick to hedge her hopes. "We're following a case of someone we believe *might* have been a member of the Ascendant Light Fellowship. So, unfortunately, we're not going after the group itself, but looking for information on one of its members."

"Oh." She presses her lips together. I can tell she's disappointed.

"I'm going to send you an image via the chat." I send over a digital copy of the artist's rendering of our Jane Doe. "Can you tell me if you recognize her?"

Sharon squints at the screen. "Hmm." She shakes her head. "She's not my kid, but I'll ask around with some of the others in the group." She gives me a weak smile. "Some of us are pretty tight, and there are a few that come to mind who might know this person. I'll put you in touch with anyone willing to speak with you."

"Thank you." I give her a sympathetic look. "So it's your child who's in the cult?"

She nods. "Kaylee." The woman looks down. "She goes by Luna now."

I raise my brows. "I've watched some of their videos. I recognize her, actually." Luna is a young woman with a short pixie cut.

Sharon looks away from the screen. "It's been three years since I heard from her." Deep emotion strains her words. "I'm really worried about her. Desperate for news. So many of us are."

I nod, my heart going out to her. I hesitate a moment, wondering if it's appropriate to share personal information, but decide to go for it. Maybe sharing will bring her some comfort and even get her to trust me more. "I know how you feel."

She gives me a doubtful look.

"No, really. I grew up in a cult, too. Zion House. It was a fundamentalist religious group. My younger sister and I escaped, but my mom and other siblings are still in. Every day, I look for information about where they could be, how they're doing, if they're still alive." I choke up and clear my throat.

Sharon looks at me with sympathy and leans closer to her computer. "I'm really sorry to hear that."

I give her a tight nod. "Thanks."

"I'll ask around and get back to you ASAP."

"Thank you."

She looks like she's about to sign off but hesitates. "Um." She licks her lips. "This young woman you're looking for. Is she in some kind of trouble?"

It might just be my imagination, but I feel like what she really wants to ask is if she's alive.

A weight settles on my chest. If Sharon finds someone who recognizes our Jane Doe, will I have to tell a parent that their daughter was murdered? Talking to Sharon makes our victim seem all the more real to me. I can't bring myself to tell Sharon she's dead, so I simply say, "She's part of an active investigation. That's all I can say for now."

The woman looks like she wants to ask more, but in the end just nods. "Talk to you soon."

We sign off, and I close the laptop. It takes me some time, but eventually I drift off to an uneasy sleep, full of the same nightmares I've had ever since I escaped the cult.

CHAPTER 29

I wake up to the acidic aroma of grandma's awful coffee burning my nose. I scrunch up my face and rub at my dry eyes, patting around for my phone on the nightstand beside me.

Shadow lets out an annoyed huff, bothered that I'm jostling him at the foot of the bed. Of course, he doesn't seem to mind that he's taking up 70 percent of it. Still half awake, I hold my phone close to my face and squint at the time. Just past seven o'clock.

I yawn, grateful that for the first time in days, I've got a decent number of hours of sleep. Still blinking away the fogginess, I unlock my phone and spot a new notifications. Instantly I'm more alert as I click on the message from Sharon, the subreddit moderator.

The message is short. She tells me that three people got back to her, saying that the artist's rendering of our Jane Doe might be their kid. She gives me their names and phone numbers. Then she mentions there's a fourth. She didn't hear back from her, but Sharon knows this woman personally and has seen pics of her daughter. She believes our Jane Doe might be her and urges me to give the woman a call anyway.

I push myself up to sitting, fluffing the pillows behind my back, fully awake now. I have a lead, a direction to follow, and that gives me all the energy I need. Well, at least until I can hoof it down to the Grind to get a mocha and a scone.

I hesitate. It might be a bit early on a Sunday morning to make the calls. Then again, I have no doubt that these people are desperate for information about their loved ones, just like I am for information about my family. I wouldn't care if it was two in the morning if someone called me with information about my mom or brothers and sisters. I dial the first number.

Fifteen minutes later, I've called the first three people Sharon referred to me, and they're all dead ends. The first father I talked to told me his daughter was in her late forties, which is totally the wrong age for our Jane Doe.

The next person I spoke to initially sounded promising, but then she told me that she's spoken to her sister within the last week. Apparently, her sister's been sneaking her phone calls more often and seems to be wavering on leaving the cult. That's positive news for the woman and her sister, but unfortunately, our Jane Doe was killed six to eight weeks ago, which means, again, not a match.

The third mother I talked to eventually described her daughter in detail, mentioning that she's missing a finger. That eliminates her as a possibility. The ME would definitely have told us if our victim was missing any digits.

Finally, I'm left with the fourth name that Sharon gave me. The one she didn't get permission to pass on but felt I should try anyhow. I dial the number, and it rings and rings. Finally, I hang up. The call never even went to voicemail.

All the hope and energy that had been coursing through me just minutes ago disappears. I let out a heavy sigh. Just more dead ends, again.

Still, I appreciate Sharon following up with me, so I decide to give her a call and thank her. After just a couple of rings, she picks up.

I hold the phone up to my face, and she does the same. She's wearing glasses, and judging by the headboard behind her, she's still in bed, too. "Hi, Sharon," I smile, sleep lines still crisscrossing my face. "I'm sorry if I woke you up."

"No, no, it's alright." She raises her brows. "Did you have any luck with the names I gave you?"

I give her a grateful smile but shake my head. "Unfortunately not. The first three didn't pan out, and I couldn't get through to the fourth number."

Sharon looks away and nods thoughtfully. "I'll post that artist's rendering in the sub," she assures me. "Just in case someone sees it and recognizes their kid—someone I didn't reach out to for you."

I nod. "I'd appreciate that, thank you."

She pauses again, sucking on her lips. It seems to me there's something she wants to tell me, but isn't sure if she should.

I'm tempted to encourage her, but stay quiet instead, letting her work it out. My patience pays off when she finally lets out a sigh and her eyes drift back to the camera. "Look, I'm not sure I should be telling you this, but Mary Ann Ackerman, that last number I gave you? She and I were close a few years ago. She's had a rough couple of years and doesn't answer the phone anymore, even when I call. I think she's become a bit reclusive." Her brows knit together in worry. "Mary Ann doesn't have any other family, and I just think everything with her daughter, plus getting older, has hit her really hard."

I give her an encouraging nod.

Sharon lets out a heavy sigh again. "But... I have her address. I always send her a Christmas card," she explains. "I'm going to give it to you. The thing is, I've seen pictures of her daughter. Of course, they're from several years ago, and it's hard to be sure judging by that drawing you showed me, but..." She gives me an earnest look through the phone. "I'd bet good money on that being Mary Ann Ackerman's daughter, Joy."

My breath catches. "Percentage wise, how sure are you?"

Sharon opens her mouth, appearing to debate within herself. "Ninety-five percent? I think you need to do what it takes to get in contact with her." Sharon gives me her address. I thank her again and we hang up.

This Mary Ann Ackerman woman lives in Simi Valley. I'm not sure where that is, so I Google it and discover it's near Los Angeles. Not exactly the easiest place to get to, but it's not halfway around the world, either.

I sit there in bed for a moment, pondering my next move. We don't have any concrete proof that Mary Ann Ackerman's daughter and our Jane Doe are the same person. However, Sharon, who's seen pictures of her, says she's fairly sure it is.

Will that be enough to convince the chief that we should follow this up in person? I'm not sure. But I do feel more confident that Hanks and I are on the same team now and that he'll hear me out.

Even though it's Sunday and supposed to be my day off, this is an active murder investigation, and I feel called to put in whatever hours necessary to get justice for this woman. I stroke Shadow's soft furry back a couple of times. "Well, boy, what do you think? You ready to go in to work today?"

He pricks up his ears, seeming to understand my words, before burying his long nose under the covers, effectively telling me to go back to bed. I chuckle and spring to my feet. "That's the spirit."

I hurry down the hall to hop in the shower before heading into the station, and walk in on Hope showering instead.

She scoffs behind the flowered shower curtain. "Don't you knock?"

"Sorry," I apologize, backing out the door before popping my head back in again. "But hurry up. I've got a lead on the case."

CHAPTER 30

It's still early for a Sunday morning, barely past nine, when Detective Hanks and I roll up at the chief's home. It's a beautiful, sprawling Victorian, not dissimilar to Grandma's house, except about twice as big, with what appears to be a triple lot that includes an enormous, landscaped lawn.

His wife, Rose, who seems like a sweet woman, shows us into the chief's study, just off the foyer, and sets cups of coffee in front of us and her husband. Shelves of leather-bound books line the wall behind Jamison as he reclines in the wingback chair, wearing a plaid button-down tucked into jeans with penny loafers. It feels odd to see the man in casual clothes.

It gives me a weird feeling, like when I was a kid and saw my teacher at the grocery store. It's as if I imagine Chief Jamison lives at the station and wears his uniform to sleep, or something. I cup my hand around the warm mug and blow gently on my coffee, then take a sip. I'm grateful for both the hit of caffeine and also the fact that it tastes nothing like Grandma Gloria's burnt sludge.

"Thank you for meeting with us, Chief. Especially at home," Hanks begins.

Jamison acknowledges us with a nod, then swallows a gulp of coffee. "What is this all about?" His intelligent dark eyes shift between the detective and me.

Hanks gestures for me to take over. "I made contact with a woman on a subreddit last night. It's a forum for family members and friends of the Ascendant Light Fellowship victims, the cult we believe our Jane Doe has a connection to."

Chief Jamison waits for me to continue.

"This woman's own daughter is in the cult. She put me in touch with a few other parents and siblings whose child might fit the description of our Jane Doe. Unfortunately, none of those panned out, but the moderator heavily suggested I try to contact a fourth woman, Mary Ann Ackerman."

"Okay," the chief says uncertainly.

"Now, I wasn't able to get a hold of Mary Ann. But Sharon, the moderator, said she'd seen photos of Mary Ann's daughter, Joy, and that our artist's rendering looks a lot like Joy."

Hanks takes over. "Mercer really took initiative on this, Chief. She was unable to reach Ms. Ackerman by phone but did get her address."

Chief Jamison lifts a palm. "All right, well, where is she?"

"Simi Valley, near Los Angeles," I answer.

Jamison arches a brow, and Hanks takes over again. "We'd like to fly down there and speak with her in person."

The chief frowns and leans back in his tall leather armchair. He glances out the window at a sprawling elm tree that shades much of his backyard. He strokes his chin, his gaze distant as he thinks it over.

He turns back to us. "This seems like a long shot, and you know we're a small department." He splays his hands. "We're on a tight budget, and it's a stretch to pay for flights and a rental car down there just to *attempt* to speak with a woman who won't even pick up her phone."

Detective Hanks leans forward, resting his laced hands on the edge of the desk. "I understand, Chief. I do. But this is a solid lead."

Jamison pulls his lips to the side. "Are we sure this woman even still lives there?"

I nod. "The moderator said she and Mary Ann were really close at one point. Then a couple years ago, Ms. Ackerman became more reclusive and distant, but Sharon still sends her Christmas cards at that address."

The chief inhales deeply through his nose, his gaze sliding between Hanks and me. Finally, he lets out the breath. "Okay." He holds up a hand. "But only one of you. We don't have the budget to fly both of you down at the last minute, like this."

Hanks and I angle toward each other. I assume Hanks will go. He's the experienced detective and lead on the case, after all. So I'm absolutely shocked when he gestures at me. "This is your lead, kid. Go down there. Get our information."

I nearly spit out the mouthful of coffee I was sipping. Instead, I choke it down, my throat burning. "Really?"

He nods. "Besides, this woman will probably open up to you more easily than me. You can relate to her plight."

I blink a couple of times, thinking it over. It's true. I was able to make that personal connection with Sharon over having family members lost to a cult. As an escapee myself, I know there's a lot of shame in the association. You get used to people looking at you differently when they hear about your background, and I suspect family members and friends of cult members get the same treatment.

If I share about my own history, there's at least a chance Mary Ann Ackerman will be more likely to hear me out.

The weight of this responsibility settles firmly on my shoulders. I know how much is riding on this, and I'm determined to follow through. I sit up straighter in my chair and set the coffee mug on the coaster. I nod at the Chief.

"I'm going to make sure this trip is worth it."

His lips quirk to a smile. "You're gonna have to leave Shadow, you know. Dogs don't count as carry-ons." He says it teasingly, but it's true. I hadn't thought of that. My stomach twists with anxiety. Shadow provides me so much emotional comfort and support. I truly wish I could bring him with me.

Chief Jamison stands, patting his desk. "All right, Mercer. I'll give Linda a call. Go home and get ready. She's going to book you a flight, and there's a good chance you're going to need to get down to Portland pretty quick. Keep your phone on you. She'll give you a call."

"Thank you, Chief." Hanks and I shake hands with Jamison and then hop back in his car. We're nearly back at my house when my phone rings, and it's the station. I pick up, "Mercer here."

"Hey, Eden, it's Linda. I hear you're going down to Los Angeles?"

I nod, though she can't see me of course, and exchange a look with Hanks, who's turning onto my street. "That's the plan."

"Well, I just booked you a flight. It's the only one out of PDX today flying into Burbank. And I've arranged for a rental car for you when you land."

"Great, thank you."

"Don't thank me yet," she cuts in. "Thing is, the flight leaves in just over two and a half hours."

I gasp. "Two hours? That's barely enough time to get down to Portland."

"Well, you'd better get ready quickly and drive fast." I can practically hear her wink over the phone. "Get going and have a safe flight. And good luck."

CHAPTER 31

I sigh with relief as I pull off the eight-lane highway onto surface streets. The navigation app on my phone instructs me to turn right. I cruise past palm trees and bright blue sky and can't believe that just a few hours ago I was on the misty, drizzly coast, wearing a heavy coat. Said coat now rests in the back seat of the rental car, and I'm perfectly comfortable in my jeans and chambray button-up.

It's been nothing but go, go, go since the chief gave me permission to fly down to southern California. I barely made it to Portland airport on time to make my flight, slipping in just before they closed the gate. Now, I'm barely keeping it together as I drive the LA area traffic. I've almost gotten into three accidents and been honked at more times than I can count. I promise myself that I'll never grumble about Nightfall traffic ever again.

Since landing, I've tried calling Mary Ann Ackerman a few more times, but have yet to get an answer. The call never even goes to voicemail, either. It just rings and rings. In any case, according to my app, I'll be at her place in less than thirty minutes now.

I'm cruising past a gas station lined with tall bushes that

bloom with pink flowers, when the phone rings through the car system. I glance down and hit a button on the steering wheel to answer.

I didn't get a chance to look at the caller ID, so I answer, "Officer Mercer."

"Eden, this is Sharon. The subreddit moderator?"

I frown. I hadn't expected to hear from her again so soon. "Hi, Sharon, what's up?" I turn left per the app's instructions.

"I have some bad news."

My stomach sinks, though I keep my attention on the road.

"I actually managed to get a hold of Mary Ann Ackerman."

"You did?" I perk up. That sounds like good news.

"Um, unfortunately, she doesn't want to speak with you."

Damn. I grip the steering wheel tighter as anxiety courses through me. "Do you know why?"

Sharon pauses. "She didn't really get into it, but I got the sense that all of this turmoil with her daughter has just been too much for her."

I set my jaw in frustration. This is not what I need right now. I try a different tactic. "Did she see the artist's rendering?"

"No," Sharon answers. "Uh, I offered to email it to her, but she didn't even want to look at it."

Great. I sigh inwardly. But try to keep my voice positive. "All right, Sharon. Obviously not the best news, but I appreciate you passing that on to me."

"Yeah, Eden. Sorry about that."

I hang up with Sharon and pull up to a stoplight. What now? I'm already here in Simi Valley, practically on Mary Ann Ackerman's doorstep. I set my shoulders, and when the light turns green, keep driving. I'm already here. There's no turning back without at least trying to talk to the woman. If she doesn't want to speak to me, then it's up to me to convince her to.

I drive for another twenty minutes down wide, sunny streets, and pull into a subdivision with similar-looking houses that all have slump block walls. I scan the house numbers, and when the app on my phone tells me I've arrived, I park in front of a blue single-level ranch house.

I turn off the ignition and sit there for a moment studying the house. I double-check the address and find that it is indeed the one that Sharon gave me. Looks like the house used to be cute, but the blue paint is peeling and faded, and the front lawn appears crunchy and dead. Shades cover all the windows, and I get an overwhelming sense of sadness and loneliness.

Checking that I have a copy of the artist's rendering in my pocket, I step out of the car. As I approach the front door, anxious knots form in my stomach.

On one hand, Mary Ann Ackermann might simply turn me away, in which case I'll have to let Hanks and Chief Jamison down. On the other hand, if she agrees to speak with me, there's a chance I'm about to inform a woman that her daughter is dead.

I feel I might nearly be sick when I knock on the door. I wait, and wait a little longer. When I don't hear anything, I knock again, louder this time. I hold still, listening intently. A shuffle of footsteps sounds on the other side of the door, and I wait for the deadbolt to unlock and the knob to turn. Instead, I'm met only with silence.

Finally, a faint, warbly voice calls through the door. "Who is it?"

"Hello, ma'am." I do my best to sound friendly, but official. "I'm Officer Eden Mercer. I'm hoping to have a word with Mary Ann Ackerman."

There's silence for a moment. "I told Sharon I didn't want to speak to you."

At least I'm speaking to the right person. I glance around the sunny neighborhood. A woman walks a dog on the other side of the street, and further down, a middle-aged guy is washing his car in his driveway. I inch closer to the door and lower my voice.

"I understand, ma'am. And I wouldn't be here if it wasn't urgent that I speak with you."

"What do you need to speak with *me* for?" She sounds irritated.

"It's about your daughter, Joy."

"There's nothing to say. I haven't seen her in years" comes her hoarse answer.

I gulp against the tight lump in my throat. Even after all these years, sharing my story isn't easy. Especially with a stranger, through a door. "Mary Ann, I grew up in a cult also." I glance around the street. No one's close enough to overhear, but still, I desperately wish she would let me inside so I could say this to her in person. "My sister and I escaped when we were kids, but my mom and the rest of my siblings are still in it. I know how draining, how all-consuming it can be to search for your family members. To wonder where they are, what they're doing, if they're healthy, happy, or even thinking of you. And I know how tempting it can be to just say the past is the past and let it go. But this is really important. And I know that if somebody came to me with information about my family, no matter how hard it would be, I'd hear them out."

I squeeze my eyes shut, waiting for her to yell at me to go away. But to my surprise, the lock clicks and the front door eases open a few inches. A frail woman peers out at me. The light inside the house is dim, but from what I can see, she has short curly hair and looks drawn, sallow.

My guess is she's younger than she appears, but she moves stiffly as she shuffles back and throws a hand inside. "Well, come on in then, I guess."

I give her a grateful smile and step past her. It's a shocking change from the bright blue sky and happy sunshine outside to the home's dark interior. All the curtains are drawn, only letting in a dim brown light that has me squinting.

She indicates that I should have a seat in the living room. I walk across a tan carpet and have a seat on a worn-looking sofa. She perches on the edge of the armchair across from me. An antique-looking wooden coffee table sits between us, topped with a bowl of candies that look like they haven't been touched in years.

Mary Ann sits with her shoulders slumped forward and her hands folded on her knees. She doesn't even meet my eyes. "What has Joy done this time?"

I raise my brows in surprise. "Done?"

She huffs. "Joy was always up to something, and you're a cop, aren't you? What is it now? She in some kind of trouble?"

I gulp. "Ma'am, Joy hasn't done anything wrong." I glance around the room. A wooden cabinet stands in the corner, displaying porcelain figurines and framed photos. There are some pictures of a man and woman and two little girls. Looks like it was taken in the eighties at a photo studio.

Other photos show young women, blond, with freckles across their cheeks. There are some others of a very cute little boy with curly hair, bright blue eyes, and tan skin. I turn back to the tense woman across from me. I want Mary Ann to feel safe opening up to me, so I try to get her talking.

I lean forward. "What can you tell me about Joy? What was she like when she was younger?"

Mary Ann sits up a little straighter. She fiddles with the hem of her long shirt. "Well…" She sighs. "Her late father and I were, well, to be honest, we were pretty strict parents." She flashes me a look, then drops her eyes again. "Joy was…" She lets out a dry chuckle. "Joy was always her own person, you know? She was a wild kid, climbing trees, getting into trouble, rolling in the dirt." She shakes her head. "As she grew up, that turned into rebellion. She pushed back against her father and me, and once it was *just* me, she and I butted heads a lot."

Ms. Ackerman shakes her head slowly. "Joy was always real impulsive, but when she got older it led her to fall in with some real odd folks. People that were no good for her, you know?" She shakes her head. "And then she ran away. At first I got some notes from her, calling herself Gaia."

She scoffs and rolls her light blue eyes. "I mean, she has to come up with a new name for herself? What's wrong with Joy?"

I nod politely for her to continue.

"Then the notes stopped coming. We didn't hear anything for a long time. My other daughter, Joy's sister, she joined, what is it…" Mary Ann rolls her wrist, thinking. "Reddit. Yeah. She helped me set up a Reddit account. I don't know, it helped for a while, talking to other people going through the same thing. That's where I met Sharon. But then it became too painful to live it over and over again." She shakes her head. "I just can't anymore."

I suck on my lips. This house and everything Mary Ann Ackerman is telling me give me the impression that she's been sapped of color, of energy, of life. "I understand. I don't want to take up much of your time or put you through the stress again, but…" I hate to do this to her, but I unfold the artist's rendering and hand it to her. "Ma'am, can you tell me if this is your daughter Joy?"

Her eyes widen, and she nods. "Oh my God." She traces a hand over the drawing. "Yes, yes, that's definitely Joy. Why?"

I can't even begin to describe the clash of emotions that wash through me. On one hand, I'm pretty sure we've just identified our Jane Doe, which is a major lead for our case. On the other hand, I know that I'm about to deliver news that will change this woman's life forever.

I lean forward and catch Mary Ann Ackerman's gaze. "Ma'am, I am so sorry to tell you this... but your daughter Joy is dead."

She doesn't react for a moment, just blinks at me as though she hasn't heard me. Then she sucks in a shuddering breath and brings a trembling hand to her mouth. "What?"

Police procedure is strict on this. There's a certain way we have to deliver the news to make sure that the victim's family understands. We can't use colloquialisms like "passed away" or "no longer with us." So I reiterate, "She is deceased, ma'am. We believe she was murdered."

"Oh my God. Oh my God." Mary Ann devolves into sobbing, her shoulders trembling. She buries her face in her hands, and I look awkwardly around until I spot a box of tissues. I gently press one into her hand. What does one do in a situation like this?

I know I wanted to do *real* police work, but this might just be the hardest thing I've ever done. I place a hand on the woman's bony shoulder. "Ma'am, I'm so sorry." I stay there for several minutes, just letting Mary Ann express her grief.

The woman is racked with sobs, and I gently rub her back. A feeble attempt at comforting her. "Ma'am, do you want me to call your other daughter? Or do you have a friend or other relative I could call who would be of comfort?"

She lifts her face, her eyes bloodshot, tears streaking down her cheeks. "Clay, too?"

I frown, puzzled, then lean forward, perched on the edge of the sofa. "Clay?"

"Clayton, my grandson. Her son." Her chin trembles, her wet eyes full of deep pain. "Is—is he gone, too?"

My breath catches. "Joy had a kid."

"Yes," Mary Ann stammers between gulping sobs. "Yes. And she took him with her when she ran away." She points a trembling hand toward the cabinet in the corner that houses all the framed pictures. I leap to my feet and rush over, grabbing the only picture of a little boy I can find.

"Is this him?"

Mary Ann's sobbing too hard to speak, but she nods.

I look at the photograph of Mary Ann holding the little boy, Clay, on her lap. He has tight, dark curls, bright blue eyes, and freckles scattered across his cheeks and nose. He's holding a teddy bear, and his grandmother is smiling broadly. The woman in the photo looks like a different person than the woman in front of me.

In the photo she's tan, plump, and has a twinkle to her eye. The Mary Ann sobbing on the couch right now seems like a shell of her former self. I bring the photograph over to the sofa with me and wait with Mary Ann until she can speak again. "Ma'am, we were not aware that Joy had a son."

Finally, the older woman looks up. "You-you mean he's…" Her voice trembles, and she presses a hand to her mouth until she can speak again. "He's still alive?"

I lick my lips. "I wish I could give you a definitive answer. All I can say is that we didn't find his body."

Pain, anguish, and hope play across her face. She gazes at the photograph in my hands. "He was four there. He'd be eight now."

I look at the cute little boy. "Do you have a more updated picture?"

She shakes her head, sniffling. "No, I haven't seen him or spoken to him since Joy took him with her up to Oregon."

I nod. "Ms. Ackerman, we will make it our top priority to find this boy."

Her pale blue eyes search mine, as though questioning if I'm telling the truth.

I stay steady and hold her gaze until she finally nods. "All right. Thank you. You find him."

"Do you have a copy of this photo I can have?"

"Take that one." She waves it away with a trembling hand. "I have others."

"Thank you, ma'am." I squeeze her shoulder one more time, then slip the photograph out of the frame. "You've been a huge help. Again, I'm so sorry for the tragic news. Our station will be in contact with you to officially identify the remains."

"Oh!" She sobs. "Will I have to fly up there and—and look at her like that?"

I shake my head. "No, in most cases that's not necessary anymore. But our department will explain everything to you, all right? We're gonna try to make this as painless on you as possible. And I'll be in touch about Clay."

"Thank you."

I think of one last thing before I leave. "Is it possible Clay's with his father or another relative or friend?"

She shakes her head. "No. In her letters, Joy told me she took him up there." She raises a trembling hand to her mouth, her eyes heavy with sadness. "She told me she didn't want to leave him with me because I'd been so hard on her as a kid." She shakes her head. "There's so much I wish I could apologize to her about. So much I wish I could say."

I give her a sympathetic look and rise to leave. "I'll be in touch, Ms. Ackerman."

CHAPTER 32

An hour later, I rush back to Burbank Airport, drop off the rental car, and crawl at a snail's pace through security. I've tried calling Hanks a couple of times on the drive to the airport, but my reception is lousy, and we keep getting cut off. I'm itching to tell him what I've found, so I try again at the gate, even though my boarding group is already on the plane and they're making last calls over the loudspeaker.

I nibble on my lip, antsy, as I mentally urge Hanks to pick up. Just as I'm about to hang up, he answers.

"Hanks here."

"Finally," I sigh.

"I've been trying you, kid."

"Me, too," I answer. "Lousy reception. Listen, I spoke with Mary Ann Ackerman, and she identified the victim. It's her daughter, Joy Ackerman."

"Way to go, kid." The pride oozing from Hanks's voice makes me feel all warm and fuzzy. That feeling quickly fades when the flight attendant at the gate shoots me a sharp look. I hold up a finger, indicating I just need a minute. She cocks her head, her expression going flat.

"That's some crack police work."

I sigh, my stomach twisting at the memory. "It was rough, telling her her daughter had been murdered."

"Mmm." Hanks makes a sympathetic noise. "Worst part of the job, kid."

I get the impression he's holding back, but I don't have time to puzzle it out. "Hey, I only have a second before the plane takes off." I show my boarding pass, then hustle down the empty gangway. "But I learned something else. You're not going to believe this, but it changes everything. Joy Ackerman has a son—he'd be eight now, and she took him to the Ascendant Light Fellowship with her when she left her mother's home."

"A kid?" Shock laces Hanks's gravelly voice.

I nod a greeting at the flight attendant, then shuffle down the center aisle past full rows. I'm the last passenger to board, and it looks like I'll be taking the last empty seat in the far back of the plane.

"Damn. You're right, this does change things."

I sidle up to one of the last rows in the back and give the guy sitting in the aisle seat an apologetic smile. He stands and we do an awkward shuffle so I can take the middle seat. I shove my bag under the seat in front of me and the flight attendant catches my attention.

"Phones need to be in airplane mode."

I nod and hold up a finger to her, pleading for just one moment. "Hanks, I gotta go," I whisper.

"Wait, kid—I can do you one better in terms of big news."

"What could be bigger than identifying our victim and a possible missing or killed child?" The woman by the window shoots me a horrified look.

"Novak just arrested someone for her murder."

"Wait, what? Who?"

"Ma'am." The flight attendant in the aisle gives me a stern look. "Phones need to be in airplane mode for takeoff."

I sigh, deeply frustrated. "Sorry, Hanks, talk to you when I land." I hang up, and the flight attendant moves on. I settle in for a miserable two-hour flight where I'll be racking my brain. Who did Novak arrest? This is *our* case. What did he know that we didn't?

CHAPTER 33

Hanks, Shadow, and I park in front of the Elk Ridge police station first thing in the morning. I didn't get back to Nightfall until late yesterday evening, but neither Hanks nor I was willing to wait another minute longer than necessary to figure out what the hell was going on over here in Elk Ridge. Hanks casts a disgusted look at Chief Novak's souped-up pickup as we get out of the car, and I grab Shadow's leash. As a united front, we march into the station.

Officer Dobre looks up from his desk in the lobby. His eyes widen as he takes us in, and it might be my imagination, but the color seems to drain from his face. He stands, eyes full of fear, and stammers, "D-Detective Hanks. Officer Mercer." He nods a hello at each of us, and Hanks and I exchange a look. It's like Officer Dobre is expecting us and fearing our arrival all at the same time.

"I got a bad feeling," Hanks mutters.

Chief Novak comes strolling down the hallway. The first time we met him, he was jovial, chummy, as though we were all best buds. Now, he steps his feet wide, as if blocking our way. The chief folds his arms across his chest and sticks his pudgy belly out, glaring at us.

"Come to congratulate us?" he asks, a smug smile stretching across his face.

I glance over at Hanks and note the red flush creeping up his neck. I'm sure he's seething, but he manages to hold a fairly neutral poker face. "Something like that," he grumbles. "Heard you made an arrest in our case."

Chief Novak splays his hands while Officer Dobre continues to look terrified. "What can I say? It's a team effort, right? Pretty sure justice doesn't care who's doing the arresting."

"Justice," Hanks mutters under his breath. "We'd like to talk to this fellow you've arrested."

Novak tsks. "I'm afraid that's not going to be possible."

A cloud passes over Hanks's face. "And why is that exactly?"

"Well, first of all, we already did the interrogating when he turned himself in and know all we need to know." He sneers. "Secondly, the man's lawyer isn't present."

A muscle twitches in Hanks's jaw. "Why don't you give us his lawyer's contact information and we'll have him join us once our suspect is in Nightfall custody."

Novak gives Hanks a faux pained look. "Ooh, afraid that won't work, either. We won't be handing him over to you." He smirks. "The suspect will be staying here in Elk Ridge."

Hanks has had it and starts forward. "This is our case and we will be taking custody of the suspect."

Novak bristles as Hanks darts closer. He holds up one hand, resting the other on his gun at his hip. Hanks stops, his face red and eyes blazing. The chief glares at Hanks. "Now, this ain't my decision." He keeps his hand on his weapon. "Our suspect's lawyer has requested he be held here in Elk Ridge, as said lawyer lives just outside of town, himself. Best to keep it local, hm?" He edges closer to Hanks. "In the spirit of cooperation."

Hanks's nostrils flare. Novak is clearly relishing his ability to stymie us, which makes me question his character. Is he just a jerk looking to take credit for solving our case, or does he have some personal interest in this? Regardless, he has a point. It's not unreasonable for a suspect to be held close to home, especially when his lawyer is local and we're not too long of a drive away.

"Fine." Hanks grinds out. "Then, in the spirit of cooperation, how about you hand over the interrogation footage?"

Novak sneers at him a moment longer, before releasing his gun, and spreading his palms with a cheery smile. "Why, of course." He jerks his chin at Officer Dobre. "Go ahead."

The officer behind the desk fumbles with his computer. As we wait for him to get us the footage, Novak folds his arms and sniffs. "Whole lotta fuss for one of those weirdos."

"'Scuse me?" Hanks challenges him.

Novak waves a hand, dismissively. "This 'victim'? She brought this on herself. I mean, joining a crazy cult like that, she was asking for trouble."

Part of me is feeling like a tea kettle, slowly coming to a boil. Maybe it's Chief Novak's stupid, smug grin getting to me. Maybe it's the fact that just yesterday I was speaking with Mary Ann Ackerman, telling her that her daughter had been murdered. Either way, I feel my hold on myself slipping. It doesn't happen often with me. It takes a lot to get me to snap. But once I do, my steady, reserved facade gives way and the anger explodes out of me. I grind my teeth, holding myself together through sheer willpower.

Chief Novak shrugs. "Waste of police resources if you ask me."

No one did. My reserve breaks. I stomp forward, my intimidating German Shepherd at my side. "Joy Ackerman is as deserving of justice as anyone else."

"Who?" The chief scoffs at me, disdain written all over his face. He barely spares me a glance.

I curl my lips back in utter disbelief. "Our victim, Joy Ackerman. We identified her yesterday." I shake my head. "You don't even know who she is, yet we're supposed to believe you cracked the case and found her murderer?"

Hanks shoots me a warning look, but once that tether snaps for me, it takes a lot to reel me back in.

Chief Novak turns his bright red face to me. "Back off, Officer."

But I don't. I stand my ground. "Did you even know she had an eight year old son?"

"I said, stand down," Chief Novak barks.

My chest heaves. "How can you call yourself an officer of the law, when you pick and choose who's worthy of justice?"

Novak points a trembling finger at the door and yells, "Out of my station!" His voice booms around the small room, and Shadow plants his feet, his lips curling back in a snarl.

Shit. I'm suddenly back to myself, and I realize how far I've pushed it. "It's okay, boy," I mutter, not wanting my dog to attack a fellow cop. "Come on." Quite unlike himself, Shadow doesn't obey the first command. "Come on, boy," I say again.

"We need to get out of here," Hanks mutters in my ear, gripping me tightly by the shoulder. He darts closer to Officer Dobre who hands him a thumb drive over the desk, then drags me toward the door, and Shadow, who's in a stare-off with Chief Novak, finally turns and follows me out.

We storm back out past Chief Novak's stupidly expensive truck and climb into the car, but before we can shut the doors behind us, Novak is standing in front of us, screaming, "I'm calling your chief!"

His face is nearly purple, eyes bulging. "I'll see to it you're both pulled from the case."

CHAPTER 34

Officer Dobre checked the status of the interrogation footage downloading on the thumb drive. Nearly there. He cringed, the tension palpable, as the officers from Nightfall went to battle with Novak. He almost felt like he couldn't breathe. Why wasn't the chief cooperating with them? Why was he insisting that Dobre lie to them about that woman, Joy Ackerman, coming into the station that night?

Dobre set his jaw, and balled his hands into fists as Officer Mercer and Detective Hanks pushed back against Novak's evasiveness. Dobre had seen some questionable actions from Novak, and he had a bad feeling about all of this. His gaze darted to the chief's ridiculously expensive new truck parked out front. The detective had made a comment on his way out last time about the truck and how it must pay well to be Novak. Elk Ridge was a tiny town. Dobre knew Novak couldn't be earning that much. Was Novak being paid off?

Dobre tuned back into the conversation as the young woman, red-faced, glared at his chief.

"Did you even know she had an eight year old son?"

It was as though an ice cube slid down Dobre's spine.

Novak spluttered something, but Dobre wasn't listening anymore. His gaze dropped to the framed photo of his family on his desk. His own little boy was eight years old, and his stomach twisted, as though he might be sick at the thought of his own son in danger.

A debate was raging inside Dobre. Follow his conscience or fall into line with Chief Novak? He knew going against the man would trigger his rage and most likely get him fired. He stared at his family's smiling faces. His wife didn't work. There wasn't much work to be found in Elk Ridge, and he needed this job to house them and keep food on the table. Not to mention his daughter was in club gymnastics. It was an expensive sport, involving a lot of travel and pricey fees. But it was her dream. And her coach said she had a lot of promise. Could go to the Olympics one day.

His actions risked not only the life he'd built for himself but his family's too. Still, his heart wrenched at the thought of another little boy, just like his own, now without his mother.

Dobre made up his mind. He darted a quick look at the group gathered in front of him in the lobby. The dog with his hackles up. Everyone red-faced. Their voices growing louder.

"Get out of here! Out of my station!" Novak screamed. *Shit*. Dobre pulled the flash drive from his computer, the footage downloaded, and handed it across the desk to the detective. The Nightfall officers retreated out the door and got into their car with Novak following them, still yelling.

Dobre made a decision. He looked around the desk and grabbed the first thing he could find, a generic blue pen, and sprinted out the door, past Novak. The Nightfall officers were already backing out of the parking lot as Dobre waved them down. "Wait!"

The car paused, idling, as Detective Hanks rolled down his driver side window.

"Dobre, what in the hell are you doing?" Novak growled from behind him.

"They forgot something," Dobre called over his shoulder, holding up the pen briefly. He could feel the heat stinging his cheeks. He was a terrible liar and couldn't bear to meet Novak's eyes. He knew he'd see right through him. Hopefully, Novak didn't realize that all he was pretending to return was a five-cent pen.

The detective frowned at him, his bushy brows drawing together, and the blond officer raised a questioning brow. Dobre glanced behind him, making sure Novak was still near the front door of the station. He bent forward. "Y'all forgot your pen."

The detective opened his mouth, as if to protest, but Dobre swallowed against the lump in his throat and lowered his voice to a whisper, cutting him off.

"Joy Ackerman came into the Elk Ridge station late one night a couple months ago. Could very well be the same night she was killed. She was worried about her son." He handed over the pen, patted the door frame and backed up.

The detective gave him a long look before rolling up his window. They backed out onto Main Street, then sped off toward the coast. Dobre could feel Novak's burning gaze on his back. Though Dobre feared that Novak was on to him, he also felt an odd sense of calm and right.

He stood up tall, safe in knowing that whatever may come, he did the right thing.

CHAPTER 35

Shadow, Detective Hanks, and I walk quickly through Nightfall Station's lobby, where a few citizens wait around on the hard wood chairs. We raise hands in greeting to Linda and Joan, but as we push through the low, swinging door to the back, they wave us over.

Hanks glances across the bullpen toward his office, clearly eager to check out whatever is on the thumb drive that Officer Dobre from handed us as we were pulling out. With a resigned sigh, he slumps over to Linda and Joan, and folds his arms. "What's up, ladies?"

They pretty much ignore him. Joan rubs my shoulder as her brows knit together in concern. "You okay, hon?"

I look from her to Linda. "Oh boy, this can't be good."

Linda winces, not one to mince words. "Chief Novak from Elk Ridge gave us an earful about you. You're in trouble."

I close my eyes and groan.

"What'd Jamison have to say about it?" Hanks asks.

"He's out doing press at the beach for that lunar eclipse watching party." Linda gives me a sympathetic look. "So he hasn't heard yet."

"Oh, right." I look up toward the high ceiling. In all the excitement with our case, I'd forgotten that it was tonight.

"Maybe it'll put the chief in a more positive frame of mind." The many bracelets Joan wears slide up to her elbows as she lifts her hands. "It's kind of fun, no? The diner's open late for a lunar eclipse early bird breakfast, and they're having the bonfire watch party on the beach."

Hanks seems distracted but asks, "What time is it at again?"

"Should happen around 2:00 a.m.," Linda clarifies.

"Alright. And when's Jamison done with this beach thing?"

Linda shrugs, and the two women, who are thick as thieves, exchange glances. "You've got maybe an hour."

"Great." Hanks tips his head back toward his office. "Come on, kid. We've got a little time before the shit hits the fan."

Once in Hanks's office, we close the door behind us, and Shadow curls up on the sofa. I pull the chair around to the other side of the desk and sit close to Hanks as he pops in the thumb drive and opens the file.

It's a video from a high camera angle looking down on an interrogation room. I recognize Chief Novak on one side of the table with Orion, the man who met us at the compound gate, sitting on the other side next to a ragged-looking older man.

Hanks hits play.

The timestamp rolls away at the bottom of the screen. The audio is a bit echoey and the footage grainy, but we get the gist of what's going on.

"Please state your names," Chief Novak cues.

"I'm Michael Johnson, also known by Orion within the Ascendant Light Fellowship. I'm here representing my client, Stephen Adams, also known as Phoenix within the Ascendant Light Fellowship."

I gape. "Orion is his lawyer?"

Hanks keeps his gaze glued to the screen.

"And how do you wish me to refer to you?" Chief Novak asks.

"Orion and Phoenix are just fine."

The man named Phoenix sits with his shoulders slumped forward, his stringy gray hair falling into his face. Despite the bad quality of the video, he's visibly twitching and scratching repeatedly at his cheek and neck. The man looks emaciated, and dark bags hang under his eyes.

Hanks shakes his head as we watch. "That Phoenix guy looks high out of his mind."

In the video, Chief Novak jots a few notes down on a yellow legal pad and then addresses Phoenix. "Please tell us why you're here today."

Again, it's Orion, the man with slicked-back dark hair, who answers. "My client Phoenix wishes to confess to the murder of Joy Ackerman, also known as Gaia."

Novak clears his throat. "Who?"

Orion splays his hands. "The woman those officers came around asking about. I believe her body has already been discovered near Nightfall."

My jaw drops. "So, the men just came in and confessed. Just like that."

"Just like that," Hanks mutters while he thoughtfully watches the interrogation.

Orion mutters something to his client, who stammers out, "I f-found Gaia on the side of the road, picked her up and took her to the woods, and then I killed her."

Hanks scoffs, leaning back in his chair and crossing his arms. "Well, short and sweet, I guess."

I shake my head. I haven't seen many murder confessions in my time on the force, but when I went through field training in the police academy, we studied plenty of videos of interrogations. Someone stammering it out like this, with no emotion, as though describing how they took out the trash, is highly unusual.

After Chief Novak jots down some notes, he looks again across the table. "Why'd you do it?"

Again, Orion mutters to his client and then Phoenix speaks. "We were, uh, we were dating." The older man scratches at the stubble on his throat. "And um, she left me and I was mad about it."

Chief Novak nods.

I frown. "We're supposed to believe this man and Joy Ackerman were dating?"

The guy appears to be in his seventies and we know now from Joy Ackerman's mother that she was twenty-five.

"Quite the age gap," Hanks agrees.

"How did you kill her?" Novak prompts.

Phoenix looks to his lawyer, who answers for him. "He shot her."

"So, where's the gun?" Novak asks.

"Gun?" Phoenix looks genuinely confused. Orion loudly clears his throat and steps in.

"He told me he threw it in a river."

Hanks throws his hands up. "Well, that's convenient."

Novak asks a few more leading questions before detailing how he's going to draft up a statement and he'll need Phoenix to sign the confession.

As they're wrapping up in the video, I shake my head. "He didn't even mention the ritual burial. I mean, isn't that kind of key? The fact that her head was removed and placed between her feet?"

Hanks nods. "No mention of the kid, either." He pauses the video as Chief Novak stands and turns toward the door. "This is ludicrous." He throws a hand up. "The man was high out of his mind, and Novak was asking leading questions. The supposed killer's answers all sounded rehearsed, and the whole 'interrogation,'" he makes air quotes, "lasted all of four minutes. I've never seen anything like this."

"You think he was coached?"

Hanks nods.

I lean back in my chair and nibble the tip of my thumb. "Why would that man confess to killing Joy Ackerman if he didn't do it?"

"You've seen the online videos." Hanks splays his hands. "Those followers would do anything for their leader, even take the fall for murder." Anger wells inside me at this miscarriage of justice. "The cult served Novak this fall guy on a platter." My chest heaves, and I throw my hands up, agitated. "How could Novak not see it?" I answer my own question. "Maybe he does, and he's benefitting somehow." Hanks drums his fingers on his desk. "Maybe the cult paid him off."

We both sit with that thought hanging heavy in the air. I nod slowly, casting back through our interactions with the chief. "You know, that Orion fellow met us at the gate after we spoke with Novak. You think the chief tipped them off?"

Hanks raises his bushy brows, thinking it over. "I think that's a real possibility. Besides, I doubt he can afford that fancy truck of his on a small-town chief's salary."

"And what about what Officer Dobre told us? Why would Novak hide the fact that Joy Ackerman had come into his station, likely the night she died, unless he was hoping to cover it up?" I huff. "There's a lot pointing to the fact that something is off here."

Hanks grunts. "Let's hope it's enough."

CHAPTER 36

"Hanks! Mercer! My office, now."

I look up from the paperwork I've been pretending to do as Chief Jamison spins on his heel, marching back into his office. My gaze drifts across the bullpen to Hanks, who's emerging from his office.

He gives me a bracing look and tips his head toward the chief's office. I've been waiting on pins and needles since Jamison got back from opening the watch party down at the beach. Even with his office door closed, I could hear Chief Novak's booming voice on the speakerphone call a few minutes ago.

I rise from my desk and hold a hand out as Shadow lifts his head. My dog can stay resting. No need for Shadow to get chewed out, too. I feel like a kid being called into the principal as I drag my feet into the chief's office, closing the door behind me. I take a seat next to Hanks and hazard a glance at the fuming Jamison.

I've never seen him so furious. His eyes are blazing and his nostrils flare as he stares us down. "Care to guess who I just got off the phone with?"

I cringe, but Hanks sits tall, adjusting his tie.

Jamison doesn't wait for us to answer him. He jabs a finger at his phone. "That was Chief Novak from Elk Ridge. And he wants your head, Mercer. Not that he's pleased with either of you." The chief scowls at Hanks, then turns his angry gaze back to me. I wither under it, unable to meet his eyes.

"He wants you not only pulled off the case but reprimanded, and ideally, fired."

At that, I jerk my head up, my mouth dropping open. I can admit that perhaps I was over the line back there in Elk Ridge, but fired? That's ridiculous. "Chief, that guy's a jerk."

Jamison narrows his dark eyes at me. "You know most detectives go their entire careers without pissing off another town's chief this much, and it's your first case." He slams a hand down on the desk, making me jump.

Hanks clears his throat. "Well, in Mercer's defense, sir, she's naturally quite irritating and pisses a lot of people off without trying."

Jamison furrows his brow, entirely unamused, and I shoot Hanks a look. What is he thinking?

He lets out a nervous chuckle. "Sorry, Chief, just an attempt at a little levity. In all seriousness, Mercer's doing a fantastic job. Sure, she may have lost her cool a little bit back there, but she didn't say anything that wasn't true."

Jamison arches a disbelieving brow.

"My read on Chief Novak is he's a man who can't stand to be questioned, much less challenged, and that's what Mercer did—with good cause."

Jamison huffs through his nose, clearly doubtful, but at least waits for Hanks to explain further.

"As we were leaving the station, Novak's own officer secretly told us that he recognized Joy Ackerman from the artist's sketch and that she came into the Elk Ridge station a couple months ago, worried her son was in danger."

Jamison frowns. "What do you mean by he secretly told you?"

"He rushed out after us," I explain. "Under the pretense that we forgot our pen. He went out of his way to not inform us in front of Novak."

I splay my hands, pleading with Jamison to see our side of things. "That very well could have been the same night she was killed."

Our chief looks thoughtful and leans back in his chair. He steeples his fingers.

"Why wouldn't Novak have told us that?" Hanks presses. "And why wouldn't that woman have brought her child to the police station if she was worried about him, *unless* the cult was keeping the kid away from her?"

Jamison's expression grows grim. "Tell me about this suspect Novak arrested."

We fill Jamison in on Phoenix's arrest, and how his fellow cult member, Orion, is acting as his lawyer and insisting they remain in Elk Ridge.

"Apparently, Phoenix decided to turn himself in." Hanks rolls his eyes. "Whole thing feels coached to me. And we couldn't even interrogate him ourselves because the man is insisting on his lawyer being present."

Jamison looks thoughtful. "That part's hardly unusual."

Hanks jabs a finger into the desk, riled up. "Okay, but Novak intentionally kept vital information from us about Joy Ackerman. And when we pressed him this morning about checking up on the kid, he blew up on us. I think the man's hiding something and doesn't appreciate us sticking our noses in it."

Jamison sighs and massages the bridge of his nose before looking up and lifting a palm. "So what? What's your next move?" He shoots me a sharp look. "*Assuming* you're not pulled from the case."

My stomach sinks, though it does seem like Hanks has convinced him to at least consider our point of view. The detective and I exchange a glance. We talked about this very thing after watching the interrogation footage, formulating our next moves.

Hanks leans back. "We want a warrant to go search the cult's compound."

Jamison scoffs and shakes his head, but Hanks presses on.

"We believe Joy's son could be in danger. At the very least, he's unaccounted for."

Jamison sits with that for a moment, his jaw set. "You realize what you're asking me to do?" His voice is tense, loud. "Elk Ridge has a confession. So for us to get a warrant, I'm going to need to go to a county judge, going over Chief Novak's head, to get a warrant for *his* jurisdiction." He shakes his head, his gaze darting between me and Hanks. "It's an act of war. I'd have to publicly accuse him at the very least of incompetence, and at the worst of corruption and actively obstructing a homicide investigation."

When he lays it all out like that, it does sound like a reach.

Hanks's throat bobs. "Yep, that about sums it up."

Jamison shoots him a death stare, and I'm shocked that Hanks can hold his gaze. Finally, the chief closes his eyes for a long moment before shaking his head. "I'll see what I can do."

I grin. I have no idea how Hanks pulled it off, but he seems to have won the chief over to our side.

"Sir, time is of the essence," Hanks presses. "The boy could at this very moment be—"

Jamison holds up a hand, stopping him. "Don't push your luck, Hanks." He throws a hand towards the window. "You realize we're dealing with thousands of tourists who've flooded into Nightfall? And considering the lunar eclipse doesn't happen until 2:00 a.m., that means we're going to have lots of partiers out on the streets, driving back to Portland or to their hotels or wherever afterwards, under the influence. We need all hands on deck for patrol." He glares. "And yet, in the middle of all this, you're asking me to go to a county judge for some kid who may or may not be in trouble, in a town where the chief just reamed me a new one."

Hanks presses his lips together and bows his head.

"Get out of here." Jamison waves us off, spinning to look out the window. Hanks flashes his eyes at me, and we hurry out of the office.

The detective closes the door behind us, and as we hurry across the bullpen, eager to get away from our fuming chief, I elbow Hanks. "Hey, thanks for standing up for me back there."

He shrugs. "Only spoke my mind."

I nibble my bottom lip. "Think the chief will come through for us?"

Hanks shrugs. "He always has."

CHAPTER 37

Mere hours later, pine trees whizz past the window as Hanks takes a sharp turn too fast. I clutch the door and press back in my seat. As we come around the bend and hit a straightaway, I breathe again. I shoot a look at Hanks, but he merely seems eager. For a moment, he had me wondering if he had a death wish.

I check on Shadow in the back seat. My dog pants, a goofy smile on his face. He's fine.

A few other cruisers precede us. Chief Jamison's in the lead car, and we've brought all the officers we can spare from patrolling the lunar eclipse parties. Hanks fidgets with the steering wheel, like he's kneading it. His sharp eyes are fixed on the road.

Though no one's turned on their lights or siren, we're speeding along at a rate well past the legal limit. "Jamison stuck his neck out for us on this." Hanks gives me a significant look. "County judge gave us a warrant to search the property," he sighs, "but he didn't see sufficient evidence that Novak was acting as a hindrance. So, he was notified and invited to join the search as a courtesy."

I shift in my seat, irritated. "If Novak is working with the cult, he's tipped them off."

Hanks nods. "Yep."

I set my jaw, a tension headache starting at my temples. I'm nervous and stressed. This is our one chance. If Joy Ackerman's little boy, Clay, is on that compound, this is the only shot we're gonna get to find him and help him. I just hope he's still alive and didn't meet the same fate as his mother.

On cue, as if picking up on my nerves, Shadow rests his heavy head on my shoulder.

Hanks glances over and smirks. "He do that a lot?"

"Yep." I slide an arm around Shadow's neck and nuzzle into him, giving him a hug.

"You train him to do that?"

I grin. "Nope. He just started doing it on his own from the very first ride when I found him."

Hanks makes a thoughtful noise, then pats the steering wheel. "Now listen, kid, we've got to do this by the book." He shoots me a significant look, raising his brows. "Novak's gonna be watching like a hawk, making sure we cross every *t* and dot every *i*. We make one wrong move, and he's not gonna hesitate to come down hard on us."

"Got it." Not only does our investigation ride on how this search goes, but it seems my job and reputation also hang in the balance. "We're allowed to look everywhere?" I clarify.

Hanks nods. "Any restriction will be listed in the warrant, and Jamison will be sure to brief us on that when we arrive."

"How much longer?" I ask.

We pass a mile marker, the thing whirring by in a blur. "About twenty minutes."

My stomach twists in a mix of nerves and excitement. I wonder what the reaction of the cult members will be. Most people in a cult have no idea they're in one. I mean, I spent fourteen years of my life in one and had no idea.

I gaze out at the thick forest all around us as I muse out

loud. "I wonder what would have happened if heathen cops stormed into Canaan Springs when I was a kid."

"Heathen?" Hanks inquires.

"It was our group's word for outsiders."

He scoffs. "So, normal cops, in other words."

I nod. "We had our own officers within the town, but they were corrupt."

"Like Novak," Hanks mutters. "Allegedly."

I grin. "Worse. If Novak is in on this, it's because they've paid him off. Our police were comprised of cult members who were loyal to the group, through and through. Their first duty was to uphold 'biblical law.'" I make air quotes. "US law came second."

Hanks frowns and makes another thoughtful noise. After a couple moments of silence, he shoots a quick glance at me. "So, what do you think the reaction would have been?"

I scoff, picturing all the men I grew up with who had well-stocked gun safes. The elders had given many talks about the coming apocalypse and how we'd need to defend ourselves. "It would have been all-out war," I say with confidence.

Hanks scowls. "Well, let's hope these new age folks have a different take."

CHAPTER 38

Hanks and I park next to the other three Nightfall Patrol cars. We idle in front of the cattle gate that bars our entrance to the Ascendant Light Fellowship's compound. Wide swaths of cleared land sit nestled among the tall pine forest, with a cluster of buildings set far back from the dirt road.

We wait as Orion strolls down the long dirt driveway toward us. This is the man who refused Hanks and me entry the first time, and the supposed lawyer representing Phoenix in that laughable interrogation. He wears his shiny hair slicked back in a low ponytail and today sports a tasseled vest over a plaid button-up, jeans, and cowboy boots.

Hanks drums his fingers against the steering wheel, impatient. "Want to pick up the pace, huh, buddy?"

When Orion reaches the gate, he tips the brim of his hat in greeting, and Chief Jamison emerges from the lead patrol car. Even though we've rolled down our windows, we can't make out their words, though it's clear the chief is showing him our warrant.

Orion peruses it, hands it back, and then unlatches the

gate. He swings it open wide and gestures for us to drive on in.

Hanks pulls a face. "That was oddly easy."

We roll up our windows to avoid choking on the others' dust and rattle down the long driveway toward the large cabin surrounded by yurts, trailers, and small shacks. We park in front of the cabin beside the other few cars already lined up and hop out, slamming the car doors shut behind us.

Hanks and I, along with Shadow, Chief Jamison, Bulldog, and a few other officers who typically work the night shift, circle up. It's all hands on deck, between the search of the cult property and the lunar eclipse tourist events happening back in Nightfall.

Chief Jamison waves everyone in close. "Now listen, county judge gave us the scope to collect evidence and take witness statements as long as it pertains to the murder of Joy Ackerman or the whereabouts and safety of her son, Clay Ackerman. Everybody got that?"

Everyone nods, and Chief Jamison continues. "Hanks is lead on this case. So what do you think? Where do we start?"

The detective gestures at the big cabin in front of us. "Seems like as good a place as any. Let's all start there. Once we make contact with the cult leaders or whoever's in charge here, we can spread out, check the other buildings."

He gestures at the rundown shelters surrounding us. A few gaunt faces emerge from yurt flaps and the doors of shacks, peering out at us. Everyone looks overly tanned, like they spend a lot of time working outside and not enough time eating.

Shadow shifts next to me, his ears pricked and gaze alert. Just as we're about to break and head inside, another patrol car pulls up, parks, and out hops Chief Novak.

Hanks and I exchange annoyed glances. While we were aware that the warrant allowed him to observe, we were hoping he'd skip out on the search party. No such luck. An older woman emerges from the passenger side of Novak's cruiser. She wears brown slacks, a loose paisley top, and her gray hair in tight curls.

I give Hanks a questioning look, but his confused gaze is fixed on the woman.

Novak strolls up to our chief and gives him a friendly handshake.

"Novak, I take it?" Jamison asks. They nod at each other, though the tension is palpable.

He introduces the woman beside him. She carries a leather satchel and hugs a clipboard to her chest. "This is Mallory Kemps."

She nods a general greeting and Jamison raises a brow. "I take it you're not an officer?"

"Oh, no." Mallory shakes her head. "I'm a social worker."

"Mal and I go way back," Novak explains with a smirk.

Hanks frowns. "And you're here because?"

The older woman blinks at him in surprise and gestures at Novak. "I was told you might be interviewing a child and if so, a parent or social worker is required to be present."

Shoot. She's right. I can't believe we didn't think of that. I suppose I just assumed we wouldn't find Clay, or at least, that the cult wouldn't willingly let him speak with us. Now Novak's no doubt brought along someone loyal to him.

"Good luck in there," Novak smirks. Finally, Orion, the man who met us at the gate, comes strolling back down the long driveway and raises a hand in greeting. "Welcome, Officers. Allow me to show you inside?" He gestures at the big cabin, and Detective Hanks nods.

The slight man leads the way up the uneven porch steps. Brambles and brush grow thick around the cabin, with scattered barrels, rusting metal parts, and random debris littered about the land.

I tightly grip Shadow's leash and join Hanks as one of the first officers inside.

"Come on in," Orion says, oddly cooperative.

This is not going how I expected it to. The interior of the cabin is large, bigger than it looks from the outside. We step into a central room with a tall, double-high peaked ceiling and exposed wood beams. Stairs lead up to a wide landing and the second story.

I glance to the side and note a kitchen, bathroom, and a few bedrooms on the ground floor. The place is oddly colorful, like a rainbow threw up inside. Alternate walls have been painted in yellows, oranges, purples, and reds. Christmas lights are strung all over.

Grandma, Hope, and I took down our decorations weeks ago. Maybe this is just how it looks all the time. I note one of the tie-dye tapestries hanging on the wall, recognizing it from their YouTube videos.

Once we're all inside, the other officers wait for Hanks's orders. Even though Chief Jamison is here, Detective Hanks is still lead on the case. Jamison and Novak stand off to the side, observing.

A few cult members emerge from the kitchen, lingering in the doorway, their eyes darting nervously around at all the officers gathered in their living room.

"Now, how can we help you, Officers?" Orion plasters on a bright white smile and spreads his palms open.

"Why don't we start with having you tell us why you lied about not recognizing Joy Ackerman?" Hanks stares the man down.

Orion is all innocence. "Is that who was featured in that drawing?" He presses a hand to his chest. "Honestly, I didn't see the resemblance."

He's lying.

Hanks licks his lips and glares. "No? How about explaining why you lied about her being missing, then?" Orion blinks, his eyes growing wide, as if he's shocked. "Why, because she wasn't missing. She left of her own accord, as everyone here is free to do any time they wish."

I bet.

"How many members are currently living here on the compound?" Hanks follows up.

Orion looks off to the side, thinking for a moment. "We're currently at fifty-seven, I believe."

There's clearly not enough room for all of them in the cabin, so I suspect quite a few of them live in the yurts, rundown trailers, and shacks. If it's true that they're all free to leave when they want, why are so many of them choosing to live in abject poverty?

Hanks cocks his head. "We'll be interviewing some of your members. We'd also like to meet with your leader." The detective narrows his eyes. "Hopefully that won't *disturb* her," he sneers, throwing Orion's reason for barring us access to the property back in his face.

"Of course," Orion says, smiling broadly, apparently unbothered by our presence.

Hanks adjusts his stance. I can tell he's growing more irritated by Orion's chipper agreement. "And we'll need to see your IDs."

Orion's face crumples, and he presses his hands together. "Unfortunately, that won't be possible." His voice is oily, smooth. "We burn them all upon initiation to the group."

"You're joking," Hanks scoffs.

"We relinquish the outside material world when we join the Ascendant Light Fellowship."

Hanks rolls his eyes. "Of course you do."

A door creaks upstairs, catching my attention, and a beautiful blond woman steps onto the landing. Her shiny blond hair flows in smooth waves over her shoulders, and she wears a long, flowing white dress. I recognize her immediately from the group's YouTube videos. She doesn't appear in the videos often, but when she does, the members react like they're receiving a visit from a world leader or a massive celebrity.

This is Source, the woman behind it all. Her electric blue eyes are even more entrancing in person. She places her hands on the banister and sweeps her gaze over all of us gathered below, like a queen surveying her subjects.

"Orion, what is this?" Her voice is melodic.

The man presses a hand to his chest and steps back, allowing Source a clear line of sight to Hanks and the rest of us. "Source, these are the officers I told you about. I believe they're concerned about Joy Ackerman."

Her blond brows knit together in confusion.

"Gaia," Orion clarifies, and Source lifts her chin in recognition.

"Ah."

Orion flashes Hanks and the rest of us an apologetic smile. "When we join the group, part of leaving the material world and our former lives behind involves taking new names. Source knew Joy Ackerman only as Gaia for the last four years."

"Until she mysteriously left of her own accord, right?" Hanks says, his voice dripping with sarcasm.

"Exactly," Orion answers, meeting his gaze.

Hanks huffs. "Our officers are going to need access to every room in this cabin. We'll be collecting evidence regarding Joy Ackerman's murder, and we're going to need to speak with her son, Clay. Is he here?"

I hold my breath. Truth be told, I expect they'll tell us he left with his mother. But instead, there's an awkward silence.

And then a young boy steps out from the room behind Source and joins her at the banister. "I'm right here." He waves and smiles as Source hugs him to her side. "But I'm not Clay anymore. I'm called Chosen One now."

Hanks and I exchange wide-eyed looks that clearly spell

out "what the fuck?" I look back at the boy. Is that really Clay?

"Let me see the picture." Hanks sidles close to me, his voice low. I reach into my pocket and pull out a photocopy of the photograph Mary Ann Ackerman let me take from her home.

"This was him at four years old. Mary Ann Ackerman said the boy would be eight now." Hanks and I study the photo, then look up at the boy standing beside Source.

I have to say, the boy upstairs looks a little older than eight years old. Closer to eleven if I had to guess, but then again, I'm not great with children's ages. Besides, it's possible the kid just had a growth spurt. Just like in the photograph, the boy in front of us has freckles across his cheeks. From what I can tell from down here, his blue eyes match those in the photo, as do his curly hair and tan skin. He looks leaner now, his jaw more square, but maybe he's lost baby weight, or is just getting meager sustenance like the other members.

Hanks glances back at Chief Jamison, whose eyes are narrowed in concern. We convinced Jamison to stick his neck out for us and go over Novak's head based on our claim that this little boy was either missing or in danger.

Now here he is, smiling and waving. Did we get this all wrong?

Hanks clears his throat. "We'd like to speak with Clay alone." He gestures to the other cops. "I want everyone to pull these group members aside individually for questioning. We need to know about Joy Ackerman, Clay, and what goes on here, yeah?"

The other officers nod and spread out across the cabin, moving over to those gathered in the kitchen entryway, while others dip back outside, no doubt heading towards the yurts and trailers.

Chiefs Novak and Jamison and the social worker stay behind with us.

Source smiles down on us, and I gaze up at her beautiful face. I notice a slight tinge of blue to her pale skin, and I'm reminded of Joy Ackerman's headless corpse. I shudder.

"Of course you can question Clay. Why don't you use my bedroom?" She gestures at the room behind her as Hanks, Shadow, Mallory, and I jog up the stairs. As I sweep past her, I'm struck by the strong smell of patchouli.

I'm glad to be out from under that woman's intense blue-eyed gaze as we step into the bedroom and close the door behind us. It's nicer than I'd have expected based on the state of some of those decrepit buildings outside. There's a large king bed under a big window. The ceiling's peaked, just like the living room, and Source has her own river rock fireplace. Bookshelves line one of the walls with a comfy armchair near the door.

That's where I gesture for Clay to have a seat. He hops up into the chair, that same wide smile on his face.

Hanks indicates for me to take the lead while he looks around the room. I let go of Shadow's leash as well, letting my K-9 sniff around. There's always the chance he might discover something useful.

I crouch down in front of Clay, hoping to look less intimidating than if I were towering over him. Mallory sidles up beside me, still clutching her clipboard. I know it's just procedure for a social worker to be present, but knowing she's tight with Novak has me annoyed with her. "Hi. I just need to ask you some questions, okay?"

He nods eagerly.

"Can you give me your name?"

"Clay Ackerman," he says.

"And your age?"

"I am eight years old."

Mallory is scribbling down his answers on her notepad.

"What's your mom's name?"

He hesitates a moment. "Gaia is what we call her in the group, but her real name is Joy."

I nod. "Okay, great." I nibble my bottom lip and glance around the room, noting the sleeping bag on the floor covered in stars and spaceships. "Is that where you sleep?"

Clay nods. He jumps off the chair and skips over, sitting criss-cross on the sleeping bag.

I exchange a concerned look with Hanks, then Mallory, and follow him. "You don't mind, uh, sleeping on the floor?" Again, I crouch down to be on his level.

"Nope, it's great," he says.

I look up to Mallory, who stays standing tall beside me. "Are these suitable conditions for a child? Sleeping on the floor?"

The social worker purses her lips. "It's certainly not conventional, but the boy appears to have a sleeping mat for cushioning and blankets for warmth." She gestures at his makeshift bed with her pen. "Besides, as a whole the place is clean and tidy."

I gawk at her. Is that really enough to prove he's safe and taken care of?

I turn back to Clay. Even though he keeps a bright smile plastered on his face, he scrubs at his eyes. He's been doing that since the moment he stepped onto the landing beside Source, and I notice his eyes are quite red and irritated-looking. Maybe it's allergies.

My gaze drifts to the bookshelf beside him. He sleeps wedged in between the king-sized bed and the shelves. I scan the spines of the books, noting a couple dozen fantasy stories. I grin. "Are these your books?"

He studies them for a moment, then nods. "Uh-huh."

I spot a couple of Tolkien tomes. I'm trying to connect with him. Hopefully, if I can gain his trust, he'll open up a little more. I gesture at *The Return of the King*. "Wow, that's pretty advanced reading for eight years old. Nice job."

He doesn't respond.

I clear my throat and try again to connect with him. "All who wander are not lost, am I right?" It's a lame attempt and I know I sound like a dork, but any kid who likes to read fantasy this much will surely pounce on the chance to talk about some of their favorite books right?

But Clay doesn't bite. In fact, he frowns at me and looks confused. Did he not get the reference? I mean, any Lord of the Rings fan, even if they'd only seen the movies, would get it. Or is he just frowning at me because he thinks I'm a dork? That could definitely be it.

He winces and scratches at his eyes again.

"Clay, is there anything you want to tell us about how you're being treated here?"

Mallory clears her throat and shifts on her feet.

He shakes his head, his perfect curls bouncing. "Nope, I like it here."

"They treat you well?" I press. "You're getting enough to eat? No one's hurting you?"

"Yep. It's great." Clay's still smiling broadly.

Shadow wanders over and sits beside me. The boy looks between me and my dog. "You can pet him if you want to?"

Clay thinks it over, then shakes his head.

I understand. Sometimes a dog this big can be intimidating to a kid. Heck, he can be intimidating to adults, too. But that's only because they don't know what a softie Shadow is. I stroke my dog's head and suck in a breath over my teeth. "Clay, why didn't you leave with your mom?"

"I didn't want to." Clay folds his arms across his chest. "I like it here. My mom was mean to me."

Mallory frowns and cuts in. "Mean to you in what way?"

"Just…" He looks off to the side. "Um, just, she would yell at me and um, she was just mean."

"Okay." Mallory scribbles down some notes.

Hanks comes over and stands behind us. He plants his

hands on his hips. "Listen, Clay, this is important. You're safe with us. We can protect you. Do you feel like you're in danger here?"

Clay shakes his head no.

Hanks isn't having any more luck with the boy than I did.

"Have they ever made you feel unsafe? Source, or Orion, or any of the other adults?"

Again, Clay shakes his head. "Nope, never."

Hanks and I exchange concerned looks.

I try again. "Clay, really, it's okay, you can trust us. We're here to help you. If you're worried about getting in trouble, we can make sure you—"

The little boy interrupts, scowling. "No, okay? Everything's fine. I like it here. That's it." He gets to his feet and pushes past us, throwing open the door and darting back out onto the landing.

I rise from the crouch back up to standing. "Well, that went well."

Mallory purses her lips and shoots us both sharp looks. "I know your objective is to prove he's mistreated, but you're pushing him in a way that's unproductive. The boy appears perfectly fine, despite your attempts to get him to say otherwise." She arches a brow and follows Clay out onto the landing.

The detective shakes his head. "I'm not sure what to make of this."

I shrug. "Me, neither."

Before we leave, I scan the bookcase. "Did you find anything in here?" I ask Hanks.

"Nah." He gestures at the nightstand. "Nothing aside from this bizarre sleeping arrangement and a lot of booze."

While the bottom shelf next to Clay's bed is full of fantasy books, I note that the rest of the shelves aren't lined in books, but in spiral-bound notebooks.

I pull one out and flip open to a random page. I can't read

half the handwriting, it's so cramped, but I manage to pick out a few words here and there.

"Source says we need to make more videos to entice new members, 1:03 p.m. 1:04 p.m. Source sneezes." I keep scanning and realize it's a detailed account, minute by minute, of everything Source does and says. This particular notebook is dated from back in October. "Holy cow," I mutter. "How many of these are there?"

Hanks has moved to the door.

I hold up the notebook. "These are detailed accounts of everything Source has been doing and saying."

Hanks nods. "I'll send some officers up to bag these up for evidence."

I put the notebook back, grab Shadow's leash, and follow Hanks back outside onto the landing.

Source is now downstairs with the others, and a few of the other officers have returned from outside. Clay and Mallory have rejoined them. Chief Jamison jerks his head, motioning for us to follow him. He steps outside onto the porch, and after sharing an uneasy look, Hanks, Shadow, and I head downstairs.

We step outside onto the front porch and join Jamison, who's holding a small stack of papers in one hand. It's chilly but bright at the moment, as many of the clouds have cleared. If it stays this way, it'll be great eclipse watching weather and the tourists will be happy.

Hanks licks his lips. "The boy says everything's fine, but..." He shakes his head. "Something doesn't feel right here."

"You didn't find *anything*?" Jamison pushes.

Hanks splays his hands and Jamison scoffs, marching a few feet away and then pacing back. "You assured me this kid was in grave danger."

Hanks's throat bobs, and I lower my gaze. We're definitely in trouble. "Has anyone else found anything?" Hanks asks.

"Not everyone's finished questioning, but so far they all say that the kid, Clay, is doing just fine and insisted on staying behind when his mom left of her own accord." Jamison continues pacing, like he's building up steam.

I clear my throat. "Surely now that his mother's deceased, we should step in and take Clay into the custody of the state until we can home him with his grandmother, or another relative?"

I thought my suggestion was reasonable, but this just fuels Jamison's wrath. He whirls on us and holds up the papers in his hand, shaking them. I can see now that they're some kind of contract. "We would, if years ago Joy Ackerman hadn't signed over Clay's guardianship to Source, aka Amanda Davis, in the event of her death or inability to care for her son."

My jaw drops. "No."

Jamison pushes the papers at Hanks, who takes them and peruses the contract, with me reading over his shoulder. He skims over the agreement. "Where did you get these?" He flips to the next page.

"The lawyer handed them over," Jamison growls. "Apparently, within the first couple of weeks of Joy moving here, she wanted to make sure Clay would be cared for if anything happened to her."

Hanks scoffed, still scanning the pages. "Right. I'm sure it was her idea."

Jamison scowls. "Orion told us Ms. Ackerman wasn't close with her own mother and didn't want Clay to return to her in the event of her death or incapacitation."

My stomach turns and I mutter, "That actually does sound like her. Mary Ann Ackerman told me she and Joy fought a lot because of her strict parenting."

Hanks pales and flips to the signature page. There's Joy's signature, Source's, and Orion's, as well as two witnesses. The detective looks up. "Have we checked with these witnesses?"

Jamison, whose eyes are blazing, nods. "They corroborated the story. The document is legitimate."

Shoot. So Source is Clay's legal guardian. We can hardly make a case for taking him away when he's telling us he's happy here.

Hanks hands back the contract, then crosses his arms, and I can see the wheels turning behind his eyes. "Even if they're telling the truth about the boy's guardianship and Joy Ackerman left of her own accord, someone murdered her and buried her in a ritual fashion out in the forest. They made special use of that symbol. If it wasn't one of these folks, who would it be?"

Chief Jamison throws his hands up. "I don't know, but I stuck my neck out for you two, and so far we've got *nothing*. You'd better hope something turns up." He stomps back inside, and my stomach twists with shame as Hanks, Shadow, and I follow him back in.

Jamison calls out to all the officers gathered. "Anyone find anything?"

Bulldog pulls up a plastic baggie of shredded green plant material. "Some marijuana."

Orion holds up a finger. "In legal amounts."

"Fuck," Hanks mutters under his breath. "This isn't looking good, kid."

"No kidding." And I don't even need Bulldog sneering at me to know what a disaster this is shaping up to be.

CHAPTER 39

The chief scowls at Hanks and me, and I shrivel under his gaze. None of this is playing out how I expected it to. The cult was definitely ready for us, and they're making us look like fools. Either that, or I am just totally way off base.

Chief Jamison pulls us aside as more officers return to the main cabin, sharing their findings after interviewing cult members. Apparently, everyone says that Joy neglected Clay. She just wasn't interested in the boy and spent her time partying.

I hate to admit it, but their accounts are similar to what Joy's mother, Mary Ann, told me when I flew to Simi Valley. My stomach twists with nerves and shame as Chief Jamison pulls Hanks and me into the kitchen.

"We haven't found squat," he grinds out between clenched teeth. Shadow sidles up close and leans against my leg, offering me comfort, but this time it's not doing anything for me.

We put everything on the line—the case, my job, Jamison's reputation—to get the search warrant, and so far we've come up empty. "That boy—" Jamison jabs a finger in Clay's direction. We left him sitting on one of the sofas next to Source and the social worker. "—is alive and well and says he *wanted* to stay here."

"What if it's not Clay?" I blurt out. Hanks and the chief shoot me surprised looks. I'm a bit surprised I spoke up also, and I'm not sure it was wise, but I press on. "Maybe they're passing him off as Clay because the real Clay's missing, or even worse..." It's a thought that's been nagging at me. The boy in front of us looks similar to the young kid in the picture, but there are some differences—his nose is narrower, frame leaner, and brows a different shape.

Jamison massages the bridge of his nose.

Short of a DNA test, I'm not sure how we'd prove this. I back up and glance at the little boy with his red eyes, curly hair, and freckles. I get an idea. "Maybe those aren't real freckles. They probably drew them on. Watch." I hustle over to the stove and rip a kitchen towel off the handle, then wet one end of it in the sink. I hold it up to Chief Jamison and march over to Clay, crouching in front of him.

"Listen, Clay. This is a little bit cold," I show the wet rag. "But I'm just gonna wipe this on your face, okay?"

"Excuse me?" Mallory Kemps interjects. "Why?"

The little boy shoots Source a nervous look, but she nods for me to go ahead. I ignore the social worker's protests and swipe the wet rag across his cheeks and... nothing happens.

I expected the freckles to smear or come off altogether. If they'd been made with an eyebrow pencil, for instance, that's exactly what would have happened. Sometimes makeup is water-resistant, though, so I try again. When nothing happens, I hold Clay's chin with one hand and scrub at his cheek.

"Stop!" He shoves my hands away.

"Officer!" Mallory Kemps chastises me.

When I check the cloth, there's only a faint brown tint to it, and all of Clay's freckles are totally intact.

"What exactly are you doing?" Source asks, cocking her head.

I hate having her intense blue eyes on me. It reminds me of the way my father and the other elders would watch me. My breath is coming faster now. "Care to explain the brown on this rag?" I'm clutching at straws, I know it, but I'm getting desperate.

Source shrugs. "He's a little boy; he likes to play in the dirt."

Mallory tsks.

My shoulders slump. Of course he does. I have to admit my fake freckle theory was pretty farfetched. I feel all eyes on me. Jamison is fuming in the doorway of the kitchen, and beside him, Hanks stands with his hand over his mouth. I glance back, where Bulldog stands smirking and some of the other officers have doubt written all over their faces.

I toss the kitchen rag aside, my chest heaving as I feel this case, and my chance to make detective, slipping through my fingers.

"You know, Officer," Source says, her eyes fixed on my face. "Sometimes we only see what we want to see. If we simply open our minds to the truth, that's when we gain true knowledge." She spreads her arms wide to take in Clay and several of the other members of the cult who are sitting around on other sofas or floor cushions. "That's why we're all gathered here. These are seekers of knowledge. We have nothing to hide." She cocks her head, watching me. "Why are you so convinced we do?"

I bristle. I know I shouldn't answer. But there's something about this woman that reminds me of my own cult leaders growing up. Something that makes me both want to obey and challenge her. I set my jaw. "Because one of your members, Joy Ackerman, was found murdered in the forest."

Source's eyes widen and the social worker gasps.

I suddenly realize how callously I said that, right in front of the boy. I turn to Clay. "I-I'm so sorry."

The little boy exchanges a look with Source. "It's okay. My mom and I weren't close." The woman reaches over and takes the little boy's hand in her own.

She looks at me, effusing ethereal beauty and peacefulness and slides an arm around the little boy, who leans his head on her shoulder.

I stagger back, bumping into a coffee table. Bulldog snickers. How did I have this so wrong?

I turn to the chief. "The kid's being coerced or brainwashed. Like I was as a kid. I'm telling you."

Chief Jamison's expression shutters. "Let's go." He's grim as he marches toward the door.

Have the other officers even finished their search of the property? There's got to be something here. I'm desperate now. My gut is telling me that something about this is all wrong. But do I trust my gut over the facts I'm seeing right in front of my eyes? Nathan, Hope, my grandma—they're always telling me to trust my instincts, to speak up for myself more.

"What about the firewood?" I gasp. "There's a huge pile of it out back." I spotted a massive pile in the field behind the cabin on our way in, covered in plastic tarps.

Chief Jamison hesitates at the door, then spins to face me. "It's winter, Mercer." He shoots me a withering look. Bulldog and Chief Novak both give me a smug grin before they file out after Jamison.

Hanks keeps his voice low as he catches my gaze. "Give it up, kid. Come on." He tips his head toward the door, and I'm about to leave after him, when my arm's yanked by Shadow's leash. I look back. Shadow sniffs at a rug in the center of the floor. His tail is stiff behind him and he's excitedly circling next to Orion's feet. My dog's ears are pricked, and his nose is glued to the ground.

He's alerting me. He's found something.

"Wait! Shadow's found something."

Chief Jamison steps past the other officers and leans back inside. "Mercer, that was an order. Let's go."

I hesitate. If I'm supposed to trust my gut and my dog, this is the moment to do so, right? Then again, disobeying the chief is going to have consequences. Still, I take the chance.

I rush over and, in a fit of desperation, shoulder Orion out of the way. Once he's off the rug, I flip it back to reveal—absolutely nothing.

My heart sinks into my feet. There's no trapdoor. No hidden evidence. Just wood planks.

Shadow stares at me with his ears perked. He's alerting me, sure, but he's not infallible. Even my amazing K-9 gets it wrong sometimes. My cheeks burn, and I'm sure I've turned bright pink with humiliation.

Bulldog, Novak, Mallory Kemps, Hanks, and Chief Jamison are all staring at me in disbelief. I've made a total ass of myself. What was I thinking?

"I-I'm sorry." I stammer out an apology to the room in general. My neck's burning, and I'm fighting with everything I have to hold back the tears stinging my eyes.

I guess I really can't trust my instincts.

CHAPTER 40

I hang my head as Chief Jamison continues to chew Hanks and me out. We sit in the chief's office back in Nightfall. I've spared Shadow the reaming, leaving him to snooze on his bed next to my desk.

The sky outside the chief's window sits dark and clear, stars beginning to twinkle against the black backdrop. Tourists and revelers in a party mood for the lunar eclipse celebrations stroll by on Main Street, laughing and talking loudly. The lights of all the boutiques and restaurants shine brightly all up and down the main drag. Normally they'd be closed up by this time of night, even though it is only just past 6:00 p.m.

I tune back into Chief Jamison's words. "That kid's just fine. And now Novak's gonna be riding my ass." I wince as he raises his voice on the last word.

I keep my gaze down. I've rarely, if ever, heard Chief Jamison swear, much less raise his voice. Now I've been treated to it twice in one day. God, I've really screwed this up.

The chief lets out a heavy sigh and leans back in his chair, swiveling to gaze out the window. His eyes are clouded over, as though he's somewhere far away in his mind.

We let the silence stretch on for a bit, until Hanks clears his throat.

"Chief, I apologize." He presses a palm to his chest. "This is on me. I was lead on the case. This is my responsibility."

I cringe. While I appreciate that Hanks isn't throwing me under the bus, it doesn't make me feel any better that he's taking accountability for my bad decisions.

I shake my head. "No, this is my fault. I'm the one who insisted that Clay was in trouble. I pushed for this, and it clearly..." My chest is tight, and I'm fighting back tears. "It clearly was a mistake."

Chief Jamison swivels back to face us, steepling his fingers together. He takes a couple of deep, calming breaths, then nods. "You know, it *was* a mistake." He pauses until I look up and meet his eyes. "But it was *my* mistake. Ultimately, I'm the one responsible here. This whole thing has been an embarrassing disappointment." His words cut to the bone.

The chief shakes his head. "Mercer, you need time. You've got promise. But we pushed you too hard, too soon."

"I don't know about that, Chief." Hanks starts to push back, but Jamison holds up a hand, cutting him off.

"Mercer, you're off the case."

My jaw drops. Somehow I'm still shocked even though I know I shouldn't be. Hanks opens his mouth to protest, but Jamison doesn't give him the chance.

"Hanks, Elk Ridge got a confession. I want you to wrap this up."

"Chief, I'm sorry," I whisper.

Jamison nods his acceptance and then dismisses us with a wave. I open my mouth to apologize further, but Hanks shakes his head then gestures toward the door. I follow his lead and step out, closing the chief's door behind him.

"Come on, kid." Hanks leads me over to his office and closes the door. He reaches into a drawer in his desk and pulls out a bottle of whiskey. He leans over, glancing behind me and checks the bullpen to make sure no one's watching. He then pours me a splash of whiskey in a spare mug, before doing the same in his own white porcelain Nightfall PD mug for himself.

I sink into the chair across from him and take the mug he offers me. I crinkle my nose at the strong fumes wafting off the liquor and then raise a doubtful brow at him. "Should we really be drinking on the job?"

Hank scoffs and leans back in his chair before taking a sip. "We're off the clock, kid." He takes another drink. "After the day we've had, I think we deserve it."

I can't argue. I take a sip. The alcohol burns sliding down my throat, and I have to admit the warmth is somewhat comforting. I'm usually a wine or margarita kind of gal, but sometimes your day is so messed up it calls for something stronger.

We sit there in silence, commiserating with each other, sipping from our mugs of whiskey. Finally, Hanks takes a deep breath and interrupts the quiet.

"This isn't the end, kid."

I shoot him a doubtful look.

"Early on, when I'd just barely made detective, there was this arson case, right?"

I lean forward, curious.

"I was convinced this one fella did it. Everything pointed to him." He leans forward. "And I pushed my theory, too, to anyone who would listen." He bites his bottom lip and shakes his head, giving me a rueful grin. "Thing was, the guy was a firefighter."

"Oh." I suck in a breath.

"Uh-huh." Hanks looks rueful before sipping his whiskey. "Yep, made a big stink about it. And it turns out, it wasn't him."

"Oof." I wince.

"Right?" He nods. "And look where I am now. You can come back from this."

I shake my head. "I'm not so sure about that."

"It's a tough blow. I'll give you that." Hanks takes another sip. "Things will look better tomorrow, though. I promise you."

I sigh. "I'll have to take your word for it."

Truth is, I've been working so hard on listening to my gut. But I messed up. I was wrong. And yet, now that I seem to have activated my instincts, it's hard for me to ignore them. And something's still telling me that we're missing something important.

There's Phoenix's confession, for one. It seemed so forced, scripted. And that Clay kid. Again, I don't spend much time around kids, but are they usually so chirpy and excited to talk to officers?

Still, I look across the desk at Hanks. He's doing his best to give me a pep talk and cheer me up. I don't want him to think I'm crazy by pushing the point. He and Jamison have already stuck their necks out enough for me, and I'm lucky to still have my job.

If I'm going to follow my instincts, I'm going to do it alone.

I finish the whiskey and thank the detective.

"I'll see you tomorrow, kid."

"See you tomorrow."

He stays in his office to finish up that paperwork on the case while I head back into the bullpen. It's mostly empty, since everybody's out on patrol for all the lunar eclipse events.

There will be speeding tickets to give, drunk drivers to arrest, bar fights to break up, and fire safety to watch out for. I'd be out there too, seeing as we need all hands on deck, if I hadn't messed things up so thoroughly that Jamison just wants me to go home.

I stand in the empty bullpen, hesitating. This next move of mine? It's beyond risky, and yet I can't seem to resist.

I wander over to the evidence locker. It's small, more of a large closet. The door's closed, but I hear shuffling and banging around inside. Clearly one of the officers is organizing things. I knock, and a moment later Red, the night lieutenant, swings the door open and blinks at me. "Oh, hey, Mercer. What's up?"

I square my shoulders and pray word of me being off the case hasn't already spread. "I want to check out some of those journals we took from the compound out by Elk Ridge. For the Joy Ackerman case I'm working with Hanks."

Red lets out a weary sigh, then gestures at the pile of evidence boxes wedged between the wire shelf racks crammed with evidence boxes and bags. "I'm just barely making a dent in cataloging them. Can it wait until tomorrow?"

I clear my throat. I'm in dangerous territory. While checking out the evidence isn't technically illegal or unethical, it *is* a breach of command and there will be consequences. If I'm found out. I should probably take this as a sign to back out now, but instead, I press on. "I just need a few of the most recent journals, from the past month or so."

He sighs again and scratches at his red mustache. "Fine. Give me a second." He grabs a clipboard off the folding table next to the door and scans the log. "Here—I've got the most recent dozen journals already logged. You can have those—that good?"

"That's great, thanks." My hand trembles as I sign my name on the line, indicating that I've checked out the evidence. There's a paper trail now, and when Jamison comes down on me, I'll have no way to deny my actions.

Red grabs an empty evidence box, piles the wire-bound journals inside, then hands it over. "Good luck." I hurry out of the way so he can close the door and get back to work cataloging.

I let out a shaky breath as I stare down at the box in my arms. I've taken a big gamble, betting on my own instincts, and I pray that it pays off. Then again, instincts come from experience, and I know cults. There's no way the Ascendant Light Fellowship is being as aboveboard as they're acting. I just hope these journals can help me prove it.

I grab Shadow's leash, then duck out, only calling goodbye to Linda and Joan over my shoulder as I hustle past them through the crowded lobby. Once I'm outside in the cold night air, I slow my pace.

I stroll down Main Street past large groups of tourists and revelers. Everyone seems in a jovial mood as I walk back up the hill towards home.

Maybe it's the whiskey that gave me the liquid courage to take the journals, or maybe it's my newfound trust in my gut. Either way, it's a stupid move. I'm already on thin ice with Jamison, and if he finds out about this, I'm sure I'll be fired. But some part of me needs to know what's in these journals.

CHAPTER 41

Once home, I jog upstairs, calling hello to Grandma and Hope. I stash the box of journals in my room before changing into comfy clothes and heading back downstairs with Shadow.

I help Grandma cook dinner, spaghetti and meatballs with a side salad, and Hope eventually comes downstairs and joins in. They each talk about their days, and when they ask me about mine, I hesitate. Part of me wants to sweep this under the rug. I'm not sure I'm ready to talk about how badly the search went, especially since my life might get a lot worse once Jamison finds out about the journals.

But Hope and Grandma know me too well. "Eden," Grandma Gloria prompts.

As I toss the ranch dressing into the big salad bowl, I sigh.

"Today was probably my worst day on the force."

"Aww." Hope gives me a sympathetic look and rushes over to wrap me in a tight hug. I lean my head against her shoulder. And before I know it, tears are streaming down my face as I recount the way I tried to stick up for myself, but it just got Hanks and me in trouble with Chief Novak. And then the way Jamison stuck up for us. I keep the story general, avoiding any specifics of the case or the search of the compound, but make it clear that I made a fool of myself.

As I share my humiliating day, it's like a weight is being lifted off my chest and shoulders. Before I know it, Hope's pressing a glass of wine into my hand and Grandma's trying to cure my sorrows by offering me more garlic bread.

We sit around the table and pretty soon I have to admit that some delicious home cooking, the company of my sister and grandma, and a little wine go a long way toward making me feel better.

Hope chews on a bite of spaghetti before frowning. "That Chief Novak dude sounds like a real asshat."

Grandma Gloria nods her agreement. Normally she'd chide Hope for calling anyone a swear word, but if they've crossed me, then she's in full support.

"Thanks." I give them teary smiles. "Truth is, though, at least in this case, he was right. I was out of line. And now I'm off the case." My stomach twists with guilt as I think of the box of evidence in my room upstairs. I shake my head, the weight of what I've done washing over me. "I'm never going to make detective."

Grandma reaches across the table and gives my hand a squeeze. "Sweetheart, it took your grandpa twelve years to become a detective." She raises her brows. "You're going to get there. Just be patient." She pats my hand.

"Yeah, hang in there," Hope chimes in. "And if you want me to beat that Novak guy up, just let me know."

This gets a grin out of me, and I chuckle. "Thanks, sis."

She tips her head toward my dog, who's scarfing dinner out of his bowl. "Or, you know, if Shadow *happened* to attack…" She trails off, raising her brows.

I shake my head at her. "Nah. We don't want Shadow to get in trouble."

"That's true." Hope coos at my dog, who stops munching just long enough to look over with his big brown eyes. "We don't want you to be in trouble, do we?" His curious eyes dart from my sister to me before he goes back to chowing down.

We chuckle, and conversation gradually shifts to the lunar eclipse this evening.

"What time is it at again?" Grandma asks.

"It's around 2:00 a.m.," Hope answers, ripping off a chunk of garlic bread.

Grandma scoffs. "Well, I tell you what, I will be long asleep by then."

She takes a sip of wine as my sister swivels her bright blue eyes to me. "How about you, Eden? Why don't you come out with me and my friends? It'll be fun. You can blow off some steam."

Part of me is tempted to go out with her. I really ought to be more social, and Hanks's words about having a life outside of the job echo in my head. At the same time, I've got those journals stashed up in my room, and I'm itching to pore over them.

"We're going to go to the pub first," Hope says with a smile, "and then wander down to the beach party. Some other people we know already have a good spot staked out. We'll make s'mores, drink hot toddies, sit around the campfire. Come on, it'll be so much fun." She shoots me a pleading look. "Please come."

I give her a smile. "I'm tempted, really, but it's been a day. I think I'm just going to take it easy tonight. Stay in. Lick my wounds."

She sighs. "All right, but if you change your mind…"

We pretty quickly wrap up dinner and clean up. It's around nine when Hope heads out to go join her friends. She checks with me one more time, and I thank her, but decline going out.

Once the kitchen's clean and Hope's gone, Grandma curls up on the couch to watch some of her guilty pleasure reality TV shows, and I head up to my room with Shadow. I make sure the door is all the way closed, grab the stack of journals, and curl up in bed with my computer. Shadow snuggles up at my feet as I begin poring through the evidence. I pull up the Ascendant Light Fellowship's YouTube channel and hit Play on their videos.

For hours, video after video plays in the background as I pore over the journals. I'm hoping something they say will help me figure out this case and what's really going on. Of course, there's a possibility that I'm totally off, that my gut can't be trusted, and that my instincts are trash. The hours stretch on as I read through the journals.

It's slow going. It's tough to make out the small, cramped handwriting and the level of detail is mind-numbing. Every single day, every *second* of Source's day has been chronicled in excruciating specifics.

9 p.m. Source lays down. 9:30 p.m. Source begins to snore. Soft snores. Little starts here and there. She rolls over. 10:15 p.m. Source wakes up, fluffs her pillow, takes a drink...

On and on and on they go. Everything Source eats, down to how her eggs are cooked and the fact that she doesn't eat the crust of her toast, is recorded. There are a lot of so-called teachings mixed in with the mundane day-to-day, all about how the Great Ascension is coming soon, where they'll all be lifted up by the elders. I'm confused about what the elders are. At times they're described as deceased humans who have passed on and now guide Source, but at other times are described almost like nonhuman beings living on another plane—aliens.

Most of it's gibberish, but it's recorded as though it's profound truth.

Source's teaching will be worshiped and studied by generations to come.

I let out a weary sigh as I turn another page filled with cramped handwriting. Notes even fill the margins.

Shadow's snoring now. His eyes are closed, paws twitching. I grin at him. I hope he's dreaming about chasing squirrels or seagulls. I look up from the journal to my laptop screen. The women in the video urge viewers to buy their crystals to help support their cause. This goes on for another hour, and I'm almost nodding off when I crack open what appears to be the most recent journal.

I spot a mention of the Great Ceremony. It's been mentioned in a few of the more recent videos, too, and has piqued my interest. I skim through the journal. Source is giving orders for how to prepare for the Great Ceremony. I prop myself up on my elbow, perking up a bit, and keep scanning the notes.

They mention chopping wood and gathering kindling in great quantities.

Source says they must be piled in the clearing behind the Mothership.

I've learned they call the big cabin the mothership and realize that must be the big pile of wood I saw out there in the field. I nibble my lip. What kind of ceremony would they need so much wood and kindling for? To me it suggests they're going to have a giant bonfire. I'm vaguely aware of traditions like this. I know they celebrate Guy Fawkes Day in the UK with bonfires. And even here in Nightfall, everyone's celebrating the lunar eclipse with bonfires down on the beach.

That thought slips something into place in my mind. The cult is also likely celebrating the lunar eclipse. Nature seems to play an important part in their teachings. When members join, they relinquish the *material* world and take on nature-themed names like Gaia, Phoenix, Luna, Terra.

It would make sense that the lunar eclipse might hold some significance to the group. I keep scanning the journal, hoping for more information about what the ceremony is and if it has ties to the eclipse.

Suddenly I find a line where it's referred to as the Great Sacrifice, not the Great Ceremony. "Sacrifice," I mutter to myself. One of Shadow's ears swivels toward me, though he keeps his eyes squeezed shut. I place my fingertip on the lined page and scan until I find another mention.

Chosen One should wear white robes for the sacrifice. Source says he is to be purified by drinking colloidal silver.

My stomach twists. "Clay said they'd renamed him Chosen One." I flip the page and find a drawing. It's the first one I've seen. Lots of wavy, vertical lines stretch toward the top of the page with cross hatching below it. Pine trees surround the lines with stars sketched above, along with a big circle—the moon. It's a giant pyre, and the cross hatching represents the kindling.

Little stick figure people circle around it. There's one smaller stick figure, and it's right in the center of the fire.

"Oh my god." I push up to sitting. I scan the journal more quickly until I come to a line that makes my blood run cold.

Chosen One will be sacrificed at exactly 2 a.m., when the lunar eclipse is at its fullest. The lunar eclipse should form a blood moon in the sky, turning it red, representative of the blood sacrifice. The little boy will be offered up to usher in the Age of Ascension.

"Holy shit." I drop the journal and leap to my feet, which startles Shadow awake. No wonder Joy Ackerman thought her son, Clay, was in danger.

I grab my phone and check the time. It's nearly midnight, which means we barely have two hours to save that little boy.

CHAPTER 42

Hanks screeches to a halt halfway up on the curb in front of my house and motions for me to get in. I open the back door for Shadow to hop in, then jump in the passenger seat and slam the door behind me. He barely waits for me to close the door before he peels out, speeding toward the highway.

"Thanks for picking me up," I say, breathless. I put on my seat belt, then glance back to make sure Shadow's settled.

Hanks grunts a reply, his eyes focused on the road ahead of him, speeding down dark residential streets. He's wisely avoiding going anywhere near downtown, which is no doubt choked with traffic and tourists in town for the lunar eclipse.

I glance up at the dark sky above the treetops. It's clear and dark, and the moon is big and round, hanging low in the sky out over the ocean. Those who traveled here to catch a glimpse are going to get a good show.

We pull onto the two-lane highway and Hanks nearly floors the sedan, throwing me back in my seat. I shoot him a surprised look.

"You going to map me?"

I grab my phone and pull up the cult compound's

address. It's still in the app from our trip out there earlier in the day.

"How long will it take to get there?" Hanks's grip is tight on the steering wheel, his knuckles splotchy.

I check the time. "Hour and thirty-five minutes."

"And how long till the eclipse?"

As soon as I read about sacrificing the boy in the journal, I called Hanks and breathlessly explained the situation to him. It took a few minutes for him to understand what I was saying, but once he did, he must have rushed out the door immediately and hopped in the car, because he was at my front door just a few minutes later.

"It's a little after twelve now, so we've got about two hours... a little less." In other words, *if* we make it in time, it'll be just barely before they sacrifice the boy.

The detective grits his teeth and pushes the car faster. The dark shadows of trees whiz past on our right, while on the left, the cliffside drops away to the ocean. The bright moon reflects on the rippling water. Then we curve right, heading inland, and leave the ocean in our rearview mirror.

"Call the chief," Hanks barks.

My stomach twists. I'm dreading this, but it's necessary. I choose his name from my speed dial and wait through a couple of rings.

"Mercer?" The chief's deep voice is equal parts annoyed and shocked.

"Chief," I rush, "you're not gonna like this."

"Oh brother," he grumbles.

"Please, hear me out. Hanks and I are on our way out to the Ascendant Light compound."

"What?" he shouts.

I pull the phone away from my ear to avoid bursting an eardrum. Hanks, who heard it too, shoots me a grimace.

"I, uh, checked out some of those journals we collected as evidence from the headquarters earlier."

"Mercer, you are beyond out of line. You were told you were off this case and you have the audacity to breach protocol and—"

I interrupt him. "I'm so sorry, Chief, you can rightfully chew me out or fire me or whatever later, but right now, I need you to listen. I found several entries describing a great sacrifice that the cult is planning for tonight during the lunar eclipse."

He's quiet now, so I press on.

"There's a drawing and lots of descriptions of building a giant pyre in the clearing behind the cabin. According to the notes, they're planning to sacrifice the Chosen One, the little boy, Clay, to further their ascension into heaven, or whatever it is they believe."

"My god," Jamison mutters. "Hanks, you there?"

I put the call on speakerphone and nod at the detective, whose eyes are glued to the road. He's got the brights on, and we're flying down the highway at a highly unsafe speed. "Here, Chief."

"Hanks, have you seen this entry?"

The detective licks his lips. "No, sir. But I trust Mercer."

I shoot him a grateful look.

Jamison sucks in a deep breath. "Alright, shit," he mutters. "I'm sending several squad cars now, but you'll get there first. Listen up, you wait for backup before you make any move. Hear me?"

"Yes, sir," Hanks and I mutter in unison.

"Good. I'll be in touch as soon as I have an update."

I hang up, and Hanks barely slows the car as we ease around a curve on the mountainous road. Luckily, there's barely any traffic. It's late, and any tourists are heading into Nightfall, not out of it.

Hanks clears his throat. "Kid, this is some crazy shit. It might get real tonight. You ready for that?"

I didn't bother to change into my uniform. I'm wearing

leggings, a sweatshirt, and my gun belt, but I nod. I understand that he means things might get violent. They're planning to kill a kid, after all. They're already intending violence. There's a lot of them and not many of us. And when beliefs get involved, people can get militant about defending them.

"I understand," I tell Hanks.

"Good," he mutters.

CHAPTER 43

Hanks kills the headlights as we turn from the dirt road toward the cult's compound. He pulls to a stop just outside the gate. "Damn, it's latched."

"Hold on." I hop out of the car, careful to close the door quietly behind me. As soon as I'm out in the brisk night air, I realize staying quiet won't be necessary.

It's dark out here in the forest, but in the clearing behind the houses and trailers, a giant pyre burns. Smoke billows towards the sky. Drums are being played. People are screaming and chanting. My stomach twists with fear. Part of me had hoped I was wrong.

Even if it would mean my career was over, part of me hoped the description of the Great Sacrifice was more metaphorical than literal. That little Clay wasn't in any real danger. But it looks like this Great Ceremony is well underway.

Above the dark treetops, the moon hangs low and round, a shadow drifting across part of it. A red tinge already seeps across the surface.

We probably only have minutes until the full lunar eclipse. I dash up to the gate, and I'm flooded with relief as I find that it's latched but not locked. They've simply looped the chain around without securing it. I undo the chain, toss it aside, and push the gate inwards, then find a rock to prop it open. We're going to want backup to be able to come straight in when they arrive. I run back around to the side of the car and hop in the passenger seat.

Hanks gives me an approving nod before rumbling forward slowly, lights off. The car bounces and jostles along the gravel and dirt driveway as we approach the dark buildings up ahead.

My heart hammers against my ribcage, and a vein pulses in my temple. "It's crazy out there," I mutter. "The drumming and screaming—and you can see the flames, right?"

Hanks nods.

We pull up to the cabin and park next to the line of cars. Then Hanks turns off the engine, and we sit in silence for a moment. Without the rumble of the engine, the chanting and singing filters into the car, and Shadow whines, his ears pricked. He turns and then turns again, uneasy in the back seat.

I lean forward, glancing up at the moon through the windshield, then turn back to Hanks. "I don't think we have much time."

He's stony-faced as he glances back out the rearview window. I follow his gaze and find nothing but an empty stretch of dirt road reaching back into the dark night. No sirens, no flashing red and blue lights. There's no sign of backup.

"I know Jamison said to wait." I nibble my bottom lip. "But I'm worried we're going to be too late to save that kid."

"Me, too." Hanks takes a deep breath and then catches my eye. "Listen, Mercer. This situation is a mess. It's dark. This ceremony over there sounds like pure pandemonium, and we've got a kid in danger. You need to stay cool-headed and follow my lead, got it?"

I nod, though my mind seems to have gone blank. I can't seem to think further ahead than just following whatever orders Hanks gives me.

"Come on." He climbs out of the car, and I follow suit, stepping back out into that dark night. Nightfall isn't a big town, but compared to this rural location out in the middle of nowhere, I feel like we can only see a small portion of the stars in the night sky. Here, they seem to all twinkle overhead, every single one a bright pinprick. A breeze rustles the trees on the perimeter of the clearing, and I tuck a strand of loose hair behind my ear before opening the back door. Shadow leaps out, and I grab his leash, then rejoin Hanks. Somewhere nearby, dogs are barking. I'm not sure if they're alerting to our presence or merely reacting to the raucous party in the clearing.

The detective keeps his voice low. "We need to get a better idea of what they're doing out there." He jerks his chin toward the towering pyre in the field. "Keep your gun ready."

He draws his own service weapon, taking the safety off, and my heart hammers faster as I follow suit.

Half crouching, we dart past the cabin to the nearest yurt and wait. It's hard to see what's happening exactly. Seems that men and women are dancing around the circle, some in long flowing robes, some stark naked. Hanks's description of pure pandemonium seems spot on.

Hanks gestures forward, and Shadow and I follow him, half-crouched, to the trailer closest to the clearing. Once there, we hunker down and then peek out from around the side. "How many would you say are out there in the field?"

I wince. "I don't know, maybe fifty, sixty."

Hanks nods. "Sounds about right to me." He lets out a quiet grunt. "In other words, we're badly outnumbered, kid." He shifts on his feet and looks back. I feel like I can read his mind. I'm also praying that backup shows up soon. But for now, we're here on our own. Staying low, I edge to the side, peeking out around the side of the trailer.

I blink against the bright orange blaze and do my best to make out individual figures. To the right of the group, I spot Source. She has her arms raised overhead, her long white robes billowing out from her. She moves closer to the flames, which illuminate her face.

Beside her is another woman I recognize from when we came to search the compound earlier today. She's got brown hair and bright brown eyes. I think that's Rainbow. And in between them is a small figure. A little boy, also wearing white robes. He looks smaller than the boy we spoke to earlier today.

Source is saying something, screaming it. I can't quite make out the words from this distance, but the kid is clearly panicking. He's trying to scramble away, but that Rainbow woman grabs his arm, and a couple of other adults circle up, penning him in. They're herding him toward the flames.

With a gasp, I turn to Hanks. "They're about to burn him alive."

The detective's dark eyes grow wide, the whites showing all around them. It's about all I can make out of his face in the darkness.

In a breath, Hanks is fully upright. "Back to the car, kid," he mutters.

We dash the short distance back to Hanks's sedan and pile inside. He levels me with a grim look. "We can't wait. We have to go in."

I nod. "I'm with you."

He sucks in a deep breath, then glances back at Shadow. "Hold on." My dog lies down on the seat, his ears perked and hackles raised.

The detective throws the car into reverse, then pulls forward and drives around the side of the buildings. He slams his portable emergency light on the dashboard and turns on the flashing red and blue signal, flips on the headlights, and grabs the microphone for the PA system. We trundle over the uneven land, threading our way between trailers and yurts. I hold onto the door as we bounce and jostle across the field toward the bonfire. Despite the flames and the headlights, I squint into the darkness, struggling to make out the figures circling around the pyre.

Hanks's voice booms over the loud speaker. "Nightfall Police Department! Everyone freeze!"

The drumming halts. Some of the dancing and cavorting carries on for a couple of moments before the rest seem to recognize our presence.

"Police!" Hanks barks again. "Everyone, down on the ground!"

My heart hammers in my chest as we drive closer. People are shouting now. Some drop as commanded, while others flee. I point at several tall silhouettes running our way. "You see them?"

Hanks nods and presses the pedal, urging the car faster and swerving further right. We're heading straight for Source and the struggling little boy. We're close enough now to see them more clearly and my jaw drops. "Hanks, that's a different kid."

Before he can respond, the nose of the car takes a sharp dip and we lurch to a stop. I slam forward, the seat belt digging into my chest, and a thud followed by a whine let me know Shadow's been thrown forward, too.

"Shadow!" I spin in my seat as my dog crawls out of the floor space behind Hanks. He licks my hand and I run my hands over his fur. Thankfully, he seems unharmed.

"You okay, kid?" Hanks asks and I nod. He peers out the windshield and tries the gas pedal again, but the wheels just spin. He smacks the steering wheel. "Shit! We're stuck in a ditch. We've got to hoof it from here."

With my heart racing, I climb out the passenger side. Sure

enough, the car's gotten lodged in a steep dip. Shadow, whose hackles are raised, stays glued to my side as I come around the car and follow Hanks out into the dark clearing. Hanks raises his badge high overhead and shouts in a booming voice, "Nightfall Police Department! Everyone freeze!"

There are definitely several men approaching us. It's hard to make them out exactly in the dark, silhouetted against the flames. The headlights cut through the dark and the red and blue emergency light strobe over the wild grass of the field. The shadowed figures continue to approach.

"I said freeze!" Hanks shouts.

My gaze darts to Source. The little boy beside her is still struggling. I'm holding my breath, praying that Source orders everyone to do as we say. Her electric blue eyes seem to turn red, reflecting the orange flames and the blood moon overhead, which is now turning a deeper red.

Instead, her shrill voice screams into the night, "Open fire!"

I'm on my belly before my brain even has time to process her words. In pure reaction, I've dropped, and Shadow drops to his belly beside me.

Booming gunshots shatter the quiet night, and I cry out as a bullet flies overhead, rustling my hair.

Hanks returns fire and then cries out. He falls to the ground with a thud beside me as more shots whizz past.

CHAPTER 44

My body moves, but my brain doesn't seem to be functioning.

I'm back on my feet before I have time to think. I scoop the moaning Detective Hanks under his arms. He's heavy, so heavy. I grunt and dig my heels in, scrambling backwards. Bullets slam into the metal car door beside me and throw up chunks of dirt at my feet. At first, I barely move, but once I get a little momentum, adrenaline surges through me, and I'm able to drag Hanks.

Shadow springs into action beside me. He grips the detective's jacket in his teeth, pinching the fabric above his shoulder, and helps me pull. I'm amazed for a moment at the bond between this sweet dog and me. Despite the bullets whizzing past our heads, the crack of gunshots, and the screaming and panic around the giant pyre, my dog is sticking by my side.

The moment of reflection is over the second we drag Hanks behind the car, which shields us, rocking as it's peppered with bullets. *Ping. Ping.* Bullets slam into the side of the sedan, and I collapse. I'm trembling and absolutely terrified. My chest is so tight I can't breathe, and I claw at my collar, trying to let more air in somehow. Tears stream down my cheeks, but I don't seem to be able to utter a sound.

Hanks groans. It's too dark to see where he's been hit, or how many times so I pull the back door open, turning on the pilot light. Shadow licks the man a couple of times right across his face.

Hanks scoffs and gently bats the dog away. "Oh, come on."

That's a good sign. At least he's speaking. I manage a sip of air before I go back to hyperventilating.

Boom. Boom. Ping. The gunshots are loud, and they're getting louder as the men move closer. It's Hanks and me against several armed men, plus the fifty other cult members now screaming and scattering from around the pyre.

In my mind, I'm lurched back to New Year's Eve. Just a few weeks ago, the bottle rockets whizzing past my head, my gun drawn, just as it is now.

I'd forgotten my gun. I glance down at my trembling hands. The second I pulled Hanks behind the trailer, I must have drawn my weapon again. I don't remember doing it. That scares me more.

"Mercer!"

I gasp and blink. Hanks has grabbed the sleeve of my jacket, and I suddenly realize this probably isn't the first time he's called my name, trying to get my attention. "Listen to me, Mercer." He speaks through gritted teeth, his husky voice laced with pain.

An involuntary whimper escapes my lips, and my hands tremble. My mind is empty with panic. He gives my arm a little shake, and I blink again, trying to focus and stay in the present. "I need you to help bandage me up. Make a tourniquet." He's holding his leg, where he's been hit.

"Okay, yeah."

My breaths are coming in short, quick pants. I gulp, and though I'm only half in control of my trembling hands, I pull out the utility knife I keep in one of the pockets of my gun belt.

I slice into my T-shirt and then rip off the whole bottom hem. It's not great, but it'll do. "Show me where," I mutter.

He takes my hand, and in the semi-darkness lit only by the pilot light of the open car door, guides me to his right thigh, right above his knee. Wet, viscous fluid—blood— warms my hands, and I recoil. I steel myself and try again. As gently as I can, I slide the fabric under his leg. He grunts with pain but manages not to cry out. Once I've got the fabric around his leg, above the wound, I tie it as tightly as I can, then wipe my bloodied hands off on my thighs.

"Good," Hanks grunts.

The gunshots are getting closer. Source is still carrying on with her disturbing ceremony. I make out a word here and there. "Lift us to ascension… noble sacrifice… Elders, I call upon thee."

I can't believe she's still pushing on with this. Bullets whizz past; others embed themselves in the metal of the trailer.

The whites shine all around Hanks's eyes. "Listen, kid, they're gonna kill that boy."

I glance up at the sky, the moon red and ruddy. It's fully in eclipse now.

"You've got this. This is all you, kid." He's panting. "I can give you cover."

I glance toward the road again. No sign of backup, yet. I've got to do this for Clay. I have to be the protector that I needed when I was a child. I take a couple of deep breaths, bracing myself.

I glance down at my dog as I slowly rise to a crouch.

"You ready, Shadow?"

His ears perk up.

My K-9 and I have trained for this. "Let's go," I mutter.

CHAPTER 45

Hanks manages to stay conscious as I help him sit up. He leans around the side of the car, sitting with his legs stretched out. He fires off a few shots. I hear cries from the men, which gives me an idea of where they are.

Shadow's off his leash, and with Hanks providing cover, the two of us sprint side by side toward the pyre.

A bullet whizzes past my head. In the surreal red light of the blood moon overhead and the giant blaze, I spin to my left. Everything I'm doing is pure instinct. Luckily I'm a good shot, and the men are somewhat silhouetted against the blaze. I aim, fire and take the guy who shot at me down. I can just make out his long hair as he cries out and drops to the ground. I fire off two more shots toward the shadowy figures behind him and keep running toward the flames.

Most of the cult members have scattered. They've either dropped to the soft dirt ground, hands covering their heads, cowering, or they're taking off for the trees, fleeing from the gunfire. Not Source, though. She and that other woman, Rainbow, are struggling with the little boy. He's screaming and digging in his heels as they tug him by the arms toward the flames.

Another bullet flies past me and embeds itself in the dirt. I turn and fire off a few more shots behind me before running on. We're close enough now, Shadow and I, that I can make out the wild look in Source's eyes. The flames flicker in them. Sweat trickles at her brow.

Shadow surges ahead. His lithe body flies through the air, paws slamming into the back of the brunette woman, Rainbow. She lets out a strangled cry as my dog knocks her to the ground and pins her there, growling into the nape of her neck.

We've practiced this in training courses before, but seeing him execute it in real life fills me with admiration and pride. I'm mere seconds behind him. The little boy now has one arm free and is trying to tug his other hand from Source. The woman is still clutching him, though her wide eyes are fixed on my dog and the woman he's pinned to the ground.

I follow my dog's lead and don't slow down. I slam into Source, knocking her flat on the ground. The air whooshes out of her, and I know I've jolted the wind out of her. I don't give her a chance to recover. In a breath, I'm kneeling, rolling her over, pinning her to the ground with my knee in the center of her back.

I pull my handcuffs off my belt, and as I'm cuffing her hands behind her back, the screech of sirens pierces the air. More screams sound from the cult members left cowering around the flames, and a few more gunshots pop off. I stay low to the ground, my knee digging into Source's back until I've got her cuffed.

Red-and-blue flashing lights peek through the trees and then come fully into view as they clear the tree line and pull forward down the dirt driveway. I let out a shuddering sigh. Backup has arrived. Hanks and I aren't alone. I just hope Hanks is still hanging in there.

I keep my gun drawn, and I'm on high alert. But whatever adrenaline surge gave me the strength to make this mad dash and save the little boy leaves my body. I drop from my crouch onto one hip, my chest heaving, as my gaze stays glued to the flashing lights. Beside me, Source coughs, but stays down.

A loud voice, Jamison's, booms over a bullhorn. "Nightfall Police Department. Drop your weapons. Hands above your head."

I'm sitting there panting while Shadow continues to pin Rainbow to the ground. A flicker of movement catches my attention. I lost track of the little boy, Clay, in all of this. He'd run off into the darkness, it seems, but now he creeps closer. He shrugs out of the white robes he's wearing and stands in front of me in a sweater and jeans.

I can tell now that this boy looks much more like the picture I saw of Clay Ackerman when he was four. He's younger than the boy who pretended to be him earlier today. His wide blue eyes look terrified, and tears streak his freckled cheeks.

I'm trembling almost uncontrollably now, my nerves giving way to the adrenaline dump, but I manage to speak calmly, despite my chattering teeth. "It's okay. You're safe now."

His chin wobbles, and then he rushes forward, wraps his arms around my neck, and hugs me tight. Tears fill my own eyes as I holster my gun and snake an arm around the little boy. I hug him tight as Nightfall officers in bulletproof vests storm across the field, weapons drawn, and defuse the situation, arresting members and kicking guns away.

I let out a shuddering sigh. We really are safe now.

CHAPTER 46

TWO WEEKS LATER

Chief Jamison stands in front of the crowded room in his dress uniform, looking polished and official. The older man gives me a warm smile.

"Eden Mercer, please step forward."

"You're up, kid." Hanks winks and, with my stomach full of butterflies, I join the chief. My cheeks burn with a mix of pride and embarrassment at standing in front of the large group of family, friends, and colleagues. I've never been comfortable being the center of attention. I nervously smooth down my dress uniform and adjust my cap and white gloves.

Chief Jamison gives me a solemn look before addressing the gathered audience. "Officer Mercer has demonstrated a rare level of commitment to justice and protecting our community. She showed unmatched courage in defending not only Detective Hanks, but also the life of an innocent young boy. She also helped secure justice for the boy's mother and went above and beyond in the line of duty."

Chief Jamison holds up a framed plaque and turns to me. "Officer Mercer, please accept the Nightfall Police Department Award for Bravery in honor of your outstanding police work."

Chief Jamison breaks out into a wide grin. "Congratulations, Officer Mercer." He heartily shakes my hand, and then we turn to face the crowd. Everyone breaks into applause, and I'm beaming. I'm smiling so hard my cheeks hurt. My gaze drifts to Hope and Grandma in the front row, who are on their feet. Hope helped me get ready this morning, doing my makeup and sweeping my hair back in an elegant but simple twist. I scan the faces in the crowd and spot Nathan, looking handsome in his dress uniform.

I glance to my right, where Detective Hanks waits beside Shadow, holding on to my K-9 for me. He gives me an approving look, and I stand taller with pride. Chief Jamison and I pose for a few photographs, and the flash leaves spots dancing in front of my eyes. "Thank you, Officer Mercer." He hands me the plaque and I retreat to the side amid more applause. I take Shadow's leash from Hanks, then rejoin Jamison.

The chief bends forward and addresses my canine partner. "And to our brave K-9 officer, Shadow, you, sir, have also earned an award for your courage and dedication."

Shadow's tail wags, and chuckles sound through the crowd. Jamison holds up a special patch the station had created to add to my dog's police vest as a symbol of his award.

"But since I know you don't love patches as much as you love these…" The polished-looking Jamison pulls a bone treat out of his pocket. "Here you go, boy."

He holds it out to Shadow, who politely takes it and then begins chomping away. Giggles sound throughout the crowd, and even the stoic Jamison cracks a grin.

"Finally," the chief continues, "I would like our own Detective Gordon Hanks to step forward."

I smile at the detective as we switch places. I offer him an arm, but he waves me off and limps to center stage. He sports his formal uniform and a new haircut. We're on the ground floor of the historic City Council chambers, which happens to be just a few buildings down Main Street from the police station. It's a beautiful old building with crisscrossing beams overhead and tall paned glass windows which let in some unusually sunny light for a February day.

Chief Jamison holds up a framed plaque and congratulates Hanks on being given the same award for bravery that I received. He and Hanks shake hands and pose for a picture. The crowd cheers, and I enthusiastically join in, with some loud whoops coming from the back row. Hanks invited the detectives from the other precincts, and my cheeks flush warm when I spot the cute Detective Wilder among them.

Chief Jamison says a few closing words, and then the ceremony is concluded. There's several dozen people gathered to watch, and they all rise from their seats as everyone mills around.

I hurry to pull Chief Jamison aside. "Thank you so much. For the award but also... for forgiving my breach of protocol."

"As I said before, Officer, while I expect this to be a one-time infraction," the older man gives me a kindly smile, "the exceptional nature of your investigative instincts and your commitment to justice outweigh your transgression."

My heart is so filled with gratitude and pride it feels like it'll burst. "Thank you."

He claps me on the shoulder. "Your grandpa would be proud of you." He moves off to speak with others as I blink back tears. My grandpa was my hero.

Grandma and Hope rush up to me first, wrapping me in tight hugs. My grandma takes my face in both her hands and blinks back tears. "I am so, so proud of you, Eden."

"I've always said it," Hope chimes in. "You're the very best."

"I'm not sure about that—"

She stops me. "You are—you are *the best*."

I chuckle at her exaggerated seriousness.

"We're celebrating." Hope bounces on her heels. "We're gonna make your favorite dinner."

"Or take you out," Grandma adds. "Whatever you want, sweetie."

"Thank you, guys."

"We'll wait for you by the door." They move off through the crowd as Shadow and I thread our way over to Hanks and his wife. She's a beautiful middle-aged woman with shoulder-length, shiny silver hair and kind eyes. Hanks is still wearing a boot on his injured leg but recovering well from the gunshot.

I've gotten to know Sue pretty well, since I saw her quite often at the hospital while visiting Hanks as he recovered from the wound. Now that it's been a few weeks, he's up and about and eager to make up for lost time.

I smile at them both. "Guess we'll be working together now." More exciting to me than the award, Jamison and Hanks have informed me that I'll be permanently assigned to aid Hanks on his cases. This with the idea that I'll receive invaluable on-the-job training and be on the track to make detective someday.

Sue grins, and Hanks shrugs. "Well, I'm getting older. Guess I could use a little help."

His wife winks. "Plus, he's a big ol' softie for Shadow, now."

It was true. I brought Shadow along on all my visits as he was recovering. The *one* time I didn't, Hanks pouted and asked where the pup was. Even now, he reaches into his pocket and pulls out some little salmon pellets that I told him were Shadow's favorites. My dog eagerly wolfs them out of his hand.

Some of Hanks's friends pull him and his wife aside, and

Nathan rushes up to me, wrapping me in a tight hug. "I knew you could do it."

"Thank you." I grin up at my friend. "I truly couldn't have done it without you. Every time I hesitated, I heard your voice in my ear telling me to trust my gut and stand up for myself."

He grins, clearly proud of himself. "And look where it got you."

I playfully slug his arm. "Exactly. It's almost like I should listen to you more or something."

He nods primly, then leans closer, lowering his voice. "All the other officers are talking about you, you know."

Heat rushes to my face, and I roll my eyes. "Well, I guess at least they know who I am now."

He shakes his head. "No, seriously, it's all really good stuff. You earned a lot of respect with that storming of the cult compound."

I quirk a brow. "Really?" Respect from the other officers. Now that would be something novel.

Nathan nods. "I'm rubbing it in, too. I don't miss a chance to remind them that I've been telling them how awesome you are."

"Thanks, friend." A few of the officers walk past and give me respectful nods or lift their hands in greeting. It takes me a moment to respond since it's so new, but I smile and wave back. How about that?

Bulldog scowls at me as he passes by.

"Except for Bulldog, of course." Nathan rolls his eyes. "He's just jealous."

"Mind if I cut in to offer my congratulations?" Dobre's mustache twitches up at the corners.

"Of course, I'll catch you later." Nathan squeezes my shoulder, then moves away as the new Chief Dobre from Elk Ridge gives me a hearty handshake.

"Congratulations, Officer Mercer."

I grin. "Thank you, *Chief* Dobre."

After Nightfall PD stormed the cult compound, quite a few of the cult members were arrested for their participation in the abuse and attempted murder of Clay. Others who were deemed to have no knowledge of the scheme have since returned to their families. I heard from Sharon, the Reddit moderator, that she's reunited with her daughter and grandson River, and they're working on repairing their relationship.

While most of the cult members are facing lesser charges as accessories to crimes, Source, Rainbow, and Zephyr are all being charged with Joy Ackerman's murder and the attempted murder of her son, Clay.

It turns out that Zephyr, who is the long-haired ex-military guy I shot in the shoulder, was the one who pulled the trigger. But it was Rainbow's presence that tricked her friend Joy into getting into their car that night. Rainbow and Zephyr had driven around looking for Joy Ackerman after she read the journal and ran away. After her unsuccessful visit to the Elk Ridge station, Joy had apparently decided to try her luck in another town, but resorted to hitch hiking. Rainbow and Zephyr had found her with her thumb out on the side of the highway, heading toward Portland. Rainbow lied to coax her into the car, promising to help Joy save her son and pretending that they also thought Source was going too far with her plan to sacrifice the boy.

Once she got in, Zephyr and Rainbow dropped the act. They drove Joy out toward the coast, marched her out into the wilderness at gunpoint, and eventually shot her. Apparently, this was all done on Source's orders. Once they realized that Joy knew of their plan to sacrifice Clay and meant to alert the authorities to it, Source considered Joy a liability. One that had to be taken care of.

Only, Source had to have some kind of mythical justification for it. So she told Rainbow and Zephyr that Joy had been polluted by some kind of dark energy, and that not only should they kill her, but give her a ritual burial to help cleanse her soul and allow her to ascend, or some such nonsense.

That explained the prayer hands and the symbol wrapped around them. Zephyr had decided to cut off the woman's head and place it between her ankles. Rainbow had protested, apparently, but he'd ignored her.

In any case, it was Rainbow's own journals that led to her downfall. She detailed Joy Ackerman's murder with her typical level of attention to detail, giving specific times, locations, and conversations. Apparently, poor Joy Ackerman had begged for her life, and when it became clear she wasn't going to live, begged for them to spare her son.

We couldn't get Joy Ackerman back. But at least we'd managed to save Clay. The journals provided an explanation for their deception when we raided the compound. As all the cult dealings unraveled, the connection to the former Chief Novak of Elk Ridge became clear, and he too was arrested. He'd tipped them off before our visits and had accepted generous bribes. They'd had time to realize we'd be looking for Clay, who was at that time, bound and gagged in the basement. Source had hatched the plan to disguise the other little boy who lived with the cult as Clay. Despite being a few years older, he'd passed as Clay due to curled hair, freckles made with henna, and a spare pair of Source's blue contacts. I guess that explained her unnaturally icy blue eyes.

Considering Novak's actions paved the way for the cult to get away with murder, he was also being charged with several crimes. We'd looked into his finances and discovered lots of large deposits to his bank accounts from a shady LLC owned by the cult members.

After Chief Novak's arrest, Officer Dobre was promoted to the new chief of Elk Ridge. I don't know the guy well, but he seems like a decent man. He stuck his neck out to get us evidence and get the truth out.

"I'm looking forward to working with you," Chief Dobre says with a grin.

"Me, too. It'd be great if Nightfall and Elk Ridge could have a friendly working relationship."

Chief Dobre chuckles. "That'd be novel, wouldn't it? Well, it is my full intention to have an open, cooperative relationship with you and your whole department."

"That's great to hear."

I greet several others, thanking them for coming, but my eyes are on a couple of people in the back. Shadow and I thread our way through the crowd and eventually make it over to little Clay Ackerman and his grandma, Mary Ann.

They stand with Mary Ann's hands resting on the boy's shoulders. As soon as Shadow and I emerge from the crowd, the little boy's bright blue eyes light up, and he rushes forward, throwing his arms around Shadow's neck. My dog sits, allowing Clay to give him a big hug and bury his face in my dog's soft fur.

"Shadow," the little boy squeals. He peppers my dog with kisses on the top of his head. I grin at Shadow. My dog closes one eye, but otherwise looks plenty happy to receive the boy's affection. His tail wags, sweeping the hardwood floor, and he leans into the boy's embrace.

"So cute," Mary Ann murmurs.

I stand beside the little boy's grandma. We watch him play with Shadow for a few moments.

"When are you going back to California?"

She gives me a tight grin. "Probably tomorrow."

I nod. "I'm glad you and Clay are getting on with your lives, but I have to admit, I'm going to miss the little guy."

I've spent time with the small boy, taking witness statements and going over aspects of the case, both in Joy Ackerman's murder and also in his own attempted murder. It's a lot for an eight-year-old, but he's a smart kid and tough, and I've grown pretty fond of him. The older woman nods. She looks night and day different from when I saw her several weeks ago.

Her hair is neatly curled, there's a light in her eyes, and she has some color to her cheeks. "Well, Clay's gonna miss you, too. You *and* Shadow." She smiles at me. "He talks about you nonstop, you know. You're his hero."

Heat rushes to my cheeks, and I look away, both embarrassed and also honored. "That's really sweet."

"Oh, Eden!" Clay spins around to look at me. He's still petting Shadow's head. "I forgot to tell you. I remembered something. Remember when they had me tied up in the cellar?"

My stomach twists a little at the boy's sad history, but I think it's a good thing that he can talk about it so easily. During our first interview, he seemed pretty shell-shocked, but after speaking about his experiences, each time the words seem to flow a little easier, like the memories are less heavy. I nod. "Yeah, I do."

"Well, remember you told me that Shadow was sniffing at the rug and you thought that maybe there was a trapdoor?"

I nod.

"I remembered that that's when I would have been in the cellar. Shadow smelled me or heard me under the floor."

I hadn't actually put the timelines together yet, but I realize the little boy's right. "Wow, Clay! You're so smart."

"Shadow was trying to save me." He wraps his arms around the dog again.

I turn to his grandma. "I hope when you're up here for the trials that you'll come say hi."

Mary Ann chuckles. "Oh, we will. You just try to stop him." After a moment, the woman grows somber. "You know, I'm so grateful to have Clay back. I really am." She shoots me an almost apologetic look. "But I'm still wrapping my head around the fact that Joy is really gone." She swipes at a tear and sniffs. "I feel really guilty."

I raise my brows, surprised.

"Guilty for how I raised her. Her father and I were super strict. Fundamentalist. I'm afraid it primed Joy to fall victim to another cult."

She's piqued my attention. "*Another* cult?" I repeat. "As in the fundamentalist group you raised Joy and her sister in was also a cult?"

Mary Ann nods. That same heaviness drifts into her expression that I saw when I visited her home in Simi Valley.

"What cult?" I wait with bated breath as she turns to me.

"It was called Zion House."

I feel like the floor's dropped out from under me. For a moment, I'm too disoriented to say anything. It's the same cult Hope and I were raised in. The same cult I've been trying to track down any information on for the last decade.

"When did you leave?" I face her fully.

She blinks, flustered by my sudden intensity. "Um, well, we started pulling away maybe... ten years ago? But it was about eight years ago that we got out for good."

"Eight years." That's a lot more recent history than I've been able to find on the group. "Did you know Anna Warner?"

Mary Ann doesn't hesitate. "Why, yes."

My stomach tightens. "That's my mother."

Her own eyes widen. "Truly?"

I nod. "My sister Hope and I left when I was fourteen. But my mom and my siblings are still in. I've been looking for them for years. Do you know where they are now?"

Mary Ann shakes her head. "No, I've lost touch with everyone, I'm afraid. You know how it is. Once you leave, they shun you."

I nod. "How'd you get out?"

She frowns. "You know, things have changed a lot since you were last there. Different dynamics. The group grew more fractured. The infighting and frequent moves got to be too much for a lot of folks. Numbers dropped—to probably half as many people as were in the group when you were a child. In the chaos of our last move, my husband and I had had it and slipped away with our girls."

"Your last move? To where?"

"Well..." Mary Ann looks thoughtful. "As of about five years ago, they were heading down south of Medford."

I gasp. "Medford, Oregon?" She nods, and we fall into silence, watching Clay and Shadow. Though they're adorable together, my mind's elsewhere, racing. Medford, Oregon.

I've been in the same state as the rest of my family and had no idea. Are they still here? Five years ago is long enough that they've likely moved.

It might pan out to be nothing, but at least it's a clue.

CHAPTER 47

It's the Monday after the ceremony. Shadow and I stroll into the station with an extra bounce in my step, now that I don't feel so ostracized from the other officers. Linda and Joan, who are both working this morning, pop up from their chairs. They're like second moms to me, and as soon as I'm past the low swinging door, I rush over to give them hugs.

They pet Shadow and, of course, sneak him a treat, though he doesn't need it since we just stopped by the Daily Grind. But I let them lavish him with praise and treats and take a little bit of praise for myself, too.

"Congratulations again," Linda gushes.

"You looked so bonita at the ceremony," Joan coos.

"Thanks." I grin. "Hope helped me get all dolled up."

Shadow and I sweep into the bullpen. I head toward my desk but stop short when I spot Hanks in his office. He's in early, just like me. He's got his booted leg propped up on the other chair and lifts his steaming mug of coffee in salute.

I wave back, then get myself set up at my desk. As the other officers filter in, they all wave and greet me. It's gonna take some getting used to, but it's nice to not feel quite so alienated anymore.

Per the usual, Jamison does the morning briefing, and I sit next to my bestie, Nathan. When it's over, though, the chief stops Hanks and me on our way out. "Officer Mercer? A word?"

A little thrill shivers down my spine.

Hanks and I exchange curious glances, then follow Jamison into his office. "Close the door."

I follow his orders, and Hanks and I sink into the chairs across from him. "We've got a new case." He slides a manila folder across the desk to us. "There's been a string of fires up and down the coast. Mostly residential properties."

"Arson?" Hanks asks.

Jamison nods. "Suspected, though not yet confirmed. The most recent one took place last night. Only this time, we've got a body."

Hanks pulls the folder closer and flips it open. We bend our heads together, ready to solve our next case.

Thank you for reading *Shattered Silence*.

Ready for more heart-pounding mysteries? Dive into *Deadly Lessons*, the next thrilling installment of the Eden Mercer Mystery Thrillers!

Also, be sure to sign up for the Paige Black newsletter to **get your free Eden Mercer prequel, *Secret Witness*.** You'll also be the first to get news on upcoming books, subscriber only discounts, and more!

GET SECRET WITNESS FOR FREE

In the misty town of Nightfall, rookie officer Eden Mercer races against time to solve a decades-old mystery and save a missing woman.
Get Secret Witness now and uncover Eden Mercer's first gripping case!
www.paigeblackauthor.com

READ THE NEXT INSTALLMENT

At Cascade Academy, the truth is as twisted as the minds it claims to heal. Officer Eden Mercer must uncover its deadly secrets before another student vanishes forever.
Dive into Deadly Lessons today and uncover the secrets that will keep you turning pages late into the night!

BOOKS BY PAIGE BLACK

Eden Mercer Mystery Thrillers

In the fog-shrouded town of Nightfall, Oregon, Officer Eden Mercer confronts dark secrets and hidden dangers. As she battles her cult past and tackles chilling cases, Eden is determined to uncover the sinister truths lurking beneath the surface.

Shattered Silence

Deadly Lessons

Lethal Lines

Treacherous Depths

Twisted Pursuit

ABOUT THE AUTHOR

Paige Black lives in Portland, OR, where the fog and rain form a perfect backdrop to her love of all things mysterious and thrilling. Often found exploring the misty, dark forests of the Oregon Coast, Paige draws inspiration from the shadowy corners of the world and the secrets they hide.

Join Paige for gripping tales of twisted cults, cunning serial killers, and the dedicated law enforcement officers who bring them to justice.

Copyright © 2024 by Paige Black

All rights reserved.

No part of this book may be reproduced in any form or by any electronic or mechanical means, including information storage and retrieval systems, without written permission from the author, except for the use of brief quotations in a book review.

Cover design by Natasha Snow.

Printed in Great Britain
by Amazon